And the world came tumbling out

RA Mitchell

AND THE WORLD CAME TUMBLING OUT

For all those who have traveled on this journey with me.

First published by RBC2 Press 2024

Copyright © 2024 by RA Mitchell

All rights reserved. No part of this publication may be reproduced, stored or transmitted in any form or by any means, electronic, mechanical, photocopying, recording, scanning, or otherwise without written permission from the publisher. It is illegal to copy this book, post it to a website, or distribute it by any other means without permission.

This novel is entirely a work of fiction. The names, characters and incidents portrayed in it are the work of the author's imagination. Any resemblance to actual persons, living or dead, events or localities is entirely coincidental.

RA Mitchell asserts the moral right to be identified as the author of this work.

ISBN: 978-1-7636560-0-0 (Print)
ISBN 978-1-7636560-1-7 (ebook)

Table of Contents

Europe
The Most Glorious Shoes in the World
Battle of the Charles Bridge
All is Rotten in 'The Garden of Earthly Delights'
The Fabled Patisserie of Brussels
A Question of Job Satisfaction
Two Sides to a Story-Part 1
Two Sides to a Story-Part 2
One Mousse, Two Mousse, Three Mousse, Four...
On a Ferry to Tallinn

The Americas
I Opened an Oyster and the World Came Tumbling Out
Death and Vanilla
What Tears Us Apart
The Grave Robber
The Lucky Bean

Australia
Icarus

The United Kingdom
A Jane Affair
The Golden Touch

Russia
A New Future
Plight of the Peacock

Europe

1

The Most Glorious Shoes in the World

The rain has been coming down in torrential sheets for hours now; the sound of it slamming against the window almost drowns out the noise of Elena's doorbell ringing. It rings once, a short burst, then a brief pause before ringing again, this time insistent, the buzzer held down with an intensity that sets Elena's teeth on edge. Another day, another delivery.

The box in her lap tilts, its contents spilling out onto the floor. Two shoes, pretty in a generic way, land deep in the rose-colored carpet, their heels making small, deep crescents.

Elena sighs. Her search has been going on for over a decade, but now, with the doctor's prognosis, it is even more crucial that she succeeds. Her very legacy is at stake. She looks down at the shoes that have been sent, her lips curling as she assesses each one. Is there a communication problem here? Has she not made herself clear? She is looking for shoes, the most extraordinary, most spectacular pair of shoes that have ever been created. Why, then, is she receiving this garbage?

Disgruntled, she tosses the box down onto the shoes and picks up her phone. She looks at the invoice, searching for a phone number before locating it and tapping it into her phone.

'Hi, yes I got them.'

A pause.

'No, they're not at all what I want. I'm sending them back.'

She holds the phone away from her ear as indignant sounds emanate from it.

'Are you done? I really don't need your hysterics right now. You may think they're amazing, and some people might agree with you, but that doesn't work for me. You should know that by now. You know what I'm looking for, so if you can't make it, don't bother.'

She hangs up, the phone sliding out of her hand onto the cashmere blanket and stands to walk across her bedroom. Her feet move slowly, purposefully, her progress further hampered by the plush carpet. She enters the bathroom and turns on the light, tentatively placing herself in front of the mirror. She casts her eyes downward and stands for a few seconds before forcing herself to bring her gaze toward her face. She stares at herself, trying not to wince at what she sees. That she has changed in the last five years would be an understatement; she barely recognizes herself now. Her eyes, which used to lure people in with their intensity, are now flat and dull. Her skin... she closes her eyes and thinks back to a day ten years ago when a man – one of many nameless, unimportant men who orbited her world – bounced a coin on her cheek to demonstrate how tight it was. That clarity and elasticity went with the arrival of the illness that has robbed her of so much. She is gaunt now, with furrowed lines that run downward, giving her a perpetually displeased expression. All that made her beautiful is gone.

The only thing of beauty that remains is her feet. Elena sees it as miraculous that her feet have been able to retain their refinement and grace even when everything else has deteriorated.

Switching off the light, she goes back to her bed and lies down. The soft mattress encompasses her aching body, and she yanks the blanket over her head. Closing her eyes, images of her life soon flash behind her lids as she drifts off to sleep.

The first to visit Elena's unconscious mind is her mother. Though she died long ago, she is there, accompanied by her constant companions: disapproval and fear. She stands in front of the crumbling edifice of their home, her mouth pursed as young Elena begs for permission to run off and play with her friends, a ragtag group who love traipsing through the woods and playing cops and robbers.

'No, absolutely not.'

'Please?!'

'I told you no. It's not your place to run wild, Elena. You are a thing of beauty, especially your feet. You must take care of them, and that does not entail running around like a little hooligan. Trust me, one day, your looks and feet will take care of you.'

Young Elena sighs. Ever since she can remember, her mother has deemed her 'special' because of her unique beauty. Elena finds it all tiresome. She just wants to play. But, as usual, she does as her mother says.

The image wavers, then flicks to another year, another Elena. By this time, they have moved from Estonia to London, a large city that she finds unsettling. In this dream, her desire to play has ended and her mother has discovered beauty pageants. She is being crowned Little Miss London City, a competition her mother has entered her in. She stands awkwardly as a man digs the crown into her head, the prongs scraping painfully against her scalp. The movement, combined with her heeled shoes, cause her to sway. She wants to snap at him, to throw barbs at his wrinkled prune-like face, but instead she swallows the churlish words and smiles. Her smile catches him unawares, and he backs off, tripping on the podium as he steps away.

In that moment, she realizes the power she has...

This realization naturally makes her rebel. The images swirl as an older Elena skips school, hangs out with inappropriate boys, and eventually leaves home to enjoy life. For a short period of time, she finds work that doesn't rely on her looks, but being a ticket inspector doesn't rely on anything besides punctuality. It isn't a particularly taxing job, nor does it pay well, but it does give her plenty of time off to go out with her friends.

'The event' happens on a breezy morning in September. The stations are teeming with peak-hour commuters, their bodies moving in unison from train to stairs and back again. Vivid autumn leaves rustle through the stations, carried in by the wind and transported onto the trains by unknowing passengers. It is one leaf that shapes what happens to her.

'It's the same shade,' a woman says as she picks up the leaf and holds it against Elena's hair.

Elena nods. 'Ticket please,' she says.

The woman hands her the ticket. 'Have you ever thought of modeling?' she asks.

'No,' Elena says. She's about to turn away to the next passenger when she feels a card being slid into her hand.

'If you do, call me.'

Elena's feet are sore when she gets home. She massages them, her fingers pressing down hard into the soft tissue. She's just finished the right foot when the card falls out of her pocket.

She picks it up and stares at it.

I can't do this job much longer.

She calls the number.

What follows is a whirlwind of activity. She has photographs taken, then goes to see clients. Before she knows it, she has handed in her notice as a ticket inspector and is working as a model.

Parties, lots of parties, lots of men. Men all over her, men wanting to capture her, possess her. All except for one, Robert, who proves so elusive, so confusing, that she is intrigued for years.

Within this revolving door of images, her mother resurfaces again, this time disappointed that Elena hasn't married and settled down like a proper woman. After all, isn't that the point of having good looks?

Her finger wags in front of Elena's face as it has done so many times before disappearing, and another face emerges – the photographer whose passion for her feet propelled her into stardom.

Elena sighs and shifts until she finally succumbs to a deep sleep.

The pain is the first thing she notices in the morning these days – that persistent ache which, over time, has insidiously transformed itself from occasional visitor to permanent resident. It creeps from one part of her body to another, sometimes bursting into small explosions along the way, always reliable in its unreliability.

For a second, her attention is distracted from the pain by the brilliance of the sun streaming through the curtains. In that moment, she has the slightest sensation of peace where everything subsides, even the pain, and she is left in the most basic form: a woman alone, greeting a new day.

Then reality takes over and she remembers that in a matter of months, weeks even, she will be no more. She has to be ready for that.

Janine, she needs Janine. She fumbles for her phone, which has magically moved from the floor to her bedside table. She plugs it into the charger and presses her PA's picture.

'It's a bit early for you, Elena.'

The sound of her PA's voice brings Elena comfort. She can feel the pressure inside of her head deflating.

'I couldn't sleep. Do we have any more shoes?'

A sigh.

'No... not any physical ones that you would approve of. But I have pictures of some you might be interested in. The designer is in Tallinn – his work is very exclusive, very niche, so I talked with him this morning...' She peters out.

'What? What's wrong?'

'If you want his shoes, you'll have to go there in person.'

'To Tallinn?' Elena asks, her voice saturating those two words with all the indignation a person of her caliber is entitled to. 'Absolutely not. I don't go to places like Tallinn, why can't he come to me?'

'I think he's agoraphobic or something... doesn't like to leave his studio,' Janine says, her voice muffled. Elena imagines her rummaging through that container of almonds that she always has on her desk, even though they both know that the nuts are a cover for the York Peppermint Patties that she has buried underneath.

'Hmm. Can you bring over the pictures? If they're good, perhaps we can meet in Paris. That's the least he can do. They better be spectacular for all this trouble... now, is there anything else? I don't have the luxury of time anymore, so it's imperative we get this done quickly.'

If this morbidity had been expressed by anyone else, there would have been an outpouring of condolences and pity. As it is Elena, Janine keeps her response to a minimum. In some ways, it is considered unthinkable by many that Elena will die. She is Elena, *the* force within the industry.

Within a few minutes, Janine is at Elena's vast apartment overlooking Central Park. She starts up the fancy espresso machine, making Elena the same soy latte she has had for years. She shuffles through a few documents that she has printed off and hands them to Elena along with the coffee. The papers consist of three designs by the enigmatic Jaak. The first is an elegant pump, its black velvety denseness contrasting with the red whimsical embroidery that darts in and out of the shoe's contours.

'Charming,' Elena says softly as she moves the paper aside to see the next one.

This one is a boot, the leather colored the distinctive reddish brown of a Stradivari violin. In keeping with the musical theme, bow-like strings twine their way up the leg, enclosing it while highlighting its sensuous shape.

Elena's mouth opens slightly as she gazes at this picture of pure seduction.

'Call him up. See if he can be in Paris by Friday.'

'Okay... but don't you want to look at the last one?' Janine asks.

Elena shakes her head. 'No, no need. This Jaak, he's gifted, anyone can see that. He has far more talent than all those other so-called designers combined.'

Janine pulls out her phone and dials Jaak's number.

'Hello, it's Janine. Yes, she loves them.' She begins pacing, her flat shoes treading heavily on the carpet. Elena glares disapprovingly at them; why does anyone wear such hideous shoes? There is no redeeming feature about them whatsoever.

'... yes, I told her. I'll talk to her again and call you back. Goodbye.'

Janine's brow is furrowed, a look that Elena knows all too well.

'What is it, what's wrong?'

'You'll have to go to Tallinn. He won't leave.'

Images flash before Elena's eyes. Tallinn, the land of her ancestors, the place where her grandparents had disappeared – translation: died – during the early days of the Communist regime. Elena's starving mother had sacrificed so much to escape that place for a better life for her baby daughter. She had remained embittered toward Tallinn her entire life. In fact, once Elena reached the high peaks of celebrity, she had made Elena promise that she would never go there – a promise Elena has kept for the entirety of her career, only to break it now.

She looks at the shoes again and sighs. She is too tired to deal with this. She just wants the damn shoes.

'Very well, book it. I hope for his sake that this is worth it.'

Two days later, Elena is flying to Tallinn, her heart leaden with the remnants of a broken promise. She can almost hear her mother's voice repeating her mantra over and over again: 'We will never return. Never. A place like that is full of evil, evil that can never be undone. We will never go back.'

Her mouth tastes of metal. She gags and sits up in the plush leather chair, pushing her cashmere wrap down. The flight has been arduous, but that is nothing new, everything feels arduous these days. She takes out a compact from her purse and looks at her face. It is still unsettling to see the haggard face before her.

'Seatbelt on, ma'am, we're just about to land.' The flight attendant's honeyed tones interrupt Elena's harsh analysis of herself. She snaps the compact shut and clicks the belt into place.

The plane lands and Elena disembarks, walking down the long corridor to customs. It is funny how customs always look the same, no matter the country. They are always so tiring. However, she is pleasantly surprised when people recognize her, so she plays it up and signs autographs for her admirers.

Janine has organized a driver to pick her up. He stands tall and young, a fresh suit smoothly encasing a muscular physique. As she walks toward him, he smiles.

If I was ten years younger... he wouldn't stand a chance, Elena thinks as she contemplates her past conquests.

'Elena, welcome to Tallinn. I am Aleksandr – I will be your driver while you're here,' he says as he picks up her luggage. She follows him to the car, momentarily blinded by the bright sun as they leave the airport building.

As they approach the car, one of those nondescript European cars that seem to be everywhere, Aleksandr stumbles and her luggage tumbles onto the pavement.

'Oh, my bags!' she cries. 'Please... they're one of a kind and can't get dirty.'

Aleksandr jumps up and retrieves her luggage. He piles it into the trunk of the car and opens her door. Elena steps in with sigh, her aching body immediately comforted by the soft leather seat.

'Would you like to go directly to your hotel?' Aleksandr asks.

'Yes please,' she replies. Her appointment with Jaak isn't until the following day, and she needs rest.

Aleksandr nods and turns on some new age music. Ordinarily, she would have hated the sound of it, but somehow, this time, it soothes her weary mind. She closes her eyes...

'We're here.' His voice breaks through her thoughts.

They are parked outside a stately building, its sandy yellow stone offset by a whipped cream trim. A plaque on the front proudly states that the building dates back to 1878. It is nice, but after so many years of travel and countless hotels, Elena's interest in them is non-existent. The only thing she cares about is comfort. After saying goodbye to Aleksandr, she checks in. Janine has booked her into the best room, a large suite on the top floor, which includes a personal tour from the manager. He twitters around uselessly for a few minutes, until she swiftly and decisively sees him on his way.

Alone at last, she orders room service. Staring out of the window while eating, she wonders what the next day will bring and whether her quest will finally be over.

Dreams plague her sleep. These aren't uncommon, but they are all the more frightening due to her seclusion. In one, a mob tears through her bedroom, screaming 'Get out! We don't want you here!' In another, she is drowning under the intense weight of luggage, with a face – Aleksandr's face, heavily distorted but still recognizable – leaning over her, his voice mocking as he repeats, 'You think they fell by accident?'

Her eyes snap open in the darkness, the remnants of the dream whirling around in her mind. She takes a ragged breath, her heart thudding painfully with every inhale. All around her is silence. It is unsettling – she is used to the sounds of New York City's perpetual traffic, the symphony of horns, the occasional screech of tires. But here, there is nothing.

Except the dream. She shuffles toward her luggage, worried now that Aleksandr did something devious to it. Had he orchestrated the whole incident just to steal from her? It would have been simple, she concedes, her attention had been elsewhere. But upon checking the bags, they all seem to be in order. She sits back, alarmed by the overwhelming fear and mistrust she has been feeling since her arrival. It is unnerving, something that she would ordinarily associate with her mother, not her.

She glances at the dainty watch that dangles from her ever-shrinking wrist and works out that it is seven-thirty in the morning. She smiles – she has plenty of time before her meeting with Jaak. Perhaps she can take a bath then do some sightseeing?

She fills the bath with hot water, the steam rising in delicate wisps in the cool air. Stepping into the colossal marble structure, her tiny frame is soon submerged, the smooth stone a soothing sensation on her skin. Relaxed for once, she closes her eyes.

Her mother is there. Elena can sense her disapproval, reaching for her, compressing her until she can no longer breathe. She knows what this is about – how could she not? She can almost hear her mother's voice, heavy with melancholy. 'Such memories I have of that place, Elena. It was hard there, for many of us. Your grandparents, God rest their souls, worked tirelessly to provide me with a good life. And then what? The moment they stopped to enjoy themselves, they were killed. For what? Something the state said they did? No, they were the victims of evil people. That is why I will never go back there. I don't care how beautiful its buildings are, how scenic its streets may be, it has brought me nothing but pain. Elena, you must promise me... promise you'll never go to Tallinn. Please? Promise your loving mother, who sacrificed so much for you, you'll never go there.'

And Elena, her young face frightened at the intensity her mother had shown, had promised. For decades, she had kept her promise. No matter how rebellious she had been feeling toward her mother, this had been the one thing she had done for her.

As the years passed, Elena asked her mother more about Tallinn and her family history. But Elena's mother remained tightlipped, saying only, 'Bad place, bad time,' and shaking her head mournfully.

But now, fifty years later, she is here in Tallinn breaking her word. From the moment she arrived, she has felt an incredible mix of guilt and fear weighing down on her like a weighted blanket. Perhaps it is time to free herself from this burden.

Slowly, she makes her way out of the tub and gets dressed. She begins brushing her hair, the bristles gently catching as she does so. She imagines the bristles are brushing away the cobwebs of her history, revealing something brighter, better.

The few impressions she'd had of Tallinn were negative – her mother painted it in a perpetually ominous light, a land of darkness and misery. But as Elena steps out of her hotel, she realizes that it's more than that.

She is greeted by a sight that's reminiscent of an illustration in her favorite book of fairytales. The book had been her constant companion when she was young. The pictures always stirred her imagination with their bright colors and beautiful buildings. The image she remembers most is a city – slim buildings of different hues and styles, their crooked lines crowding the cobblestoned streets – that she had always dreamed of visiting.

And here it is, in the flesh. Quaint buildings, their styles ranging from Medieval to Baroque and Rococo, charm the eye, their varying styles and colors never clashing, always complementing.

'How delightful!' She laughs as she spins around to appreciate the views. Her spin is short-lived when her four-inch heel catches on a cobblestone, but she quickly rights herself and struts onward with a lighter tread.

She begins her exploration on the main roads, then veers off down an enchanting lane. It is quiet, lacking the throngs of tourists that have started to invade the busier streets. She ducks her head as she passes some houses, their window boxes dripping with greenery and flowers. Soon enough, the lane comes to a dead end, and she sees a small restaurant on the corner.

It is a marked contrast to what she is used to. In New York, she wines and dines at only the most prestigious and urbane establishments. For someone who loves food, it is one of the pitfalls of fame, but it has been a necessary one. At least she can enjoy herself now.

She chooses a table in the shade of a small tree just as a waiter approaches.

'Can I please have a cappuccino and a slice of that,' she says, pointing to an intricate cake that is being handed to another customer.

'A kringle. Anything else?'

'No, thank you.'

He leaves and she takes a book out of her bag. It is one of those vacation books, heavy on page numbers but light on plot, so engrossing in its own way. She has just finished chapter thirteen when the waiter returns with her order. The delicate smell emanating from the cake makes her mouth water. She sips her coffee then takes a small bite of the cake. Bursts of cinnamon and raisins explode in her mouth, and she sighs happily. It has been weeks since she has eaten something so delectable.

She eats slowly, enjoying every morsel. Once she has finished both the coffee and cake, she glances at her watch.

'Ten forty-five! How is it so late?!' she groans. She throws her book into her bag and leaves a handful of euros on the table before rushing out. Away from the protected courtyard, the air feels hot and sticky while the sun beats down on her shoulders relentlessly.

'I know it's in here,' she mutters to herself as she rummages through her bag before triumphantly whipping out a black sun hat. The stylishly broad brim dips down, giving her a sense of mystique that she relishes.

She looks at her watch again. Eleven am. Oh Christ! Her appointment is at noon, and it would be disastrous if she was late. She plugs the address into her phone and begins walking in what she hopes is the right direction.

It is not the right direction, a fact she discovers only after she has gone several blocks in the wrong way. She taps her phone in frustration, turns around, and begins walking in the opposite direction. Finally, her movements line up with the blue arrow on her phone.

Supposedly, it's only a twenty-minute walk, which isn't too far... *is that a blister I feel?*

Her pace, which had been moderately fast, slows to a crawl. Blisters are the bane of her existence. They had bothered her when she was younger and couldn't afford expensive, well-made shoes, but now... she rarely suffers. There is a reason why she spends a fortune on her footwear. She glares at the offending boots – they are new, supposedly the best in comfort and style, or so the designer had said. He had assured her that blisters were a thing of the past with them. Clearly, he was wrong.

The blister is causing a great deal of discomfort by the time she minces her way to her destination – a small, elegantly appointed building, its façade painted a lapis blue, a J and V delicately intertwined on a lead-glass transom window that hovers above the door.

It is one minute past midday when she reaches for the brass knocker, a whimsical peacock with a stone-studded tail, and lets it fall against the door. She waits as the sound echoes before reaching for it once more. Before she can let it clang again, a woman steps into view and points toward a sign that Elena has missed. Elena peers at it, her eyes squinting as she tries to decipher the words without the assistance of her reading glasses. After several seconds squinting at it, she realizes the glasses wouldn't have helped as the sign is written in Estonian rather than English.

Elena glances up, hoping to catch the woman's eye, but she has disappeared. A shot of panic spreads through her; has she missed her appointment? Are they closed?

'No, no,' she says, grabbing hold of the knocker in a moment of desperation. She drops it against the door and waits until she hears the sound of footsteps.

The woman is back. This time she opens the door.

She speaks for a second in Estonian before noticing Elena's look of confusion, then switches to English.

'Yes? We are closed for lunch, unless you have a private appointment.'

'Yes, I'm sorry. I'm a little late. I have a 12 o'clock appointment with Jaak.'

The woman smiles. 'Ah yes, you are American lady? The one who needs a special shoe?'

Elena nods, and the woman gestures to her to come inside. 'Am I too late? Is Jaak still here?'

The woman laughs. 'No, you are fine. Jaak's here, but then he's always here. He never leaves.'

'Thank you...' Elena pauses.

'Sofia, I'm Sofia. His right-hand man, so to speak... isn't that right, darling?' she says to a man who has silently appeared behind Elena.

'Yes,' he says, his tone perfunctory.

This can only be Jaak. Elena turns to him, her body unconsciously changing to a more provocative pose, and says, 'Well, I'm very happy to meet you.' With those few words, her voice takes on a sultry tone, the one she has used for decades to seduce thousands of men. 'Your shoes are absolutely incredible. I've spent the last couple of years looking for something truly unique, and up till now, I haven't found a thing. Then I saw yours... I really believe you can create the shoes that I need.'

He takes one step closer to the door, the beveled glass transforming his body into a convoluted jumble of angles and lines so that he resembles a cubist painting brought to life.

'You understand the price for my commissions is very high,' he says. 'It takes time, and I only use the best materials.'

'Money is of no concern to me. I'm prepared to pay whatever it takes to have the most amazing shoes.'

He inclines his head. 'Would you like to follow me into my studio?'

They move from the foyer into the showroom. It is a well-lit room, the sunlight beaming on the blonde wooden floorboards that run the length of it. Dotted throughout the room are a dozen white boxes that hold single shoes. These creations are glorious, their ingenuity evident in every line, every stitch.

'You like?' Sofia asks.

'I love. I've never seen shoes like his before, and I've seen a lot.'

Sofia nods. 'Yes, he's a genius. I'm lucky to be here, it's such a privilege to work here and see how he thinks. So, your assistant said you are very well known in America?'

Elena waves her hand languidly. 'Yes, I've done some modeling and acting... but to be around this, well, it makes all that seem rather insignificant.'

One of Sofia's eyebrows lifts delicately. 'I know what you mean. People like Jaak are so rare. They can take the simplest of materials and use them to make something extraordinary. Jaak's shoes are pure art.' Sofia gazes appreciatively at a pair of stilettos carved entirely of wood.

Elena looks at Sofia, assessing her. She sees herself in Sofia, which is comforting. 'So, where does that leave you?'

Sofia smiles. 'In the learning process. And what can be better than learning from the best? Perhaps one day I'll make something worthwhile but, for now, I learn.'

They approach a set of carved wooden doors.

'And now we enter the inner sanctum,' Sofia says as she pushes the doors open.

It is chaotic. Shoes, finished and unfinished, are scattered all over. Ribbons of fabric snake their way across workbenches, their tendrils waving with every small gust of wind that blows in through an open window. A bird, its feathers as bright as the objects surrounding it, squawks and flutters its wings as it moves from one part of a large, gilded cage to another. Sketches are strewn across the floor. Elena bends down to pick one up, a pump covered with the vaguest of checkerboards, the white queen composing the heel. She gestures toward it. 'Where's this one? It looks fascinating.'

'Ah, that one. It's still up here...' Jaak points to his head. 'I never resolved some of the issues that I had with it. Sofia, can you bring us some tea?' He guides Elena to a chair and sits down opposite.

'Well, I think it's time we talked about what you're here for,' he says.

She nods slowly. 'I need to have the most wonderful shoes in the world, and I need them quickly, because... I'm dying. My doctors say I only have about six months left, which is probably generous... it's not that I want to die, I'm just worn out. But, if I'm going to die, I'd like to go in style and have the most glorious pair of shoes to celebrate my feet, since they're what made me famous. But I need something that will last an eternity. Let me show you a picture of my coffin so you can understand what I mean.'

She pulls a document from her purse and hands it to him. He looks it over thoughtfully for several minutes before speaking.

'It will be above ground, then?'

'Yes, and it'll be temperature controlled. I will, of course, be embalmed, and the glass will ensure that your shoes and my feet will be on display for years to come.'

He nods. 'Can I see your feet now?'

She slowly unzips the dainty boots that encapsulate her feet. Removing the special cashmere and copper-threaded socks she'd had made especially for her, she stretches out her feet, the sunlight highlighting every inch of them.

She watches his face as he looks at them. She has seen every emotion before when unveiling her feet – lust, appreciation, covetousness, but on Jaak's face, is an expression of complete joy, so much so that she smiles too.

'They are truly magnificent,' he whispers.

She smiles wryly. 'Which is why they're insured for twenty million dollars.'

Jaak's left eyebrow goes up and he whistles in shock. 'That much!'

'Yes, well they've done nothing but improve my life, so it was the least I could do. Without them, I don't know what I would have done.'

'I understand. Now, if you'll allow me to touch them, I'll take some measurements, so I know what I have to work with. Then we can talk about what you have in mind.'

She nods, and he begins measuring the length and width of her toes, the height of her arch, and the circumference of her ankles. As he measures, he takes notes in a small leather notebook.

Elena remains quiet as he works, enjoying the feel of fingers that move so delicately on her feet. When he puts his notebook down on the ottoman and moves back into his chair, a sigh escapes her mouth.

'I really don't have anything specific in mind,' she says. 'I just want it to be something spectacular that's never been made before... something that will show off my feet to their best advantage. I've been looking for so long... I can probably tell you more about what I don't want than what I do want.'

Jaak nods. 'Alright then, why don't you tell me what you don't want.'

'I don't want someone's interpretation of what a shoe is... I've had too many strange pieces that resemble table centerpieces rather than footwear. And the hideous promotional samples I've been sent, I don't want anything like those either.'

'And is there anything in particular that you like? In terms of material or themes?'

'I've always been drawn to the fantasy world, which is one of the reasons why I was so compelled by your pieces. In fact, I've been so impressed with your work that I'd like you to make these shoes as a surprise for me.'

From his facial expression, she can tell he wasn't expecting that.

'That's quite unusual... are you sure?'

She nods. 'Absolutely. I have a good feeling about you.'

'But what if I disappoint you like all the others?' he asks.

She looks at him. It is a good question. She studies him so intently that it seems that he wants to look away but can't.

'You won't,' she says simply. 'So, let's talk about money and a timeline. How much and how long?'

'Well, usually it takes me six months or longer to create something, but given your circumstances, I'll try to do it in four. Do you think you'll be around for that long?'

She nods. 'I've been fighting this disease for so long... I'm sure another four months won't kill me. Unlike your commission price... which is?'

'Why don't we say sixty thousand euros? At that price, I can work exclusively on your shoes.'

'Done,' she says. They shake hands and he takes a mold of her foot and calf before she prepares to depart.

'I'll see you again in four months' time,' he says while escorting her out of the studio and into the showroom.

As she leaves the building, a feeling of serenity infuses her body. She knows this is the right decision. Jaak will ensure her vision is realized.

Returning to her hotel room, she changes into wedges and begins exploring Tallinn. She walks down to Town Hall Square and admires the Gothic town hall before stopping at a florist's stall to purchase a large bouquet of cornflowers. Thinking of Janine, she stops at a tourist shop that specializes in handcrafted soaps, an obsession of Janine's. Elena never understood it – why use a clunky piece of soap when you can use the finest octuple-milled French soap that Elena has shipped in from a little-known monastery in the south of France? After smelling several bars, she purchases Janine a set that includes lavender, rose, and vanilla. Leaving the store, she stops at a few churches then makes her way up to Toompea to see the castle. However, by the time she arrives she is utterly exhausted, so she settles on a park bench instead and closes her eyes. It is so peaceful, a tiny sliver of her wants to stay instead of going back to New York. But she knows that her return is inevitable.

She loses track of time. When she opens her eyes, it is dark. She trudges back to the hotel, orders room service, and turns on the bedroom TV. There's nothing interesting on, just a few soap operas, so she takes a bath before slipping into the soft embrace of the bed.

Unlike hundreds of nights before, sleep comes instantly.

Elena's alarm goes off at five-fifteen the next morning. She groans as she stretches and begins packing her belongings. Her flight back home is scheduled to depart at ten, and Elena, always the punctual one, is determined to be at the airport by six forty-five. She gazes out the window after showering and is disheartened to see rain pelting down against the panes. The drive back to the airport takes significantly longer because of the weather, and it is six-fifty when she approaches the check-in counter.

'Where are you going?' the woman behind the counter asks.

'New York,' she replies, digging her ticket and passport out of her handbag.

'Hmm, I believe your plane is going to be delayed.'

She doesn't go into further detail, and Elena is too frazzled to ask for clarification. She's on edge without Janine. There isn't a single problem Janine can't fix. Without her, Elena is lost, and everything seems more complicated. She goes to the lounge and drops into a chair, looking at the screen. The woman was right – her plane has been delayed. Elena wastes time flicking through magazines, then consumes several coffees and a small sandwich. Once she has finished the last bite, she stands, ready to leave... only for the flight to be delayed again. She sighs heavily and reaches for the book she had been reading earlier. At this rate, she's on course to finish it.

The flight is delayed for two more hours. By this time, Elena is torn between thoughts of staying in Tallinn and worry that these delays are part of her mother's retribution.

When the plane finally arrives, she dismisses her fears. Surely her mother would understand why she had to return – why she had to break her promise.

She boards the plane and settles in for a peaceful flight.

They take off, Elena wrapped snugly in her travel blanket, her body and mind

ready for respite.

It starts subtly, a gentle rocking that lulls her into a feeling of safety. She's slowly drifting to sleep when the rocking intensifies and transforms into erratic jolts. Her eyes dart open to see the flight attendants rushing to their seats.

'Ladies and gentlemen, this is your captain speaking. We are currently experiencing some turbulence, so please stay in your seats with your seatbelts securely fastened.'

It's her mother. She wants Elena to die. More importantly, she wants Elena to die before she fulfills her legacy.

They try to rise above the jet streams, but the turbulence increases, its effects brutal. Never the best flyer even in good conditions, Elena grimaces with every shake and shudder of the plane. This goes on for hours. At times, the plane settles, only to seize up again. They're in the middle of the Atlantic Ocean when the plane lunges downward suddenly, causing several people to scream and everyone to clutch their armrests.

That's it, I'm going to die... Oh God, please don't let me die, she thinks, recognizing the irony of a dying woman worrying about her mortality.

Somehow, miraculously, the plane manages to right itself, and the flight ends uneventfully. For most passengers, the turbulence will soon be long forgotten after the story has been shared a few times; for Elena, it's a reminder of how little time she has left.

It's late when they land, and the lights of New York stream across her face in a welcoming glow. By the time she arrives home, she's exhausted. She can't remember being this tired before, not even when she had been awake for 32 hours in Italy for a commercial shoot.

Once she falls asleep, she sleeps for two days uninterrupted. On the third morning, Janine stops by her apartment with supplies.

'You okay? You don't look okay,' she says after Elena opens the door.

'Just tired.' She yawns. 'The trip was more tiring than I expected.' She turns around and picks up a box. 'Here, this is for you.'

Janine opens it and removes the soaps from their tray. She sniffs them appreciatively. 'Thank you. I do get tired of smelling your super-exclusive soap. I don't know why you keep buying that stuff.'

Elena laughs. That's one of the best things about Janine – she doesn't take Elena too seriously.

Once Janine leaves, Elena wanders from room to room, a sense of listlessness threatening to overpower her. She knows what's happening – her body is saying 'Your search is over, now what?' And she has nothing.

She tries to combat this emptiness by filling her days with pointless activities – daily trips to her favorite smoothie store, several appearances at charity events, and appointment after appointment.

Interspersed with these exercises, she calls Jaak. Contrary to her inertia, he has been working all hours of the day to create prototypes.

'Would you like to see them?' he asks one day, three months after her visit.

'No, no... I trust you. How much longer do you think?' she asks.

'Well, I'm waiting for a few materials, so maybe three or four weeks. We are so close... I can feel it.'

'Good, good,' she says before hanging up the phone.

That night, she dreams of her mother again.

'Why did you break your promise, Elena?'

'I didn't, not really. I was only there for a day... I had to go, there was no other way...' The pleading tone in Elena's voice takes her by surprise.

'You still went. A broken promise is a broken promise. You can't change that fact, no matter how hard you try.'

'But momma, I had to do it...'

Elena wakes early to air that is fraught with her mother's disappointment. She tries to justify her actions, tries to suppress the feelings of guilt, but her mother spent a lifetime teaching her the value of a good guilt trip. It was, in fact, the one thing her mother had truly excelled at.

Time passes and the guilt eats away at her as intensely as the cancer. As October moves to November, the sleet commences, drenching the city in a barrage of icy precipitation. The sky is perpetually gray, and moods plummet as drastically as thermometers. Then the sleet stops, bringing an unnatural quiet that muffles the usual city sounds. Amidst this silence is a feeling of anticipation, which is soon realized when the first snowflake falls, followed promptly by another, until the city resembles a snow globe with thousands of flakes swirling down to the ground.

The day the flakes arrive, Janine wipes her boots on the mat before entering Elena's apartment. She is late, thanks to her car, which decided not to start that morning.

'Hello?' she calls out. It is toasty in the apartment, always a mild 70 degrees, which makes a nice contrast to the weather outside. She walks to Elena's room and knocks on the door. Hearing no answer, she quietly opens it to find Elena still in bed. She walks closer, noticing that Elena's fingers are reaching toward her bedside table, where the portrait of her mother rests.

Janine touches a finger. It is icy cold. There's nothing to be done.

'Well, you're at peace now,' she says, patting the hand gently. 'Your mother can't haunt you anymore.'

She pulls out her phone and calls Jaak.

'About those shoes...'

'They're almost ready, I told her last night.'

'She's dead.'

'What? But that's impossible... I just spoke with her last night...'

'I'm with her now. She's dead.'

'But she didn't see the shoes, she must see the shoes... she would have loved them,' he groans.

'Right... well, we still need them for the funeral. When are you free to come?'

'But I've never left my apartment, let alone the country,' he splutters.

'You're doing it.' Janine's tone implies it's best to do what he's told. 'I'll book your tickets, first class of course.'

Once she hangs up on Jaak, Janine makes a few more calls, then sits down to keep Elena company until the necessary people come. There is little else to do; Elena purchased the all-inclusive, premium funerary package, which means that the directors handle everything.

Elena's funeral is scheduled to take place on a Saturday. Jaak arrives on Friday, full of laments and palpitations, his judgments on New York's shoe style flowing freely.

'Honestly, don't they want to wear something that's remotely attractive?' he asks, eyes fixed on a pair of generic rain boots splashing through a muddy puddle.

Janine, who always wears sensible shoes like New Balance or boots like Sorels, shakes her head and rolls her eyes.

'Can I see them?' she asks Jaak.

He looks coy for a second before shaking his head. 'Sorry, Elena was the only person who could see them before the ceremony. That was our arrangement. But you'll see them soon enough.'

On Saturday morning, Janine wakes early. Her body rebels against being up before nine am on a weekend, but then she opens her window to a perfectly clear blue sky.

New York's elite are at the funeral, ready to be seen and judged by each other. Whispers abound as everyone speculates on the famous shoes; everyone knows a tidbit about them, but no one knows everything.

The speeches are short, and everyone waits impatiently for the most important moment to arrive – the coffin's grand unveiling.

Elena's oldest love, Robert, accompanies Jaak down the path to the coffin. In true Elena fashion, where things aren't what they seem, it is Robert, in his 80s, who is propping Jaak up as he walks toward the coffin.

Jaak steps up to the platform and stares down. The coffin was made specially for Elena, just so that her whole body could be admired and preserved.

And there they are.

Her beautiful feet, in all their glory.

His breath catches as he stares at them.

And the shoes.

Silky golden threads twine their way around her feet, so naturally, so delicately, that it makes it seem like her feet have been embraced by rays of sunlight. And there lies the genius of the design, for the light infuses her feet with life, and the shoes' simple beauty enhances the beauty of her feet.

They are the perfect shoes.

His heart jumps for joy and, for a second, he swears that when he looks at Elena, he sees her mouth curve into a smile before staring down at the shoes with an appreciative gleam in her eyes.

2

Battle of the Charles Bridge

Night is descending slowly on the Charles Bridge in Prague. Lamplights dotting the length of the bridge cast their shimmery golden rays onto the flowing Vltava River below. The tourists, who have been walking all over the city this mild September day, debate whether their feet can last a few more hours so they can tell everyone back home that they have 'done Prague... a nice city, but far too many tourists.'

A man sits on the bridge, his chair warped and uncomfortable from years of exposure to the elements. He watches these tourists intensely, his targets, wondering which music will make them loosen their purse strings. A touch of home? Or something so brilliant that their awe manifests itself as payment? His hand drapes over the well-worn bow nestled in his lap as he tries to gauge them, but it's hard work when he's already on edge.

'You alright?' asks Caroline, the Australian artist whose highly detailed cityscapes draw in the tourists. 'You seem to be very tense these days.'

He glowers. He knows things have changed drastically. Before, he had been renowned not only for his love of music but also for his generosity and easy-going nature. But he'd had so much back then – a future to contemplate, a faith in humanity. It is only within the last couple of months that everything has fallen apart, mostly due to his nemesis. Yes, it is true – he, Marick, the finest cellist of Charles Bridge, has a nemesis.

***

June

Though it is only noon, it is steaming outside. The sun has been playing hide-and-seek with the clouds all morning, but now it beams down with the brilliance and intensity of a dentist's LED light. Marick can feel the wetness under his arms as he sets up his spot. Eyebrows furrowed; he opens his cello case. Hopefully, the humidity has not wreaked havoc on his beloved instrument.

He smiles at a tourist walking by, then raises his bow in greeting to that nice Australian girl who is preparing her displays.

Today is going to be a good day.

Marick does a series of scales, his fingers moving with certainty and precision, only stopping sporadically to tune the instrument. Once he has completed his preparations, he begins playing Boccherini's 'Cello Concerto in G,' a merry tune that twirls and dances through the air, enticing tourists and others to draw closer. Marick smiles and closes his eyes, waiting for that inevitable moment when his body transcends reality and melds with the music. He's never really understood this phenomenon, but as it has happened to him since his first music lesson at the age of three, he has learned to accept it. However, he has learned through painful experience not to share these events with others – the few he has deigned to tell looked at him afterwards with a skeptical eye. The last thing he wants is to be viewed as an oddball.

He follows the wave of music, his fingers flying until they reach the crescendo then come back down to the finale.

His trance is broken by the sound of clapping. Opening his eyes, he is heartened to see a crowd of people standing in front of him, their faces lit with an appreciation for his music. He smiles and bows, waving his bow around with a grand flourish.

He goes through a quarter of his repertoire before breaking for lunch. He walks to his favorite street vendor and buys several grilovane klobasy with sauerkraut, which he eats enthusiastically before wiping his hands clean. The heat has intensified, so he seeks shade, even the scantest, alongside buildings. Thankfully, he doesn't have far to go and, before long, he is back, drinking his carbonated water and looking around at the others. The number of tourists has dwindled dramatically. Marick imagines they are tucked away in air-conditioned museums and hotels, waiting for the heat to abate.

He has just finished tuning his instrument when he hears a sound. It is not any old noise... no, this is the sound of sublimity. He pauses, listening in raptured silence to the music coming from another cello. Marick puts down his bow in appreciation for this angelic music, the quality of which he has admittedly, never heard coming from his own instrument.

When the music stops, Marick is left bereft. And curious.

He gets up and inspects his side of the bridge immediately, trying to discover the mysterious cellist who played so beautifully.

Five stalls down, he finds him.

The sign in front of the cello case simply reads, 'Kazamir: cello.' It rests near a tower of twenty CDs, their bright covers vivid against the black instrument case.

The man sitting behind these is young. His eyes stare directly at Marick, their aqua blue contrasting with his olive skin tone. Wisps of curly hair spiral out of a knitted hat, making him appear younger than he undoubtedly is.

'Yes?' he says as the silence drags on.

Marick jerks his head. 'Sorry, head-in-the-clouds moment. I'm Marick,' he says, stretching out his hand.

The man nods and gestures toward the sign. 'Kazamir.'

'I heard your toccata, it was beautiful.'

Kazamir inclines his head. 'Thank you. It is rare to meet a man who knows his music. It is a beautiful piece, a bit simple, but it was my warmup, so I didn't want to exert myself too much.' He stops abruptly and looks at Marick as if waiting for him to say something else.

'How long have you played?' Marick asks, his curiosity getting the better of him. Deep down, he has a nagging feeling that he does not want to know the answer to this question.

If Kazamir is surprised by the question, he doesn't show it. 'A few years,' he says. 'It's something I picked up when I grew bored with the piano. Not sure how long I'll stick with it though. I like trying new things.'

Marick's jaw drops in shock. To hear the cello being referred to so nonchalantly is unnatural. From the tender age of three, he has had the utmost respect for the instrument. True, he had wanted a truck rather than a cello, and true, his first memories of using it involved his parents slapping his fingers every time he made a mistake, but that's beside the point. What his parents had known – and what he understands now, years later – is that the truck was temporary, a fleeting diversion. A cello, especially when played correctly, is forever. Eventually, those lessons had paid off. He had been hailed as the new child prodigy when he was twelve and, several years later, he had been given a place at the prestigious Academy of Performing Arts in Prague.

Kazamir's voice interrupts Marick's trip down memory lane before it veers into more depressing avenues.

'How come you know Frescobaldi?'

'I play.'

'You play what?'

'Cello,' Marick says, his voice infusing the word with all the due deference that it deserves.

'Oh yeah, you good?'

'I've been playing for twenty-four years, and I studied with the best teachers in Prague.'

Kazamir shrugs. 'Well, you probably think you're pretty good then. That's fine. You can be good. I'll be the best, and we'll make some wonderful music on this bridge. And money too.'

'Right, okay...' Marick furrows his brow, wondering how the conversation has moved in this direction. 'I should get back to my spot.'

Marick walks back, putting thoughts to his confusion. He has been on this bridge for several years, ever since his father's passing and his mother became sick and needed someone to care for her. When the doctor had given them the diagnosis, Marick had heard a death knell for his career. In a matter of days, he had given up his place within the Orchestral Academy in the Czech Philharmonic, the hardest decision he had ever made in his life. His mother's disdain for strangers made hiring a nurse impossible, so he was left to care for her during the day. His savings only lasted so long before he had to earn again, and so he became a busker. At first, he only did it at night while his mother slept, but once she died, he started doing it full time. With no partner and few close friends, playing the cello has saved him. It has given his life meaning and companionship through the camaraderie among his fellow buskers; in some regards, they are his support system.

Not that he wants to be a busker for long. Marick has dreams. Aspirations. He wants to be a professional musician – it is only a matter of time before his extraordinary talent is rediscovered and his real career begins once more. After all, Marick is still brilliant, one of Prague's best cellists.

However, until that moment occurs, he is here, the messiah of the Charles Bridge, bringing music, proper music, to the masses. In that regard, he sees himself as a generous revolutionary.

As he sits and begins playing, all thoughts of Kazamir flee his mind. His body, his mind, everything, fixates on the music.

Tourists come and listen, their hands dipping into wallets and purses, ready to free the notes and coins that had been held hostage for so long. Day fades into night and peace descends over the bridge.

The difficulties begin the following week.

That Monday is terrible. Not only is the weather overcast and dreary, but the Czech Republic football team has been beaten, yet again, by Brazil in a World Cup match. It was a brutal comedown for a team that had once been thought of as potential Cup winners. As Marick strides to the bridge, he can't help but feel like the overriding sentiment on the street is one of general discontent and gloom.

His own feelings soon match these when he approaches his spot, a part of the bridge that he has occupied for four years and discovers that he has an intruder. Kazamir.

'Hey, what are you doing here?' Marick asks.

Kazamir shrugs. 'You get more tourists on this side of the bridge, so I moved.'

'This is my spot, you'll have to find another,' Marick says, his tone casual apart from the slightest tinge of annoyance that creeps through.

'Hmm, now what is that phrase? First come, first serve... yes, that's right. So, I believe you will have to find a new place, my friend. After all, we are just the entertainers of this fine bridge, not the owners. Now if you'll excuse me, I have music to make.'

Marick seethes. All past appreciation for Kazamir slips away, and he is left with a rage he has not felt since his father's death.

If he thinks I'm going to let him get away with this, he is crazy. He will never take my site again, even if I must sleep here overnight.

He turns around and stalks off, taking a spot further down the bridge. He unpacks his instrument and sits, trying to dismiss the aura of negativity. After a minute of meditation, he tunes his cello and begins playing.

By the end of the song, he has gone from smiling to frowning. Something is off. Although he played well, brilliantly, in fact, there was something amiss. It had all the intensity and passion that his audience expects, but it lacked soul. There wasn't one second during the performance when he had become one with the music, and there definitely had not been a moment of transcendence. This realization leaves Marick sick and inflamed. What if it never returns? What will he do if it is gone forever? He scowls. This is Kazamir's fault. He has only been on the bridge for a matter of seconds and already he is threatening Marick's craft with his shenanigans. The sheer audacity of the man! That he plays well is not in doubt, but besides talent, what else does Kazamir have?

Marick keeps playing, trying desperately to retrieve what has been lost, but to no avail. His connection to the music is gone, severed... at least for this night. He packs up, puts his understandable but lamentably low earnings in his wallet, and creeps away, his departure witnessed by none. Marick shakes his head, the sound of his footsteps muffled by the mocking tune of Kazamir's cello.

A determined Marick rises the next morning, his alarm clock going off right as the sun begins its ascent. Marick, not a morning person, grumbles as he slams his fist on the noxious device.

The grumblings continue as he makes his way to the bridge, however, they lessen when he realizes that Kazamir is nowhere in sight.

Happily, he sets up his chair and begins working.

Unhappily, it turns out that Kazamir isn't far behind.

Five minutes later, he arrives and begins setting up, just diagonally from Marick. He smirks as he tips his hat.

Marick can't believe this isn't personal. This isn't the type of behavior one associates with the buskers on the Charles Bridge. Yes, there is rivalry, but it has always been congenial. This is downright nasty and confirms one thing – Kazamir must go.

As June moves into July, relations between Kazamir and Marick worsen. At first, their argument centers on location – Kazamir wants Marick's spot, which Marick refuses to give up. This means that, on occasion, Marick sleeps on the bridge just to ensure that Kazamir doesn't steal his spot. Then, there is the issue with volume. Kazamir, his chair positioned diagonally from Marick, plays the loudest, most obnoxious cello piece right when Marick is about to play a soothing, melodious one.

With every grievance, Marick feels his anger rising. Outwardly, he attempts diplomacy. He has tried speaking with Kazamir multiple times, but the man shuts him down, he has made adjustments to his program... but nothing has worked.

Then, Marick begins to suspect Kazamir of something worse – sabotage. Strange things begin happening to him. One of his newly purchased Larsen cello strings breaks under the most minuscule pressure. Marick examines the destroyed string with his flashlight only to see the markings of a cut. This incident is promptly followed by another – his chair goes missing during his lunch break, only to be found several hours later by a tourist. Finally, and most disturbing of all, is the occasion when he opens his case and finds dog excrement within. Not only does the smell deter tourists, but it also takes days to get the smell completely out of his case.

No, Kazamir isn't just a competitor, he is trying to destroy Marick and take over the Charles Bridge. But Marick refuses to give in, so he fights back in his own way. Pranks and sabotage are beneath him, so he ups his game and plays better and better, choosing songs that accentuate his brilliance.

The first night of this strategy ends triumphantly for him. He fights for the attention of every single tourist, their mouths gaping with astonishment at his skill. Euros rain down into his case, the notes creating a colorful rainbow and the coins' metallic clanking a symphony inside Marick's head.

That night, unfortunately, was an anomaly, and Kazamir soon prevailed. He brought new tools to the battle, namely an overwhelming repertoire full of classic favorites and pop hits. Night after night, he plays popular tunes, and the tourists, lured by sentimentality and oblivious to the simplicity of the pieces, flock over to him, eyes welling and mouths open, ready to sing along.

In Marick's eyes, there is nothing worse than a singalong. Why on Earth would anyone want to hear the sounds of a dozen reedy voices when you can listen to a professional performance? It is beyond belief. But sadly, the tourists do, and they love Kazamir for catering to their desires.

Marick knows he isn't alone in his despair. Some of the buskers, used to the tranquility that Marick's performance brought, have moved elsewhere. Others have quit altogether.

***

September

Tonight, Marick is going to finish this once and for all. He wants Kazamir gone, he wants life on the bridge to revert to the way it was.

That is why he challenged Kazamir to a duel.

It had been simple, really.

That morning, he had made Kazamir an offer he couldn't refuse – the chance to prove once and for all who the best cellist is. The prize is the Charles Bridge.

The loser can never busk on the bridge again.

He had appealed to Kazamir's pride, and it had worked perfectly.

The rules are simple. Both contestants must play three songs – the first will be a duet, Vivaldi's 'Concerto for two cellos,' then each person will have the opportunity to play two pieces to showcase their talent.

The bridge's buskers and tourists will be their judges. Whoever gets the most applause and money by the end of the night wins.

The duel is scheduled to start at eight in the evening. At seven forty-five, Kazamir and Marick are standing next to each other, the tension between them palpable. Marick glares at Kazamir and Kazamir glares back, his curly hair swooping down boyishly over one eye.

Marick hates that piece of hair – he has dreamed of hacking it off, mostly because his own hair decided to abandon him long ago.

They sit. At least Marick does; Kazamir squats, but somehow misses his chair and falls flat on his back. Marick's face maintains a neutral expression, but inwardly he's chuckling. Kazamir hurriedly rights himself and sends a scathing look toward Marick, who takes it all in his stride. Marick tunes his instrument. Kazamir tunes his. The tourists settle in, half in front of Marick, half in front of Kazamir.

The opening notes sound and the cellos begin their intricate weaving. The music dips, its tone thunderous, then rises. Marick closes his eyes, his fingers moving with a fierceness that he has never known before. As his bow flies, he feels the music claiming his body, and soon he is weightless, consumed by the notes and rhythm.

A sharp pain in his foot releases him from his trance. He opens his eyes and looks down to see a small hole in his shoe. As if that isn't bad enough, a trickle of blood streams from the shoe onto the pavement. He looks at Kazamir, then gazes down at Kazamir's cello spike, which has a smear of red near the bottom.

'What the... YOU STABBED ME?!' he shouts, lashing out at Kazamir with his bow. The tip hits Kazamir in the eye and Kazamir falls back, landing on his cello. Under his weight, the cello splinters, and Kazamir jumps up and launches himself at Marick. Marick steps back awkwardly, his foot now gushing blood, and feels the balustrade against his back. He tries to duck, but Kazamir comes at him with such force that they both go over the bridge.

'NOOOOOO!' They scream as their bodies move with speed toward the opaque midnight-blue waters below.

As he falls, Marick's fingers begin playing his favorite piece, which he had been going to perform that night – Bach's 'Concerto in D minor, BWV 974'. He sighs, disgruntled. He knows he would have won with that piece.

He glances at Kazamir, who is glaring at him. *What a prat, if he'd just stayed in his spot on the bridge, none of this would have happened. Greedy, that's what Kazamir is.*

A few minutes before they had fallen, a cruise ship had been making its way toward the bridge.

Sonia, a tourist from Australia, is ecstatic. After months of none-too-subtle hints, her boyfriend of four years has finally proposed. She gazes down at her engagement ring, the lamplights from the bridge making the fire within the diamond dance and sparkle. By her estimate, it is a bloody good diamond... she hadn't seen any minute inclusions when she had looked at it earlier. Thank God she brought her jeweler's loupe on this trip!

She stands there, lost in admiration, completely oblivious to her surroundings... particularly the two bodies that are heading straight for her.

The tourists from the bridge go through a torrent of emotions as the night progresses. Happy at first to witness such phenomenal performances, their contentedness slips away when the first bout of violence breaks out. Their dismay transforms into horror as the musicians fall from the bridge and land on a petite woman on board the ship, the three collapsing like dominoes.

'Oh, my lord, call the police, call the ambulance!' one woman screams. There's silence within the flurry of activity as people switch from video to phone mode to make the necessary calls.

Later, once the two men have been taken away and Sonia has been treated for shock, the tourists disappear into the night, leaving the buskers and artists on the bridge. They all stare at each other – mimes, caricature artists, painters, musicians – and take a deep breath. Then, one by one, they remove the earplugs they had been wearing for the last three months and enjoy the beautiful sound of silence.

3

All is Rotten in 'The Garden of Earthly Delights'

The Man

'Bless me, Father, for I have sinned. It has been... thir... three years since my last confession. During that time, I have lied and cheated my way up the corporate ladder.'

'Do you feel remorse for your actions, my son?' the priest asked, his low voice resonating in the delicately carved wooden confessional, the pious tone perfectly pitched after decades of guiding lost souls.

The pause lengthened as the sinner debated whether lying to a priest was something he would regret later.

'Yes, yes, I feel remorse,' he stated, convincing neither himself nor the priest. 'What do I have to do to fix this?'

'Ten "Our Fathers" and a "Hail Mary" each day,' the priest declared, a note of exasperation barely disguised in his voice.

The man smiled briefly, a sense of happiness that this was going to be far, far easier than even he had anticipated. Nothing like an imaginary solution to a non-existent problem.

His mind preoccupied, he left the confessional and the church, walking along the Gran Via through the Plaza de España, stopping to look at the Cervantes memorial. He never understood the love for Cervantes; not only was Don Quixote painfully long and tedious, but the main protagonist was an annoying character. Who the hell wanted to be a dreamer like Quixote when you could be successful?

***

The Priest

After the man left, the priest sighed and rubbed his neck. He hated confessions like those – the complete insincerity of it all drove him crazy. It was clear that the man had no remorse whatsoever. It was an indulgent waste, pure and simple: waste of time, waste of energy, waste, waste, waste.

Fortunately, the man was quickly replaced by a more repentant man who actually cared about his immortal soul. The moment the man entered the confessional, he began sobbing quietly, distressed that, yet again, he had fallen off the wagon and had succumbed to his worst nature.

The priest looked up and silently thanked God for giving him this lost soul. These were the troubled people that the priest lived for. These were the ones who needed him, needed the church.

A week later, the man returned. The priest could tell it was him by the smell... a cloud of expensive cologne permeated the confessional, its woodiness filtering through the screen and climbing up his nose. He coughed. Then he sighed and ran his hand over an intricately carved finial, his fingers gripping it so tightly that the rounded ball left an imprint on the soft, fleshy part of his palm.

'Patience,' he muttered to himself. This was, after all, one of God's children. And perhaps he would find his way back to the fold.

He could always hope.

***

The Man

The man hated coming. It reminded him of his youth, of being back in *that* place – Valladolid, that shithole. He didn't care what anyone else said about the city, he despised it with a passion. It might have been fine for some people, but he had grown up in a filthy little hovel that smelled of onions and despair. By the time he had turned five, his father had left, taking all hope of a better life with him. From that moment, his childhood soured even more as his mother, embittered by his father's departure, took her ire out on him and dragged him to church on a daily basis to atone for the sins of his father. It didn't take long for him to hate the church. In fact, going to confession was the first time since his wedding that he had been in one. He wished he could just throw some money into the donation box, but something told him his wife would know if he did. No, deep down, he knew he had no choice; he had to keep coming.

'Bless me, Father, for I have sinned. It's been a week since my last confession. It's been a massive week at work. I managed to close the biggest deal our company has ever had. Although, between the two of us, the agreement wasn't completely above board... I had to indulge in a bit of industrial espionage... which is no big thing, I mean, everyone does it these days, but I imagine it wouldn't sit well with you-know-who.' He gestured upwards.

'And what has been the effect of your actions?' the priest asked.

'What happened? Well, we closed the deal, like I said.' The man tapped his fingers on the screen's ledge, the golden rings on his fingers making a rapping sound that would set anyone's teeth on edge.

'I understand that you won. But I'm wondering about the losers. What happened to them?'

The man shrugged and snorted. 'Who knows? Or cares, for that matter! Maybe if they were better at their jobs, they wouldn't have ended up in that position. When you think about it, they have only themselves to blame.'

The priest's eyebrow went up. 'Well, why are you here then? You clearly have no regrets over what you've done. In fact, you seem rather proud of yourself and your actions.'

'Well, there was something... what was it?' The man asked, toying with the priest.

'Hmm,' the priest said, the one word imbued with a very strong sense of doubt.

'Well, it must not have been very important,' the man said. 'So, what is it this week?'

'Twenty "Our Fathers" and five hours of community service,' the priest said.

The man's lip curled in response.

'Community service, Father? I'm a busy man, I don't have time for that stuff. Can you give me something else to do?'

'No, my son, you must make the time.'

***

The Priest

The man's seat was soon taken by a broken housewife who had snapped at her husband over his latest infidelity. The priest soon forgot about the man as he sought to alleviate the woman's pain and suffering.

The man came for months, Saturday after Saturday. His transgressions became more outrageous as he insinuated himself into the top tier of the company by making himself invaluable to his boss, who also happened to be his father-in-law. Greed and ruthlessness underscored all his interactions, but even these character flaws soon paled as the man detailed his machinations. It was becoming clear to the priest that this man had no intention of returning to God... if he had ever come from God in the first place. The priest was starting to wonder if the man was coming to confession with the sole purpose of tormenting him.

Today's confession was about adultery. The man was describing, at length, the lurid details of his latest conquest – the CFO's wife. He was admiring the flexibility of her body when the priest, Heaven help him, reached the end of his tether.

'Enough,' he said, slamming his hand on the screen, which rattled at the pressure.

'Why do you come here? All you do is make a mockery of this holy sacrament. You don't have any remorse for any of your wrongdoings. You only seem to care about yourself... if you were truly repentant, I would welcome you with open arms, as would my Father, but the only thing you're doing is preventing me from helping those in need.' The priest looked around his room, his gaze landing on a brochure from the Prado that a well-dressed young lady had given him the day before. 'From now on, your penance is this: you must go to the Prado every day and sit in front of *The Garden of Earthly Delights* by Hieronymus Bosch for an hour. That's it. You look at a painting for an hour every day – that should be easy for you.'

'I don't go to art museums,' the man said, his tone short.

The priest shrugged his shoulders. 'Well, you do now. That's your penance. And don't bother coming here again until you feel remorse.'

'Maldita iglesia,' the man said as he got up and left.

The priest's eyes rolled heavenward. Thanks be to God that divine inspiration had struck.

***

The Man

His first mistake had been marrying her. He had hesitated at the time, but still went through with it. By marrying her, he was leaving his past life behind him. Gone was Valladolid, now he was in Madrid, the epicenter of everything that he cared about – power, money, and security.

Marrying her had helped with those. But equally important was his entrance into her family. As the owners of the country's largest PR firm, they were Madrid's wealthiest and most powerful family, whose friends ranged from musicians to top politicians and royalty.

Who could blame him for marrying her? He couldn't resist being lured into a world that was so opulent, so different to the one that he had grown up in. How was he to know that he had married the one religious freak in all of Madrid? She had seemed relaxed when they first met five years ago, after all, she loved parties and going out. Yeah, she went to church, but didn't everyone? But when they got married, she changed, transforming into some annoying holier-than-thou woman, a freaking Mother Theresa figure. He couldn't stand her now; she was like his fucking mother. Unfortunately, he still needed her. For now. Later, he would be in a position where he could fuck her off. He dreamed of that day.

In the meantime, he worked his ass off to make himself invaluable to his father-in-law. Day after day, he was the first in the office, the last to leave. He raced through paperwork, making sure that he was fast and thorough, schmoozing with clients when they came in. He earned himself the nickname of 'El Dorado,' which made him joke that if his words were gold, then the office would be filled to the brim.

His dark side remained hidden. Although ambition in the company was commendable and largely rewarded, he knew that there were limits on what was acceptable. He also knew he probably breached those limits. His ruthlessness continued unchecked in his pursuit to ascend the ladder. He eavesdropped on private conversations, one of which led to the dismissal of two managers engaged in an affair that went against the company's strict dating policy. He didn't care about upholding stupid policies but, in this case, it worked in his favor. Another eavesdropped conversation led to the discovery of a hidden pregnancy. The victim was his soon-to-be boss, and when she was given the boot instead, he couldn't have been more delighted. The man who replaced her was weak and inefficient; it was only a matter of time before he was taken down, leading to the man stepping up another rung on the ladder.

His wife witnessed his promotions with a look of suspicion, her mouth perpetually sucked in with disapproval. Even worse, someone must have told her about his antics, leading to her demands that he go to church and pray for forgiveness. When she had first told him this, he had laughed, thinking that she was joking. Then he remembered saints lacked a sense of humor. She told him in no uncertain terms that he would be demoted if he didn't start going to church. Finally, he agreed to confession. But there wasn't a chance in hell of him cleaning up his act and joining his pious wife in a life of good deeds and words. He just needed to be more careful.

Having brokered this deal, he kept his gleeful laughter and contempt inside, presenting a serious image to his wife, all the while plotting his future misdeeds.

Soon, the affairs began. The man perused Madrid, taking pleasures where he could, the women as seductive as the food and wine. That this was happening without his wife's knowledge made it all the more enjoyable. At least there was one thing she couldn't control.

But one thing he couldn't shake was the priest's reaction to his latest confession. The whole thing had been peculiar – it was almost like the priest knew his fears, but that was impossible, wasn't it? No one knew about his fear of paintings except for his mother, and she was dead. He shuddered as he recalled those times when she had taken him by the ear up to the attic, where she had thrown him in and locked the door. He had sat there, forced to stare at the wall upon which Velázquez's painting *The Crucified Christ* hung. At first, the painting had scared him, but then he had seen similar images in his church, and, over time, his fear had diminished. His mother had sensed this and had brought a new piece to the room – Goya's *Saturn*, a painting that showed the deranged Roman god eating one of his children. Sitting there in his chair, watching as those crazed eyes stared back at him, that cavernous mouth mid-chew while devouring a human being, had terrified him. The damn painting had haunted him for years and, since leaving Valladolid, he had vowed never to set foot in the Prado. But now, it looked like he was going to have to.

The Monday after his last confession, the man dressed in his best suit and went to work. After a long day, he headed in the direction of the Prado, strolling through the Buen Retiro Park. He watched as tourists rowed on the lake, their oars splashing through the water and catching the last rays of the summer sun. Continuing, he paused at the Crystal Palace, his favorite building in all of Madrid. Not only did he admire the aesthetics and design, but he loved the pure opulence of the building and the way it gave the illusion of warmth. As a person who didn't enjoy the cold, he appreciated anything that promoted warmth. He always struggled with winter in Madrid and just the thought of dropping temperatures was enough to make him shiver. After staring at it appreciatively for a while, he decided it was time for the Prado and proceeded onward, cutting through peak-hour traffic and irate drivers.

Despite his distaste for museums, he had to admit that the Prado was an impressive building. As he approached it, he could feel something he hadn't experienced in a while – a sense of smallness, a question of his worth. This institution had been around for so long and would be here still long after he had died. As usual, this kind of thought didn't last long. He quickly squashed it and prepared himself to enter the building. It was time he took this phobia in hand. He owed it to himself.

He started slowly, sweeping through one gallery after another, their colorful walls full of priceless artworks. Upon entering these rooms, he scanned the walls, looking for anything disturbing. Fortunately, the paintings displayed were relatively benign: they were mostly religious, the likes of which he had seen in his wife's rooms.

His breathing, which had been tense since he had entered the museum, began to loosen up, especially when the announcement came that the museum was closing.

He did not make it to the Bosch. He did, however, treat himself to a sumptuous meal at a nearby Michelin-starred restaurant before he walked home.

A week in, he still hadn't made it to the room housing *The Garden of Earthly Delights*. He thought it would continue this way until one Thursday, when an unseasonably cold day decided to work against him. He arrived at work late, flustered, and had had problems with someone's assistant threatening to make complaints against him. He had hurried to the museum and walked distractedly from room to room when he walked straight into the room that housed Goya's Black Paintings, including the infamous *Saturn* painting that had terrified him so profoundly. He ran out of the room, and somehow ended up in front of *The Garden of Earthly Delights*. With his heart pounding, his mind trying to suppress all memories of Goya's horrific painting, at first the strangeness of Bosch's painting barely registered. It wasn't until his breathing slowed and he really looked at it that he became alarmed. His first impression of the painting was that the artist had been crazy, or on some heavy drugs, because it looked like one bad hallucination.

He stared at the left panel: an innocuous scene of Adam and Eve set in a surreal background. Strange, but nothing that he hadn't seen before. Then he moved to the center panel, which was far more peculiar – kinky, in fact. There were tons of little figures, all involved in various sexual activities. Even for him, some of these activities were bizarre. The whole thing conveyed a sense of chaos, a feeling of madness. But the last panel was far more disturbing. In contrast to the previous two, this one's palette was dramatic and lacked the surreal garden background. The final panel showed Hell and the multitude of tortures that awaited sinners. The man stood there, horrified, but unable to turn away from it. He only managed to tear himself away when the museum closed for the night.

But he came back, day after day, staring at the painting and that last panel. There was something about it, its darkness and depravity, that rekindled the fear within him. As he stood there, he was transported back to that gloomy attic room and his mother's tight grip as she thrust him into the room and slammed the door, leaving him all alone in the dark with that horrific painting. His mind temporarily fractured knowing that it was in the Prado but feeling like he was trapped in that attic. His heart began to thump, and his breathing shallowed as panic set in. He tried to look at something, anything, but slowly, insidiously, the painting began working its way into his mind, a seed that festered, rotting into the very nerves of his brain.

Over time, the painting began consuming him. He lost all interest in everything, no longer went to work, no longer chased women, no longer cared about prestige or wealth. All he cared about was that painting. And so, during the day, he sat there staring at it. His nights were long and harrowing due to the constant nightmares that plagued him. His body thrashed around, his skin fevered as the dreams became more realistic, the depictions of torture and pain becoming increasingly vivid. As his night terrors progressed, his wife moved to another bedroom, fearful of what he would do in his sleep.

As winter's pale and icy grasp took hold of the city, the man's behavior became even more erratic. He rarely slept for more than two hours at a time, his terrified screams echoing throughout his wing of the mansion. During the day, he would sit in a comatose stupor, only getting up when forced to. The room soon took on his putrid smell, and what staff remained in that wing had been advised to steer clear.

Soon, he was left for days, weeks, months, alone, all alone.

One day, a year later, two men, as wide as they were tall, took him away.

***

Five years later

The Priest

He looked outside his window and exhaled softly, a sound of true contentment. What a beautiful day God had given him, a perfect day to go to his favorite place to help God's unfortunates.

He dressed, then walked quickly to the local psychiatric hospital. Saying hello to the receptionist, he made his way to the wards, visiting the inhabitants and praying for their souls. Stopping in the garden for a brief respite, he was surprised to hear a familiar voice, one that he hadn't heard for quite some time. It was the man, the one who had tormented him so greatly all those years ago. The priest wondered what he was doing here. Due to the nature of confession, the priest had only seen the vaguest suggestion of a form in the confessional. The man he had seen and pictured in his mind was powerful, confident. The man before him was frail, hesitant. This man fidgeted with a piece of string while mumbling to himself and looking around nervously. A loud clanging from the door opposite the garden made the man jump and scurry over to a large olive tree. The priest shook his head, shocked at the change, and concerned whether he had played a part in the man's ruin. He vowed to pray fervently for the man's soul.

***

The Wife

She sits at peace for once, the paperwork for her annulment finally complete. It has been five years since her husband was taken, and her life has improved dramatically. Are there times when she wants to shake her younger self for marrying such an awful man? Yes, of course. But, over time, those became less and less frequent as she found her own strength, her own life. And now, at times, she almost wants to laugh at it all. Who would have thought that her duplicitous husband would provide her with the very solution she needed to get rid of him? If he hadn't gotten drunk that one night and spoken in his sleep, she would have never known about his phobia of paintings. And then she wouldn't have had the divine inspiration to get him into the Prado. Her assistant Maria, had been quite useful there, giving the priest a brochure at exactly the right time.

Looking around the garden, she spies the priest. Though they have never met formally, Maria had given her a detailed description of him. The wife smiles and approaches him.

'I never thanked you properly for helping me with my husband,' she said, taking a checkbook out of her purse.

'Oh?' he asked.

'My husband came to you for confession, and your thoughtful penance helped him greatly. In fact, his trips to the Prado were particularly invaluable.'

'I did only what I could do for my child. But I never imagined that he would end up in a place like this.'

A look of satisfaction flickered in her eyes before it was quickly replaced by her usual expression of extreme piety.

'Yes, well, he was a troubled soul. This is the best place for him, I think,' she said decisively.

'Yes, yes of course.'

She gestured toward her book, which was now open, a gold pen in hand, waiting to write.

'Is there anything the church needs?' she asked.

Any questions regarding her husband's deterioration died on his tongue as he ruminated on his elderly parish and crumbling church.

'Well, the wall does have a rather large crack in it, which does need to be fixed soon, otherwise it'll affect the lovely stained-glass windows. But that'll cost a lot to fix...' he trailed off.

She looked at him, then wrote a large amount on the check before signing her name with a grand flourish. 'We can't have the church falling down on us. I think you'll find this more than enough,' she said as she handed him the check.

His eyebrows went up as he looked at the small piece of paper in his hand.

'You have been most kind my child, most kind indeed. The good Father will know of your generosity.'

She smiled serenely. 'Thank you, Father, but it was nothing. After all, you helped me tremendously with a problem of my own,' she said, looking at her soon-to-be-former husband. 'Funny how life works, isn't it.'

4

The Fabled Patisserie of Brussels

Pasquale the pigeon was bored. It was another day, another boring, tedious day, in Brussels. He frowned and pecked distractedly at a speck of baguette that someone had dropped on the ground. He ate the morsel, the dryness invading his throat and setting him off again. 'Why is there no decent food in Brussels?' he grumbled. He was starting to wonder why he had come here in the first place. Recently, he had been hearing about his siblings, the ones who had stayed in the more touristy cities of Venice and Rome, and they were feasting bountifully, whereas he was barely surviving. Why was he here?

But he knew why. The legend had enticed him, just like it had so many others before him – the fabled patisserie of Brussels.

Stories of this patisserie had spread far beyond Belgium's borders. Pasquale had first heard about it when he was in Germany visiting cousins. He had been eating a bratwurst in Munich, enjoying the sunny weather, when a flock of pigeons arrived, their beaks a-wobble with tales about this wonderful bakery in Brussels, which not only made the best cakes and waffles, but whose owners set out food specifically for pigeons. It was, as one pigeon described, 'as close to paradise as one could get.'

At least, that was the story. Upon further questioning, none of the pigeons had been there themselves, not even the one who had described it as 'heavenly.' They just repeated everything they had heard. Unfortunately, the story didn't provide the name of the patisserie, just a symbol of three triangles set within a sun on a brown paper bag, so it was all a mystery.

Pasquale liked mysteries.

Or so he had thought.

As he began preparing for his flight to Brussels, he felt confident in his ability to solve this puzzle quickly. After all, hadn't he found that café in Marienplatz that made the best Baumkuchen? And he had only been in Munich for a week when he discovered it. So, finding this patisserie in Brussels would surely be easy.

The following week, he left Munich for Brussels and began his search. He started in the northern districts, quickly passing over Sint-Agatha-Berchem due to its soul-less appearance, and pausing briefly in Sint-Jans-Molenbeek, transfixed by the sounds of the markets and the smells of the food. He continued southward to Watermael-Boitsfort, which seemed more like a village with its sprinkling of tiny cottages, huge trees, and beautiful lakes. He passed a pleasant afternoon near Lac du bois de la Cambre, listening to relatives from Quebec as they settled in and greeted each other familiarly in French. However, his attention span, which was longer than some of his friends', waned and he grew tired of their cooing. He left with little fanfare and had only begun flying to the heart of Brussels when he was caught in a huge wind that took him further north to Sint Joost, an area full of tall, shiny, luxury buildings, which Pasquale struggled to navigate through. Several times, he narrowly avoided flying into expansive windows that confused his sense of direction even more. Finally, he made his way south, flying over the Parc de Bruxelles, whose rectangular symmetry entranced him, and ended up at the Grand-Place, staring down at the elaborate Baroque buildings surrounding the square.

After all the searching he had done, and the bits of waffles and cakes he had eaten – the pieces so small he wondered whether Belgians were big eaters or miserly – he was still no closer to finding the elusive patisserie. In fact, he was beginning to worry that he was going to waste away in this concrete cesspool because of his desire to find it.

He was sitting in front of the Town Hall, the medieval structure a sanctuary to birds from all over, sighing and fluffing out his feathers, debating whether he should leave this boring city, when something happened.

He had little warning – a sudden rush of air and a slight pressure on his wings was all he felt before the man ran past him. Pasquale smoothed down his feathers, which lifted again as two policemen thundered by, their pursuit of the man hampered by the tourists who had gathered to witness the police chase.

Pasquale was entranced; he had never seen anything this exciting before. He flew up and over, soaring toward the three men, who had already covered a lot of ground in the brief time they had been running.

Pasquale looked back at the Grand-Place, the square already filled with tourists, their cameras and phones outstretched as they snapped pictures of the guild halls, whose spires reached up toward the late morning sun.

Despite the time of day, the air was surprisingly clear, and the usual pollution and congestion were absent. Pasquale flew in relative comfort, looking down to keep tabs on his entertainment. Pasquale thought the man must be in good shape as he was still running with ease, maintaining the same gap between himself and the police. It looked like he was going somewhere in particular as his stride didn't break until he came to the Canal de Bruxelles. The man ran alongside it, his hand sliding along the railing as he glanced behind him at the police who were only now beginning to catch up. Pasquale watched as the man looked up and down the canal, obviously watching for someone or something to appear. Pasquale followed his gaze, stopping for a moment on a suspicious-looking person dressed completely in black pleather, like one of the characters Pasquale had seen on the big screens in shop windows. This man looked up and down the canal too, but then leaned over and vomited into the water below. He delicately wiped his mouth before continuing on his way.

The running man was still looking around, his confident manner dissipating before Pasquale's eyes. He now seemed uncertain and impatient. The police, who were now a few meters from their target, stopped for a second before approaching him.

The man, his mind apparently made up after a quick deliberation, stepped up onto the railing and climbed over to the other side.

From above, Pasquale watched as the man held on, preparing to jump. Just as he was about to jump, Pasquale felt an all-too-familiar urge and did what birds, particularly pigeons, so inelegantly do — he crapped. Sadly, his crap landed on the man's face, destroying his moment of peaceful concentration. The pungent white goo, of which there was a copious amount, landed squarely in the man's eyes, rendering him temporarily blind and causing him to lose his balance. His foot slipped and his hand shot out, only to be grabbed by an officer. The man sighed and held out his other hand, accepting that his attempt to escape had failed. Pasquale swooped down closer and landed on the canal bridge where he heard the man lamenting that the lousy phone he had taken hadn't even worked.

Pasquale watched from his perch as the man was handcuffed. He felt terrible. He had never meant for the man to be caught; after all, he had provided a year's worth of entertainment in a single morning. Pasquale shook his head in disappointment, wondering how he was going to fill in the rest of the day. He was already bored.

Dropping down to the pavement, he pecked listlessly at a few crumbs as the man was led to a white van with red-and-blue markings. He was pushed into the back of the vehicle, and a policeman jumped into the front seat and started the engine. The vehicle moved abruptly, its force creating a sudden and powerful gust of wind that blew toward Pasquale and sent some trash dancing down the street.

One small object fluttered in the air, a small, unexceptional brown bag. It floated for a few seconds before a rogue breeze sent it flying directly toward Pasquale. A few specks of food dropped from the bag and landed in front of him. He pounced on the morsels and devoured them. As he ate, the flavors danced along his tongue, leaving him craving more. He grabbed the bag and looked at it. Behind a large grease stain on the bag, he could detect the faintest outline of a sun encircling three triangles. It was the symbol he had heard about from the other pigeons. He opened the bag wide to his beak and breathed in, the delicious aroma surrounding him. He breathed in again, as deeply as his lungs would allow, as a feeling of elation merged with the delightful smell, leaving him giddy. He finally had evidence of the fabled patisserie of Brussels. Now he just had to find it.

Clutching the bag tightly in his beak, all thoughts of boredom gone, he set off, his heart aflutter at the thought that he was one step closer to finding paradise.

Maybe Brussels wasn't so bad after all.

5

A Question of Job Satisfaction

Hades' legs were getting cramped. Shifting his weight from one foot to another, he tapped his hand impatiently against the arched window in the campanile, gazing down at the buskers and pigeons who gathered in St Mark's Square ready to fleece the tourists from both money and food. Hades looked at his watch, a gold piece gifted to him by a grateful client the previous month. Originally, he had been impressed by it and had appreciated the sophisticated gesture. It was only when he took the timepiece to be insured that he discovered it was a fake. Not even gold, let alone 24-karat. This had, as was to be expected, altered his relationship irrevocably with the client. He had thought about leaving the watch on the man's grave but felt that might draw a bit too much attention to himself and, since he had brought about the man's demise, he decided that a low profile was necessary. So, he kept the watch and led the man to Cerberus, who took him to where he belonged.

To its credit, the watch kept excellent time. It was reading six forty-five, which meant that his target was fifteen minutes late. He sighed heavily; his large frame crammed in the small space that he had been hiding in. Why couldn't people be on time anymore? He couldn't help but wonder if, somehow, his targets subconsciously knew that he was waiting for them.

Granted, he had arrived early for this job, but that was due to necessity more than anything else. Not only did it take time to set up, but he had only been recently diagnosed with a visual processing disorder by a specialist doctor. This diagnosis explained why he had struggled for years to understand the written messages sent by the other gods. It also highlighted the difficulties he had been having since coming above ground... his disorder made reading briefs and signs difficult, to say the least. However, needs must, and since the Underworld was on the lowest pay scale in the realm, he needed to supplement his poor income somehow... at least this job meant he could give his wife Perse a nice vacation.

It was only now that he realized just how much his primary role in the Underworld relied on verbal communication. Ensuring that souls remained there required little more than a few well-selected words. As he was able to do this effectively, under his rule the Underworld had been an efficiently run organization for the last seven millennia. So well run that, at times, it could be monotonous.

His venture above ground contrasted greatly with the Underworld. Gone was the tedium – since his arrival, he had been met with nothing but challenges. First, he'd had difficulties finding a job. Fortunately, Hermes had known someone who knew someone who needed a person like Hades. Another complication was that Hades had never worked for a human before. It was a revelation and a nightmare. Had humans always been so demanding? So petty? And so completely disorganized? He couldn't help but wonder how they had thrived for so long because, from his perspective, they were a hopeless bunch. His boss Morris, the founder of Easy Solutions, was especially bad. The number of errors, in conjunction with the overheads... one could hardly believe that the company was still operational. Frankly, if Hades had managed the Underworld like this, it would have been empty. But, as he was above ground, he decided to keep his mouth shut.

And if dealing with humans wasn't challenging enough, he'd had to navigate through their towns and cities. Based on this trip alone, Venice could win the title for the world's worst city. He would love to know who designed the place. Not only did all the street signs look identical, but the streets themselves did too – narrow, winding laneways lined with tall buildings in what he had heard described as the Venetian Gothic style. Many of these backed onto canals that he had traversed countless times already, often crossing a canal only to find himself back to where he had started. Venice's whole set-up made the Underworld look like a paragon of logical design and maneuverability. After two weeks here, he knew that Venice was a new form of hell.

Hades sighed, glaring at a solitary pigeon that had perched on the ledge next to his hand. It cooed, blinking at him with a profound blankness, pecking pointlessly at a stone near its feet. For a moment, Hades contemplated getting rid of it, but decided it wasn't his place to exterminate something so small and meaningless. The bird, perhaps sensing that there was something amiss with this human, looked at him intently. Hades took this as an invitation to share his thoughts.

'I hate this place. You probably hate it too. I'm sure everything looks the same from where you are.'

A vacant expression somehow managed to convey agreement.

'If you were me, and had to live one place for the rest of your life, where would it be?'

The bird's head jerked backward, its beak working as a small, wonky compass needle pointed north.

Hades nodded. 'Just as I suspected. I, too, would go north.'

Just as Hades made this pronouncement, the bird took flight, its body circling the intricate lamp posts with their pale rose glass, before soaring higher.

North… the word teased him, bringing tantalizing images of a different place – Bruges. For a moment, he was transported to another time, another tower, where another death had transpired. That one had been an uncomplicated and punctual affair, a simple matter of eliminating the CEO of a small tech company whose wife had discovered that his 'all-inclusive' business trips included his mistress. The wife, showing her ruthless yet practical side, had bypassed her lawyer and hired Easy Solutions instead, bringing Hades into the equation. Fortunately for Hades, the CEO had been early for his appointment, and in the dwindling hours of the night he had gone tumbling down the stairs of the belfry. In the minutes following the CEO's departure, Hades had leaned against the railing and enjoyed Bruges' peaceful ambience.

It really was his favorite city. The food was good, the architecture pleasing, and, because of its size, it was a relatively easy place to navigate. Admittedly, there had been a few times when he had lost his way, but he had eventually worked it out. Except for that one time.

It was the day after the hit, and the weather was remarkably fine. Hades had twelve hours to fill until his departure and he was at a loss of what to do. He had done the usual sightseeing, drunk his weight in beer and eaten enough waffles to soak up the alcohol. All it took was a chance remark on the street and, before he knew it, he was renting a bicycle and heading toward a beach. Or so he had thought. The moment he started pedaling, his wheels going heavily and rhythmically over the cobblestones, the movement jarring every single bone in his immortal body, he felt he should have known better. Teeth clanking as he followed the canal, he wondered how humans kept their bodies intact when their main form of transportation was cycling. He had thought that chariots had been rough, but these bicycles were another thing altogether.

Once he left the town center, the trip worsened and his confusion amplified. He tried to remember the directions he had been given but he had forgotten them. He tried looking at the map but couldn't work it out. So, he kept going down the road, that endless road with bumps that came out of nowhere and hoped to come upon something of interest soon. As time passed, and the sun continued pummeling down on his already-sore shoulders, he became increasingly alarmed at the surrounding landscape, which was growing more bucolic. The last straw was when he swerved off the path to avoid hitting a stray cow. Attempting to regain control of the bicycle, his pant leg was caught up in the chain and he came crashing down.

As injuries go, he had seen worse in the Underworld. Far, far worse. He had often thought he could pen a book on the most horrific wounds that he had seen. He had even come up with a title, *Lacerations of the Deep,* but Perse was adamant that no one would ever read a book that ghoulish. Hades didn't agree. He understood humans enough to know that they were fascinated by all things grotesque and morbid.

He stared at the bone that jutted out, its sharp contours visible above his ankle, and sighed heavily. This was unfortunate. Down in the Underworld, he was immune to human weaknesses. Above ground, he was vulnerable, and he didn't like it. He took his phone out of his coat pocket and scrolled through his contact list before pressing call next to the picture of a well-dressed man.

'Pius.' A deep voice answered once the phone had rung.

'It's Hades. I've broken my ankle.'

'How do you know?'

'The bone's sticking out. I think that's a big enough indicator.'

An irritable sigh before an abrupt order. 'Hold the phone near it.'

Hades did as requested and, within seconds, the phone began emitting a warm yellow light that infused his leg. Soon enough the bone was back in its place, all signs of the fracture gone.

'Not bad,' Hades said when he brought the phone back to his ear.

'I can always undo it if you want me to,' Pius said tersely.

'No, no, that's quite all right. Thank you.'

'Try not to bother me again.'

Hades rolled his eyes as he put his phone away and got back on the bicycle. He had never been in contact with the god of medicine before, so he didn't know if Pius was normally that rude, but his demeanor seemed a bit off-putting. Hades thought that doctors were supposed to be more sympathetic.

Feeling disgruntled, he turned his bicycle around and began the arduous trip back to Bruges. Fortunately, his journey back was far more simplistic; he followed the same street back into the city center. Two hours later, he reached the bicycle shop, his body aching from the cobblestones' onslaught. He left the bicycle in the returns area and went to comfort himself with pasta in a box, which went a long way in supporting his stomach and his budget.

He wished there was an equivalent in Venice, but he hadn't discovered one yet. His stomach had remained empty since his arrival.

Where the hell is this guy? he thought once again as he adjusted his legs. He knew the target was on vacation with his family, so there was always a chance that schedules could vary but, so far, this guy always went for the same run every morning, finishing up in St Mark's Square.

As Hades crouched down once again, he ran through the man's dossier in his mind. He could describe the man, Jamie X, perfectly – six-feet tall, light-brown hair, a five-o'clock stubble that emphasized his chiseled jawline. Hades rubbed his own jawline, which the other gods had jokingly referred to as equine. He closed his eyes and completed the picture, the Roman nose, which made an aristocratic statement below a pair of penetrating cerulean eyes. Hades didn't know the full story about Jamie X, but something told him he was dangerous.

At seven-thirty, a man sprinted into the plaza. Hades pushed his legs, ready to stand and take position, when a figure ran up to his target and clapped him on the back. Hades watched as the two men came closer, his momentary hesitancy transforming into shock when he saw that the two men were identical. Same hair, same stubble, same eyes. The only difference that Hades could see was the color of their clothes. One wore gray, the other wore black.

Hades looked again, analyzing each man as they slowed down to a walk. He looked frantically for something, anything, that would set them apart. Nothing. In the three years he had been doing this, he had never seen two people who looked so much alike. It was eerie. And it made his job impossible. Which man was he supposed to kill?

He thought back to the brief, trying to recall whether there was any distinguishing feature that he had missed. He was positive there wasn't and that he would have remembered if something like twins had been mentioned. No, the only family that had been included was a wife and two kids. This was problematic. What was he supposed to do? Which one should he kill?

His hand shaking, he eased his finger off the trigger. No, this wasn't right, there was something off about this.

Holstering his gun, he got up slowly, his feet and legs making him all too aware of how long he had been crouched there. His left foot spasmed as he straightened and stomped down to get the blood circulating.

Hades looked down at the square. The two men had turned around and were now walking away from him. Hades took out his phone and called his boss, something he rarely did.

'You done already?' Morris asked, a surprised note in his voice.

'No, there were two of them... I couldn't tell which was which.'

'Yeah, about that... they're twins. We thought you'd take them both out, you know, the easiest solution to the problem. And it just so happens that they both hired us to take the other one out.'

'And you didn't think to tell me this?'

'Well, you didn't really need to know. You're hired to kill, not think.'

'That's bullshit.'

'It is what it is. I had to make a change to our usual policy and request full payment upfront, so I hope you took care of them. They paid a premium price for our services.'

'Go to hell.' Hades jabbed at his phone and stalked over to the elevator.

He pressed the down button, his breath coming out in irritated puffs as he reflected on his current career path. Perhaps it was time for a change. Did he really want to keep working for Morris? He knew what Perse wanted; she had recently become friends with an ambassador's wife and was forever going on about the amazing parties that her friend attended. It was inevitable now that when he checked his emails there would be a job posting with the words 'diplomat' or 'foreign services' included. He didn't quite understand this; they had been married long enough for her to know that diplomacy, people relations, and analyzing subtle communication were not his strengths.

Leaving the tower, he walked along the piazza, his long strides cutting through a swarm of pigeons. He went left and through a number of mis-turns, particularly when the road name changed from Marzaria San Zulian to Ponte dei Bareteri, eventually made his way to the Rialto Bridge, where he stopped to analyze his situation and plan his next move. One that, sadly for Perse, did not require diplomacy.

Easy Solutions was a viable company with a sound basis. However, Morris was a liability; his poor management of the company was negatively impacting the business, and Hades needed the work. Therefore, it was time to remove Morris and take over the company himself. He could make everything paperless, more streamlined, and increase efficiency and security. And, who knew? If he did it right, he could make it bigger... could even look at franchising. The possibilities were endless.

He was Hades after all, and he had plenty of time.

6

Two Sides to a Story – Part 1

Bastille Day - 14 July 2024

It was a night of celebrations. The Firemen's Balls had begun hours ago, music pumping through the streets of Paris, everyone dancing and drinking with sheer abandon. Though the fireworks had ended, the bright embers long faded into the sky, Champs de Mars was still full of people, the feeling of fraternity and goodwill lingering in the air.

Everyone was celebrating. Everyone except for the Groupe de Sécurité de la présidence de la République, who currently had a crisis on their hands.

They were in the Palais de Élysée, the atmosphere of which was decidedly somber. The president had just been discovered dead in her bath, her head tilted back against the white marble, jasmine and sandalwood perfuming the air. As M. Frontier moved toward her, towel in hand to shield her body, he almost stepped on a book labeled 'Journal.' He bent down to pick it up, disturbing a sheath of papers that had been carelessly tucked within the book. They were covered in the dead president's writing, her bold, distinctive style instantly recognizable. He was about to put them back when he saw the word 'Confessions' across the top of one page.

Handing the towel to his next in command, he took the book with its papers and strode to the library. Closing the door, he sat at the modernist blue table, a mother-of-pearl streak cutting across the surface like a wave, and placed the papers on top. The chair was digging into his thigh. He fidgeted, but the movement provided no relief. He hated furniture that was more about style than comfort.

The papers sat there, waiting for him. He hesitated. There was a feeling emanating from them, a sense that these papers were potentially dangerous, that the information they contained could undermine everything. But he knew he had to read them... it was a matter of security, after all.

He picked up the first page and began to read.

***

Confessions

Gerard, I am dying. Of this, I am certain. The doctors say the opposite, but I know better... I can feel the cells in my body breaking down. I know that my time is limited. This, therefore, is my confession – of everything. As my husband, some things you know, but others you are unaware of. I had, long ago, learned the value of keeping certain matters to myself, a rule that I clung to with an obstinacy you know only too well. Recently though, I have felt myself drowning under the weight of these secrets, which have been a necessity for so long. The constant battle between my professional face and personal one has drained me.

I know what you're thinking – I was never one to dwell on the difficulties of life. I was a born fighter. From the moment I pushed my way out of my mother's womb to the day I left school, I was always most comfortable when I was arguing. My parents thought I would be a lawyer, but while that suited me for a time, it didn't go far enough in terms of my ambition. You knew that about me, that there was one thing I had been craving all along: power. You understood how important politics was to me.

I'd like to believe that you'll understand everything I've done, even if you don't agree with the actions I've taken.

One last thing. Destroy this once you've read it.

Let my legacy remain unblemished.

***

2014

Do you recall that year? It was the start of me. But it began rather unpleasantly for someone else. She's rarely in the news now but, back then, she was everywhere, much to my annoyance – Valerie Blanc.

I remember the morning after the incident. I woke to the manic rushing of the newspapers, their headlines screaming about Valerie Blanc's little accident at the Louvre. Of course, they didn't know the full story, no one did... except me. And perhaps Valerie, but even she didn't know *everything*.

Do you recall when the press came that day? They were so predictable with their formulaic questions: Had I seen Ms. Blanc's fall? What did this mean for the election? Did I have anything to say? They even asked you questions, which I felt was a bit rich given that you hadn't been there.

We didn't say much that day. But now, now I can say anything, everything. My road to greatness has been a lonely one, even with you by my side... not that I would admit that to anyone but you. Now my compulsion drives me to talk, to treat this paper like a confidante of flesh and blood.

Did I have a hand in her political demise? Yes, of course. Who else would mastermind what happened to her? Who else had so much to gain from her departure?

She had many supporters. They obviously did not know the woman very well, and they certainly did not have the dubious honor of running against her in the mayoral election. No, that was a trial only I experienced.

So, when they spoke so fondly of her, I shrugged my shoulders sympathetically – with all the elegant nonchalance of my long Gallic ancestry – and said all the right platitudes while inside... inside, I just wanted to scream.

Just another example of maintaining a professional exterior and suppressing the truth within. Then again, we politicians are known to have a certain flexibility with the truth.

Up to that point, I had been, for the most part, fairly honest. My qualifications, my background... all above board. The only thing I was less than forthright about was my reason for going into politics. Let's be honest, whoever is naïve enough to believe that people go into politics for the betterment of humanity or to 'make the world a better place' deserves what they get – your average politician, who's in it for the money or the power. I already had money... I just needed the power.

But I forget myself... I forget you, Gerard. You already know this. How many times have we sat in the garden laughing over the naïve idealism of our constituents? Somehow, it never grew old.

What grew tiresome, however, was knowing that I was the ideal candidate for the Mayoress of Paris, but I still had to compete... and who knew that I would be up against someone who was, in many ways, more manipulative than me? Still, these things happen, and you take care of them and move on.

***

I am so weary these days... this illness is taking everything from me.

Where was I?

Oh yes, Valerie.

From the beginning, she was a formidable match. Her carefully curated image was everywhere: from the local bakery to art galleries and bus stops. That classic portrait illuminated her face perfectly, highlighting the delicate features that enthralled the public. It didn't matter who you spoke with, everyone fell under her spell. They all saw her as an authentic woman whose nurturing and pragmatic nature would solve the city's problems. As one businessman stated, 'She will fix everything that is wrong in Paris... and then Paris will be wonderful again.'

How are people so gullible, Gerard? Sometimes even I am astounded at how easily swayed the population is, how quickly they can believe what is presented to them without delving under the surface. Which makes me wonder -- were you so easily tricked? I like to think not, but it would be presumptuous of me to think I knew what was going on in your mind.

As for me, it was quite simple to decipher her. From the start, I could tell that, appearances aside, this woman had a mind like a steel trap and the cunning of a crow. I also knew that I would have to keep her on my radar and watch my step with her.

Of course, I was right to do so.

In the beginning, we barely interacted. A few interviews and her melodic voice seduced listeners, making her ratings skyrocket. Then, as the campaign went underway, everything changed, intensified. Ours became a combative dance that both of us were trying to lead. Two steps forward, one step back, she led, then I did... the unwieldy dance continued. She struck gold by helping a pensioner with his shopping. I got a lift when I was 'spotted' volunteering at a food shelter... now that I think about it, that was your idea. Gerard, Gerard... you knew I hated those kinds of events. They were simply awful. So wearisome, trying to pretend that I cared about those little people and their little lives. I think you were amused, watching me as I interacted with them, all the while hiding every negative thought that was racing through my head. I was a consummate actress that day, even you would have to admit it.

Then she upped the stakes again. The very next day she treated an entire class of primary school students to a hot air balloon ride. It was, frankly, ridiculous. You and I were in the Jardin des Tuileries, planning our next strategic move, when we saw the balloon's white orb soaring higher into the air. We could see it float to the Eiffel Tower then circle around to the Parc André Citroën. I was flabbergasted. I think I turned to you and asked, 'How could anyone even compete with that?' You shrugged without ever really answering. But this gimmick signaled the beginning of her end. She was playing a dangerous game, an American one. And this, most assuredly, was not America.

Even now, I wonder what you thought about Valerie. Were you drawn in like the others? Or did you see her as the villain of this tale? At times, I thought I detected a hint of sympathy toward her, but then, like a flicker of light, it was gone.

For me, she was far from a benevolent person. Am I supposed to believe she wasn't behind the exposé that detailed my father's dealings with the Nazis? I mean, that secret had been so heavily guarded within the family that even I didn't know about it until I was forty. I can't fathom where she found that information... not even you knew it. Thankfully, I was able to spin the story so that, instead of being a treasonous collaborator, my father was transformed into a heroic swindler who sold the Nazis defective equipment.

Then, if that wasn't bad enough, she tried to ensnare my father in an adulterous affair. A bold move on her part given his advanced age. Of course, she picked her 'victim' with care. The French don't usually care about affairs, but when a candidate's campaign is all about family values, it doesn't look good when a relative is sleeping with a young lady seventy years his junior. After all, who likes a hypocrite? Thankfully, he was too oblivious, consumed with whatever bottle of wine he had under his nose, to succumb. Thank God for small mercies. If he had been twenty years younger, it would have been a different story.

That was the moment when I realized Valerie would stop at nothing to be Mayoress. I knew I had to do something drastic.

***

Well, we both know that I've never really been a huge fan of classical art. You used to drag me to some exhibitions, and I would be bored in a matter of minutes. Contemporary art is far more exciting, whereas this stuff is so... bourgeois. I'm always surprised that anyone in France likes it. It is a waste of time, a waste of resources, and, well, just a waste of everything, really. However, in this instance, it actually helped me, so perhaps there's something positive to say about it after all.

I had heard that Valerie was holding an event at the Louvre, something to do with fundraising for her campaign, and I received an invitation. I went, not because I wanted to, but because I was curious as to what she had in store for me. It didn't seem like the type of affair that a person would invite their rival to. Then again, who knew what was going on in Valerie's mind?

You had a business dinner that night, which I resented at the time. It was only later that I realized how fortuitous it was that you weren't there.

Walking up the steps of the Louvre, I shuddered. It contained so much that I despised – tourists, pomposity, and that art. I dreaded going inside, but the thought of winning the election spurred me on. I worked my way through the crowds to greet Valerie, who was surrounded by her adoring minions. She looked good, her body draped in a scarlet couture gown that fit her perfectly. She was wearing her highest stilettos. I stared at her shoes. They gave me an idea. You see, Valerie isn't the only cunning one around. Once I had a plan, it was only a small matter of waiting for the perfect opportunity.

That arrived later.

The champagne was flowing as quickly as the conversation, and waiters were making the rounds with canapés the size of a fingernail, when Valerie went off to do a photo shoot. I heard the photographer mention the Napoleon rooms, only for her to say 'No, there's only one place I can be photographed, and that's next to *Victory.*'

The sheer impudence of the woman! Lauding herself as the winner when the election itself was weeks away. But I knew this was my one chance.

The Louvre was full of people, making it easy for me to follow Valerie and her small entourage unseen. We were walking down one of the many staircases, the *Winged Victory* in sight, her marble body full of forward momentum, her wings reaching back and enticing all to look at her, when I struck.

Valerie's head was tilted, her eyes fixated on the phone in her hand when I gave her the slightest of nudges. She was so focused on her screen that she barely noticed until she was crashing down the stairs, her stilettos proving no match for the slippery marble surface. Poor thing – she tried in vain to catch herself, as did her sycophants, but those shoes, well, frankly, they're a killer. I don't know why women continue to wear them. But I won't be too critical, after all, they did help me achieve my goal.

One of her lackeys called the medics, her voice fluctuating from calm to frantic as she tried to administer first aid. Soon, the medics arrived in a flurry of activity. They spoke in hushed voices, taking Valerie away on a gurney. Then the press, that committee of vultures, spread out, trying to ascertain what had happened.

Amid the confusion, I melted away.

The tension in my shoulders, which had been increasing as of late through my dealings with Valerie, dissipated instantly.

Goodbye Valerie Blanc.

Her exit was not permanent of course, that would have been ghoulish. However, the coma she was in obviously eradicated any dreams or aspirations she'd had. Apparently, she ended her days on a lavender farm. How banal.

***

Then, I was Madame la Maire. I think we can both agree that I performed my role admirably... so well, in fact, that within a few years I had the presidency in sight. I just had to take care of a few people...

Don't worry Gerard, everyone else was minor. Valerie was my most challenging obstacle, so she had to be dealt with harshly. The others, well, there were only three or four... remember M. Citron? His mouth, so continuously pursed like he had just eaten a sour lemon. He was the second person who tried to impede my progress; unfortunately for him, I had some rather sensitive and damaging photographs that I threatened to take to the press. His death two months later had nothing to do with me.

And then, of course, who could forget L'œuf? That ridiculous woman, she tried so desperately to get the big scoop on me based on a few suspicions... I don't know how she ever thought she would get close. She was the easiest – I just made a few calls, and she was no longer working for the newspaper.

So, you see why these things had to be done. In the name of Paris, in the name of France, these people had to be dealt with. Only I could see the bigger picture and only I could envision ways of bettering France.

But now my time has ended, I am choosing to leave this world at the peak of my reign. I can only hope that my successor continues my good work as I have left this country in a position of power: a position of pride. Let that legacy, my legacy, endure.

Celeste

***

2024

The papers dropped from M. Frontier's hands and landed on the slippery surface of the table. He sat there stunned, unsure of what to do. Part of him wanted to burn them, but the other part, who had known and liked Valerie Blanc, wanted justice for her. But in the end, he knew he only really had one choice – the one that was best for France.

He gathered the papers and strolled out of the library, prepared to do what he knew he must.

7

Two Sides to a Story – Part 2

Sunlight creeps in, the rays reaching toward my pillow, their fingers coming ever closer, bright beams creating fluid patterns on the pillowcase.

I relish these moments, when all is quiet and still, an abnormality for a place like this. One never thinks of hospitals as noisy; however, they seem to thrive on endless sounds – beeps from the machines, the endless pacing of visitors and staff, and somber conversations led by earnest doctors, all busy passing judgments and making prognoses. God, how I hate doctors. I never used to have much of an opinion about them, but now I find their self-importance more irritating than being here.

From what the nurses say, it was night when they brought me here. Apparently, I had been in the Louvre, which seems odd because, generally speaking, I don't like museums. I find them tedious and pretentious, and I haven't stepped inside of one for ages. It's very perplexing; I can't figure out what I was doing there. When I flicker through my memories, I have the faintest sensation of flying, but nothing more.

According to the doctors, I have been here for more than two weeks. I'm not fully aware of my situation, but sometimes images pass through my mind, making me wonder if subconsciously I know more than I realize.

The sunlight flickers once more and my eyes droop. I find myself tired again, tired even though I've done nothing but lie here.

I have just drifted off, my fingers imbued with that light tingle that always precludes my descent into slumber, when my door opens. I don't stir, hoping that whoever it is gets the point that now is not the time to visit. But as the person lets go of breath that has been held for too long, I know instinctively that they aren't going to leave. I also know who it is.

Celeste.

Her fragrance infests the room, the pungent oud perfume assaulting my senses. I can see her in my mind, that statuesque figure that dominates every space so easily. I imagine she is dressed, as always, impeccably, perhaps a midnight-blue Lanvin dress draped elegantly, its color offsetting her perfectly coiffed platinum hair. I can feel her eyes on me, those cold, calculating green eyes that never seem to emit any kind of warmth or humanity.

Selfish, spiteful Celeste embodies everything that I detest in today's society. Her self-obsession, coupled with a complete lack of a moral compass, makes her extremely dangerous. I've heard stories of her destroying people just for her own personal enjoyment. In fact, I know someone whose career she completely ruined. The man's crime? He had simply pointed out an ethics issue in a case she had accepted. One small thing, and she went at him like a terrier after a rat. The woman is a menace, a master of manipulation, particularly when it comes to her ambitions. It wouldn't be hard to imagine the streets of Paris lined with the carcasses of people she has used and discarded, their dreams and aspirations of no importance to her. The one thing that matters, the only thing that matters to Celeste, is Celeste.

Not that I should be surprised, given her family history. War has a way of bringing out the best and worst of people, and Celeste's father showed his true nature when he became a leading Nazi collaborator in northern France. After the war, he tried to hide his past by moving to Paris, but it wasn't hard to uncover his crimes, especially when I had a good investigator.

Yes, that's right. I was the one who revealed her father's history. I saw it as my duty; the citizens of Paris deserved to know who they were voting for.

Her PR team worked overtime to spin the story, but something tells me they weren't completely successful.

'You are looking better, I suppose.' Her low, melodious voice fills the room, its intensity hurting my ears. 'I didn't want to visit, but you know what the press can be like. If I hadn't come, my polls would have suffered, and I can't have that. We are so close to election time, and I'm in the lead. You should see your replacement, he is a work of art. I don't know which board room they dragged him from, but the man is a hopeless politician. He won't last a second after this election. I'll see to it. Just like I took care of you.' She laughs mirthlessly. 'Hmm, maybe this trip wasn't such a bad idea. It's probably the one chance I'll have to be completely honest with someone. And based on what the doctors have been saying, it doesn't seem like you will ever wake up, so whatever I say will stay with you.' There is a rustle of fabric, and pressure as she sits down on the bed next to me. 'So yes, you're here because of me. I don't know if you remember your little accident in the Louvre. Well, obviously not an accident at all. I must say, I wasn't expecting it to be quite so successful.'

Images flash through my mind. A phone in my hand, with something... upsetting. A message? Photograph? There's the Niké of Samothrace, her body striding away from me, until the lightest of touches sends me flying, my fingertips reaching out to touch those delicate wings.

Then, there's nothing. A swirling vortex of blackness threatens to suck me under, but I fight it.

Eyes still closed; I detect her movements as she opens a window – forbidden – and lights a cigarette – strictly forbidden. After listening to the gentle puffs of her smoking, I hear a thud as she brings the window down, filling the room with a pungent fog, the distinctive smell of her cigarettes leaving me nauseated.

My thoughts are broken off by the sound of metal clanging; Celeste always played with her cuff bracelets when she was restless. 'Although this has been lovely, I should get going. So much to do. I expect the next time I see you, it'll be at your funeral. Won't that be nice? It will have a wonderful sense of finality. One can only hope that that day comes sooner rather than later.'

She leaves in a flurry of sounds – the rustle of packages as they are gathered, the click of her shoes on the tile floor, and the door that stops short of slamming shut.

My next visitor is my nurse, who's sweet but, at the same time, terribly old-fashioned. She rearranges me, then oh-so-gently runs her fingers through my hair.

After a minute, she steps back and says, 'That's looking much better. We can't have you looking disheveled for your husband, can we? He should be here any second now.' I can sense her glancing down at her watch. My heart sinks. I wish she wouldn't go, that I could stay within the secure confines of her fingers. She reminds me so much of my mother, and the thought makes me want to weep.

But soon, Louis, my husband... or should I say ex? We have been together for so long; it is difficult to think of us as separate entities. My feelings toward him have undergone a serious transformation. But one can't always predict the future, and I certainly couldn't when I rushed to meet him at our favorite café in the 1st arrondissement, on the afternoon of the Louvre event. It was our wedding anniversary, the thirtieth to be precise, and I was late.

In my hand, I grasped a beautifully wrapped package containing Louis' present, a luxurious azure cashmere scarf, the brilliant blue his favorite color since it contrasted so well with his graying hair. Not the most creative gift, I know, but at least it was something he would use. After all, when you've been married for that long, the romantic gestures tend to diminish and gifts veer toward the utilitarian. Little did I know the 'gift' he had in store for me.

I had just crossed Rue Montorgueil, my head tilted upwards to appreciate the unseasonable warmth of the afternoon sun, when my thoughts were interrupted by the screeching of an engine followed by a thud. I glanced over, sure that there had been an accident, only to be knocked over by the solid mass of a body from the opposite direction. My knees slammed into the pavement, the upper part of my body cushioned by the man below. My eyes narrowed as I studied him; he didn't seem to be the type to assault an unknown woman, but one could never tell. Words of indignation sprang to my tongue, but, before I could utter them, my attention was drawn back to where I had been. It was chaos. A bollard that I had walked next to seconds before was now lying on its side, its uprooted base crumbling under the impact of a sleek black-and-red motorbike. People scattered as the bike righted itself and the driver took off once again, its departure as startling as its entry.

'I'm sorry, but would you mind moving? It's just that I'm having difficulties breathing.' The voice underneath me was sincerely apologetic in the way that only British people could be, particularly when they are not the ones at fault.

'Oh yes, I'm so sorry. Thank you,' I said, getting up carefully.

He stood, his tall frame crammed into an ill-fitting suit, which was now horribly wrinkled. 'Ah, that's better. Thank you. Are you okay?'

'Yes, thanks to you. I can't imagine what that was all about.'

'Nor can I. But trust me, he was coming straight toward you.'

Those last words reverberated through my mind as I spoke with the police about what had happened. During that time, I tried calling Louis, but his phone automatically went to voicemail, leading me to believe he was having one of his 'very important' business calls that never ended.

Once the police finished, they dropped me off near the café before racing off. I weaved through tables on the pavement until I reached ours.

As predicted, he was on the phone. Yet, his mannerisms led me to believe this was not a business call. Not the usual one at least. The downward tilt of his head was altogether too secretive, and he fiddled with his wine glass, something he normally didn't do. My suspicions intensified as I approached the table, for he abruptly ended the call and looked up. I saw surprise in his eyes before the expression was quickly shrouded.

'Hello, I was wondering where you were,' he said, rising and kissing my cheek.

I frowned. 'There was an incident. Which you would have known if you had answered your phone. This is for you,' I said, shoving the once-pristine package into his hands.

'You shouldn't have...' he said as he sat down. 'Wine?'

'Yes, thank you.' Fatigue hit the moment I sat down, and I felt like going home and having a nap. The warmth of the sun, the taste of the wine, and the gentle murmurs of the other diners had a soothing effect on me. As Louis talked, I could feel my eyelids begin to droop.

'Valerie!' My eyes snapped open. 'Did you hear what I said?'

'No,' I snapped back. 'I've had a long day, and I still have my event tonight. So, forgive me if I missed something. Wait, are you leaving already?'

Well, I had certainly missed something. And now, now that I'm sitting in this room, in silence, I can finally remember the message that upset me so much on that fateful night.

I meant what I said in the café. I want a divorce now.

When you've been married as long as we have, it's difficult, if not impossible, to keep the momentum going. For me, it had been gone long ago, yet I still cared deeply for him. Clearly, he did not reciprocate.

The moment Louis enters my hospital room, the atmosphere in the room changes: a sense of hesitancy and shared history infuses the air. As he approaches me, his eyes focused intently on me, a trickle of apprehension works its way down my spine.

'You look good.'

I can't say the same about him. I have heard the nurses talk about his appearance; apparently, he has aged considerably in the last two weeks. There are shadows underneath his eyes, his hair is unkempt, and his suit is rumpled.

He steps forward, his coat brushing up against my blanket, and leans over.

'I'm so sorry...' he whispers in my ear. 'It wasn't supposed to happen that way... he said it would be painless. Painless and permanent. That was the agreement.'

Painless? Permanent? What agreement?

'But maybe this is for the best. I should have known it wasn't the best way to end our marriage. I just got caught up in the drama. I guess that's what happens when you fall in love with somebody like Antoinette. And getting rid of you seemed like a good idea at the time, but now, now I'm not sure. I mean, it makes you think, doesn't it?'

Yes, I think you are crazy. Do you honestly hear yourself Louis? You tried to kill me so you could be with this Antoinette. It's outrageous!

'I spoke with the doctors, they're optimistic about your recovery. I was thinking, maybe we should move you somewhere nicer. You always said you wanted to live on a lavender farm. And if we don't do it now, when are we going to do it?' He patted my hand. 'And I promise, I'll be here for you. Even after everything, it turns out that I still love you.' He glances down at his watch, some overly expensive thing that I'd gotten him. 'Well, I'll leave you for now, can't stand hospitals, but I'll see you again soon.'

He turns and leaves, the cloying smell of cologne that I had not purchased lingering long after he had gone.

I'm exhausted now. My two visitors, not content with trying to kill me, have just drained me of energy. I wonder about drifting back into that peaceful nothingness, but I can't. Even if my body wants to, my mind refuses to comply.

I open my eyes, the light-filled room coming into focus and spurring me into action. In my mind, I can see myself stepping from my bed, ready to defend myself from any more terrible visitors.

'Beep! Beep! Beep!' The machine next to me comes to life, its shrillness piercing the air, and a doctor comes running in.

'We're losing her!' he shouts, before it flatlines.

As I begin levitating, I look down at my body and shrug.

Which one should I haunt first? I wonder while I float away.

***

Bastille Day 2024

My death lasted three minutes and fifteen seconds. I will never understand how they managed to bring me back to life, but I am profoundly grateful to the doctors who resuscitated me.

Because of them, I am living a peaceful life on a lavender farm in southern France, the entrancing smells wafting through my windows and bringing me much joy. Occasionally, when I feel like it, I walk through those fields, feeling the cool grass underfoot and reveling in the fact that on this day, the 14th of July 2024, I can celebrate that even after all her plots and machinations, I have outlived Celeste Rouge, former mayor of Paris and president of France.

8

One Mousse, Two Mousse, Three Mousse, Four...

It was a bittersweet irony that Tristan Harrington's end occurred at the beginning of a festival, although by all accounts, it was no ordinary festival. No, this event had the backing of the Spanish government, along with the rather suggestive name 'Seductions of the Chili Pepper,' which, as a seasoned food critic, Tristan deemed ridiculous. But as a writer from a certain generation, there was much in the world that he found ridiculous.

Including his boss, the new editor of the *Your Way, Today* newspaper.

Tristan had been with the newspaper since its inception forty years ago; he had started at the bottom as a lowly reporter, then worked his way up. At the beginning, he would waste his days lurking outside courts, interviewing low-level thugs and burying himself deep in the pits of the newspaper archives researching for the more senior reporters. Over time, he progressed, and once he had completed his studies at a prestigious culinary school, he merged his two loves – food and writing. He began writing restaurant reviews – unpaid, of course. But he used the experience to build up a portfolio. After a year of unpaid reviews, he presented his extensive portfolio to his editor.

The editor saw something in him and gave him a chance; six months later, Tristan had his dream job – food critic. He gained the editor's trust and was given free rein to review anything. Tristan was allowed to go wherever he wanted and eat whatever was on the menu with however much money was required for the experience.

Some would have taken advantage of this freedom, but Tristan did not. For the most part, he was a man of principles and believed the unbiased truth took precedence over everything else.

Unfortunately, this long-anticipated freedom would not last. It transpired that his editor did not share his principles. In fact, his truth was so far from the actual truth that it would take a bridge to join the two. It had taken a whistle-blower and months of independent investigation to determine that he had taken monies from several questionable businessmen in return for burying certain stories.

Tristan was saddened but not surprised by this turn of events.

For a while, he remained largely unconcerned. He was, after all, the best food critic in the country and still in his prime.

Then, he met his new editor, Augustus.

'Just call me Gus,' he told Tristan as he stretched out his hand. 'Gus' leaned back idly in his chair, his other hand tapping a pendulum toy that swung irritably on his desk.

Tristan shook the proffered hand, eyes narrowed. Being a journalist required certain talents, and the ability to sniff out a wanker was one of them. 'Just call me Gus' was not fooling anyone. Beneath that chummy, laid-back façade lurked your stereotypical public-school graduate, complete with a permanent sense of entitlement and arrogance.

It didn't take long for Gus to reveal his true nature. Though his predecessor hadn't been perfect by any account, he had, at least, been dedicated to his job. Gus had no such compulsions; it was clear that he was doing the bare minimum required to keep the newspaper running. In the three months he had been editor, his lunch breaks had lengthened exponentially. Tristan had won fifty pounds in a bet on

Gus's last lunch break, which had started at ten-forty and finished at two-fifteen.

Normally, Tristan wouldn't mind this laissez-faire attitude, but it was more complex than that. Because while Gus didn't do his job, he thrived on telling people how to do theirs. He was an irritant, not just to Tristan, but everyone at the paper.

It was a Friday afternoon when Gus sprang his news on Tristan.

'Have you finished that review yet?' he asked, dressed in a suit that was meant to be ironic in its cheapness but failed since Tristan was able to spot Savile Row a mile away.

'Yes.' Tristan waited. He knew there was a bombshell coming; that was the way Gus operated. He always saved his unpopular requests and orders for Friday afternoon when everyone was on their way out.

'I need you to go to this,' Gus said, handing him a shiny brochure.

Tristan looked at it.

'I don't do festivals,' he said.

'You may not have in the past... but you're going now,' Gus said, all traces of congeniality gone.

'But... chili peppers!' Tristan spluttered.

'They're flaming hot right now – it's all about the chili peppers. Besides, the festival is in Barcelona... and, if I'm not mistaken, Barcelona was just voted number one for world's sexiest food. According to *Our Way, The News Highway,* it's the "pulse" for all the current food trends. So, it's crucial you go... after all, you aren't getting any younger, but your readers are, so you have to stay current. Speaking of which, I need you to sex up your reviews a bit, they're feeling a bit stale.'

With every word spoken, Tristan found his will to live depleting. He struggled to keep a neutral expression on his face. Deep down, he knew that, in a way, Gus was right. New readers demanded new ways of writing and reviewing. If he wanted to stay in his job, doing what he loved, he would have to adapt.

Tristan looked through the brochure again, hoping another peek would make the festival more appealing. It didn't. They had done their best to make the festival seem seductive yet high end, which he was sure enticed some, like his boss, but he knew the true food aficionados wouldn't bite. He shook his head. Back in the day, festivals were fantastic: vibrant, affordable gatherings of like-minded people exploring new tastes and sounds. Nowadays, they are over-hyped, overpriced, underperforming ventures with money being thrown around by people who were richer but not wiser.

At least he was going to Spain, a country he had enjoyed tremendously in the past, although now it had the nickname 'Britlandia' due to the alarming number of Brits who had immigrated there. He hadn't noticed at first, but then, about a decade ago, he'd had the unfortunate luck of running into several people he knew from London. He considered this first instance coincidental, but he soon determined that Spain had been 'discovered,' and the hordes of British had multiplied, much to his ever-growing dismay. Like most nationalities, there were Brits and there were *Brits*. He was of the former, the tourist who embraced another country's culture... as long as it was of a certain standard, of course. The latter category were the Brits who took Britain with them on their travels. They were the tourists who constantly asked for a full English breakfast and were not happy with anything else. However, even with these narrowminded travelers and the increased foot traffic, Tristan knew that Spain was infinitely better than some of the other destinations that he had been sent to under Gus's editorship. Places like Budapest.

Several months ago, Gus had stopped by Tristan's office with a book in his hand and said, 'Budapest.' Tristan had been wary; although he had traveled throughout Eastern Europe extensively, he had always managed to avoid this particular city. He knew several food critics from Budapest, and quite simply, they were nasty pieces of work. He'd taken them out for dinner one night and their bullying toward the hospitality staff had been disgraceful. That had been years ago, and by all accounts, the men had only gotten worse. Tristan tried to convey his thoughts about Budapest to Gus, but in typical Gus fashion, he bulldozed through the conversation.

Once he arrived in Budapest, Tristan realized that the trip was a test on Gus's part; not only had the food been poor, but the Hungarians he had met had been thoroughly unpleasant. Then, there had been the not-so-small matter of his accommodation. He was used to staying at four-star hotels, which was more of a necessity than a perk because of his age and need for certain amenities, but this trip had been last minute, and his accommodation had been booked the day he arrived. That Hungary had miraculously made the semifinals for the World Cup didn't matter to Tristan, nor did the fact that there wasn't availability anywhere else in the city. The hotel was substandard. It started with the gloomy lobby, continued with several black hairs found on the pillow (Tristan was bald), and finished with two early wake-ups generated by several rowdy children next door.

He had arrived back in London in a particularly vile mood; he hated Gus, traveling, and life in general, in that exact order. He began to wonder if he was getting too old for the travel part of this job. He had been doing this for so long, he was starting to feel weary. Truthfully, he now preferred staying on his own terrain – West London, to be precise, in his beautiful terrace that he had purchased in the eighties when prices were still reasonable. Back then, it had been a recently vacated squat. After several years and considerable work, it had finally been transformed into the elegant abode that it was now – a peaceful sanctuary that was becoming increasingly difficult to leave.

So, it was with a sense of irritability that Tristan dragged his luggage from the wardrobe and began packing. In went his travel suit, a bespoke piece that had cost a week's wages but looked good no matter what and, more importantly, made him appear svelte even after he had consumed a four-course meal. His Derek Rose pajamas were next. Contrary to some of his contemporaries, Tristan believed in presenting a stylish appearance twenty-four hours a day. A second change of clothes, a few essential toiletries, and he was done. He topped his carry-on with a cashmere blanket: a necessity when traveling, even if it was business class.

The flight was forgettable, as was the food, and he was content to reach his hotel, The Wittmore, in record time. It was, by the look of it, a proper hotel, with none of the nonsense you would find at the cheaper establishments. He was pleased to see a sign that discouraged children and pets from staying there. As he approached the desk, he heard the receptionist enforce this rule; Tristan silently applauded the man's strength of character before signing the guest book. He had just finished screwing the cap back on the pen when his phone pinged.

'You there yet?'

Gus was not known for his patience.

'Just checked in,' Tristan responded.

'Great. Now remember, seduce me, seduce the reader. I want something original; I want something sexy.'

'Sexy,' Tristan scoffed. 'The cheek of the man.' He glared at his phone, the temptation to respond with a cutting remark rising with every second. But before he could do so, a low battery warning flashed before his screen switched off.

'Peace and quiet,' he said as he took the elevator up to his room. He unpacked his luggage, prepared his palate cleansers for the festival, then indulged in a relaxing bath. Draining the water from the bath, he glanced outside his window, debating whether to go out and enjoy Barcelona's nightlife, but his body resisted, its aches and pains making him all too aware of his age and increasing limitations.

He awoke just as the sun was rising, his mouth desiccated from the dryness in the room. He whipped off his eye mask and drank some chilled cucumber water before donning his lightweight suit.

The sun was peeking through the canopy of leaves as he walked down La Rambla toward the site of the festival – the Plaza de Catalunya. As he walked, he noticed the subdued aura of the street – in previous years, he had enjoyed the intoxicating mix of music, food, and drink that defined La Rambla's nightlife – but all was quiet this morning, the chaos of the previous night gone. A few stragglers, their legs unsteady, weaved from one side of the street to the other, singing snippets of song. Their progress was watched with amusement, and a few cheers went up as they passed. Tristan lost sight of them as they turned down a small lane, no doubt on their way to one of Barcelona's famed street festivals.

He was nearing the plaza when he saw the festival's sign. It stretched between two large poles, its perfection marred by the presence of several pigeons who perched above it, their eyes fixed on the food below.

The earliness of the hour translated into a handful of attendees; the few that were present walked around aimlessly, their brochures waving furiously to alleviate the heat and high humidity. Tristan pushed his straw fedora up before patting his forehead with a handkerchief. He gazed around, trying to count the number of stalls but losing track after sixty-two. It was going to be a long day.

He began with the drinks – teas infused with chili, the steam rising to caress his cheek; sparkling waters, their effervescence held in check with the darkness of a smoldering chili; alcoholic beverages, their fiery flavor intensified. With each item, he lingered, taking note of the appearance, composition, and, lastly, the flavor. He rolled the liquids around in his mouth, seeing whether they had accomplished their lofty goals. The tea came close, the alcohol wasn't bad, but the sparkling water failed abysmally. He jotted down some notes, then drank some of his peppermint-flavored water before moving toward the food.

And what could he say? He stopped at over forty stalls, tasting everything from oysters to salsas, stews to croquettes. The stalls were admittedly well presented, the food was displayed in creative ways, however, the quality of the food... well, that was another matter altogether. If he was being kind, he would say it was mediocre, but most offerings were simply ghastly. They were all wrong; if the texture was fine, the flavor was off, or vice versa. Tristan dabbed at his mouth with a napkin before flinging it into a bin in disgust. He wondered if the stallholders had actually tasted their own dishes, or whether they were too busy chasing profits.

He continued down the line, his mouth in a state of displeasure, when his eye caught a glimmer of light, a touch of something magical. Through the now-massive crowd, he could see a glimpse of a stall whose delightful and whimsical decorations gave him a sense of nostalgia. He rushed forward, jostling through a constant stream of people until he reached his destination. For once, he was speechless as he approached the stall. In truth, it was not as fancy or stylish as the other stalls, but that's where its charm lay. It possessed an elegant simplicity; rich burgundy fabric draped over the table, its color enhanced by long branches entwined around the sign that read 'Sweetness of Life Dessert.' Interspersed here and there were little glass raspberries that moved with every breeze. Tristan drew closer and was greeted warmly by the owner, who invited him to try her specialty, a delicate chocolate raspberry mousse infused with the oil from the Gibraltar Naga, a pepper commonly grown in Spain.

Tristan took the small glass bowl, unaware that his fate was sealed as he took a spoonful of the airy brown mass. The second the spoon touched his tongue, the flavors burst, and he knew it was the most sublime dessert he had ever had. The beautifully rich chocolate merged perfectly with the tangy sweetness of raspberry, with the heat of the chili underpinning the whole thing. It was decadent yet contained layers of such complexity and delicacy. Tristan's taste buds sang as he ate, and he felt invigorated with every spoonful.

It was only when he heard the caustic sound of his spoon scraping the bottom of the bowl that he realized he had finished. He put the spoon down, looked at the owner, and did something he had not done in years – he ordered another mousse. And, twenty minutes later, another one.

By the end of the day, he had eaten eleven mousses – the last tasting as sublime as the first. True, there was the matter of his stomach;

once he had finished the tenth, it had been making some rather alarming grumbles. As he left the festival, the grumblings became fiercer, and he touched his stomach gingerly, his face scrunched up in pain.

'¿Todo está bien?' a street artist called out, the lamplights casting sinister shadows on her face.

'No, no...' Tristan muttered as he bent over. A sharp pain in his stomach, radiating toward his ribs, stopped all thought. He crouched down and tried to breathe slowly. 'One... two... three...' It took until ten for the pain to subside. Once it had, he walked to the nearest taxi stop and hailed the first available taxi he saw.

Tristan ignored all attempts at conversation that the driver made; his only concern was returning to the hotel, taking some Gaviscon, and going to sleep. After what seemed like hours, but was in reality only fifteen minutes, he was back in his hotel room. He trudged to the toilet, where he had several unpleasant dry heaves before taking his medicine. Then he crawled into bed.

His teeth felt furry when he woke up the next morning. He ran his tongue across them, the taste of Gaviscon still present.

'Bleh,' he said, as he got up and walked to the bathroom. He showered then brushed his teeth, determined that last night's sickness would not affect today.

But in that, he was wrong.

It happened in a restaurant. Not just any restaurant, *the* restaurant. It was a small restaurant that had opened several months ago to wild acclaim. According to reliable sources, its unpretentious menu coupled with its surprising pairings, one of which he was having today – their famous seafood omelet with a dark chocolate reduction – made for an exciting dining experience.

'Chocolate again,' he murmured as he downed some preventative medicine, all pains from the previous night now gone.

The restaurant was certainly small, its entrance tucked away between two more ostentatious establishments. He walked down the steps, ducking under a darkened cross-beam before entering the main dining room. It was an intimate and enclosed space, the exposed brick walls and subtle lighting creating a warm haven filled with enticing smells. He sat at the middle table and perused the menu before gesturing toward the waiter.

'Sí,' the man said as he approached the table.

'Una copa de vino blanco, y una tortilla de marisco española por favor,' Tristan said, closing the menu decisively.

'Por supuesto,' the waiter said.

People poured into the restaurant and soon it was awash in Spanish and Catalan, the conversations flowing around him like a gentle, persistent river.

'Very atmospheric – intimate, yet refined,' he wrote on his phone.

He continued taking notes, his brow furrowed, until he smelled something amazing next to him. His meal had arrived. If the review was based on presentation alone, it would have been five stars. It was a visual delight – bright lemony yellow with flecks of dark coral that contrasted with the deep mahogany of the chocolate reduction.

'Lovely,' he said before picking up his fork.

He cut off a sliver of omelet and ate it.

Then another.

And another.

He frowned.

Something was wrong.

He cut the omelet on the other side, ensuring that this piece was brimming with smoked salmon before placing it on his tongue. He waited for the flavors to explode in his mouth, but there was nary a fizzle, let alone an explosion. In fact, he couldn't detect a single hint of flavor.

His frown deepened. He dipped a fork tine into the reduction, waiting for the bittersweet taste to arrive, but it never did.

Next to the plate was a bowl of fresh fruit. The strawberries glistened under the soft globes overhead, the oranges heavy with their own succulent juices. Tristan contemplated both before spearing an orange slice and placing it in his mouth. He chewed, his chewing more audible now as he became increasingly desperate. Finished with the orange, he dropped his fork on the plate and his face crumpled in distress. The waiter, who had been watching him, rushed over.

'Está bién?' he asked. People generally did not frown at *this* restaurant, the staff made sure of it.

Tristan gave up all pretenses of speaking Spanish.

'No, no it's not all right. I bloody well can't taste a thing. Where is your chef? This is completely unacceptable!' Tristan threw down his napkin in disgust.

The waiter grimaced, speaking in heavily accented English. 'I'm sorry you're unhappy with your meal, could we entice you to try something different? Perhaps a lovely crepe?'

'I suppose so. Let's hope, for your sake and the sake of this restaurant's reputation, that it's better than this,' he gestured toward his plate, which was still nearly full.

'Yes of course,' the waiter said, a smile plastered on his face as he cleared away the offending items. Tristan took a sip of his wine and scowled as the cool liquid flowed from his mouth to his throat. This too lacked any kind of flavor. How on earth had this restaurant received such hype?

Ten minutes later, the waiter floated back, his ingratiating manner now submerged under a layer of smugness as he placed a dainty plate onto the table. Two crepes crisscrossed, their delicate forms topped with a feather-light dusting of powdered sugar and three plump raspberries, a smear of raspberry reduction making a vibrant crimson path across the bottom portion of the plate.

Tristan cut a piece and chewed... while the texture was right, there was no flavor. He frowned and pushed one of the raspberries, which rolled back toward his fork in a beguiling manner. He stared at it, and his stomach began turning over, a turbulent force that he had not encountered before. With a groan, he heaved himself up and rushed to the lavatory, barely making it in time before he began spewing. He lost all track of time as he leaned on the toilet, every cell of his body aching, his throat raw from vomiting.

Finally, after he had heaved his last, he stood weakly and flushed the toilet. He turned on the taps and washed his face, then stared bleakly at his reflection in the mirror.

'Drip... drip... drip...'

He jammed the tap, but the noise continued.

'Drip... drip... drip...'

He hit it again, but instead of stopping, it accelerated.

'Drip, drip, drip,'

With both hands, he wrenched the tap, only for it to fall away in his hands. The drip stopped.

'Phew,' he said.

'WOOOOOSH!'

A geyser gushed out of the broken tap's hole, quickly filling the sink before flowing onto the floor.

'BLOODY HELL!' he shouted. What next? He grabbed the tap and tried to put it back on, but it was too late. The water pressure was too strong, and he was still feeling weak from the vomiting. He lurched to the door and debated what to do. From his perspective, there were two courses of action: the right one – inform the staff and stick around – and the wrong one – to stay silent and leave.

His mind decided to follow the path of righteousness, but failed to alert his body, which decided it was going to leave right bloody now. Before he knew it, he was outside in the street hailing a taxi.

The journey back to the hotel was long and challenging. Random pains shot through his body, and his mouth was as dry as a cup of flour.

He knew what was happening. It was as clear as the cracked faux leather underneath his head. He was the victim of sabotage. This had been planned from the very start. Gus wanted to be rid of him, so he had made him go to that damned festival where those damn mousses had annihilated his taste buds. If it hadn't been for those mousses, that whole thing in the loo would never have happened.

Yet, even as he cemented his new victim status, a small portion of his mind rebelled against this direction. His taste buds had always been robust: how could a little mousse destroy them? His face clouded over as he remembered the vast amount of mousse he had consumed, and his face turned ashen. It wasn't sabotage after all; it was an uncharacteristic spell of gluttony. He shuddered. This never would have happened when he was younger. It was him; he was deteriorating. He, who had always been known for his professionalism, his discipline, was crumbling into a gluttonous mess.

Agonized, he tumbled out of the taxi into the street. He staggered into the hotel, went up to his room, and packed his bags. Then, using all his frequent flyer points, he booked the next flight back to London.

Home, he needed to be home.

Once he was safely ensconced in his house, relishing the sanctity of his space with all its meticulous order, he sank into his writing chair and whipped out his laptop. He stared at the back garden and contemplated his career. It was over. He knew it, and soon everyone else would too. After all, what good was a food critic who couldn't travel, wasn't disciplined, and, more importantly, couldn't taste?

He grimaced. Gus would be thrilled. This was the perfect opportunity for him to replace Tristan with some bright young thing. Probably some hipster whose face was plastered all over the internet and who used 'socials' rather than 'social media.'

Christ, he felt old. And tired. And defeated.

He glanced at the 'Seductions of the Chili Pepper' brochure and chuckled dryly. If ever there was a misnomer, that was it. The festival should have been named 'Death by a Thousand Chilies.' More poetic and more honest.

'Death by a Thousand Chilies,' he said. 'I quite like that.'

He began typing.

9

On a Ferry to Tallinn

Frost had delicately etched the oak leaves one October morning when Sylvie Stoddington descended the staircase in her cottage. Her feet, snugly encapsulated in sheepskin slippers, moved of their own accord toward the benchtop where the kettle sat. Sylvie flicked the switch and reached up into the cabinet for her favorite mug. She made herself a cup of tea and sat down at the kitchen table, its surface covered in the usual accruement of daily life – junk mail, keys… and underneath it all, a journal, well worn, its leather supple and creased. She pushed an envelope out of the way and pulled the journal toward her, stroking the cover, its smoothness transporting her back to when it all began.

***

The ferry was late. Sylvie looked at her watch for what felt like the hundredth time that hour, her heart twisting at the sight of the rose-gold face, its circle offset by four seed-pearl butterflies. The bracelet links entwined her slender wrist, which had become even more fragile in recent months.

The death of Sylvie's husband Jack the previous year had been an overwhelming blow. They had both been due to retire, and she had envisioned many happy years traveling together. Sadly, the universe had had a different idea, and he was killed on his way to work when his bicycle was hit by a white van.

The shock she had felt when the police knocked on the door to tell her had lingered for months. It was simply inconceivable that Jack, who had been her life, someone who had made every day an adventure, was now gone. So quickly and easily, his life, their life, their dreams, had all been extinguished.

For a while, some of these feelings were kept at bay as life continued and practical matters had to be managed. The funeral was planned, the finances were sorted, and the usual mundane daily tasks had to be completed. She began streamlining her life. Did she really need such a big house? The decision to sell wasn't an easy one; she was in her mid-sixties, so moving was harder than it had been decades ago, but there wasn't much point in having something that required so much maintenance. And yes, although it was her daughter's childhood home, and Lizzie was upset, she had her own life. In the end, the decision was made, and another six months passed. Sylvie tried not to think of Jack and how much she missed him, but though she immersed herself in the sale of the house, hoping that something would diminish the grief, nothing happened. At times, the grief threatened to consume her and drag her deeper.

Before she could succumb, her daughter acted. Lizzie booked Sylvie a solo trip, saying that she needed to get out for a bit, live a little.

So here she was, Sylvie Stoddington, on a pier waiting for a ferry to take her across the Gulf of Finland to Tallinn, a place she knew very little about. She had wondered why Lizzie had picked Tallinn, but Lizzie hadn't shed any light on the matter.

Sylvie glanced at her watch again, then looked around at the other passengers. She was watching one family in particular, the toddlers shoving crayons into their mouths while the mother desperately tried to stop them, when a loud horn sounded, and the ferry could be seen in the distance. It was bigger than she had expected, its massive bulk moving steadily toward them. As it moored, the crew running from one end of the ship to the other, a line of people ready to disembark could be seen through the windows.

Sylvie stood and began to move toward the ship as the passengers began leaving one by one, their faces alight with happiness and excitement, with Sylvie wondering if she'd ever feel like that again. As she entered the ship, she was taken aback at how large it was. When she had traveled around the US, her experience with ferries had been vastly different. They had been simple, small crafts. This, on the other hand, was more like a luxury ship. Restaurants, shops, recreational activities this ship had it all.

She chose her seat carefully, one that promised a good view. She stared at the water, its blue so bright that she reached for her sunglasses.

'Doesn't seem quite real, does it?' A voice asked from behind her. 'I don't think I've ever seen that shade of blue before.'

She nodded politely, never sure how to respond to strangers when they spoke to her. That had been Jack's specialty. He'd had the gift of the gab. She was far more likely to flee from anything resembling small talk.

'Is anyone sitting here?' the man asked, gesturing toward the seat directly across from her. She thought about lying but, looking around, she noticed that it was the only vacant seat.

'No, it's free,' she said, and he sat down, his large and well-worn suitcase touching her leg briefly before resting against the small table between the chairs.

She examined him surreptitiously from behind her sunglasses as he fidgeted in the chair. Her first impression was positive; he looked kind. The second thing she noticed was his size, how his massive frame was crammed into the chair, his legs jutting out in a way that reminded her of a praying mantis. As he shuffled through various books in his bag, his demeanor became more flustered as he flipped through one after another, dropping them on the floor.

'Everything okay?' she asked, as he retrieved a notebook that had fallen underneath the table.

'Ugh... I thought I was more organized than this,' he said, a pile of books resting haphazardly on his knee.

'Don't we all,' she murmured.

'Sorry, didn't mean to make a mess all over the place. My name is Luc, by the way,' he said, reaching out with his right hand to shake hers.

'Sylvie,' she replied. His hand engulfed hers, the unexpected touch giving her a strange sense of security. She slid her sunglasses up and asked, 'Have you been to Tallinn before?'

This seemingly innocuous question opened a flood of conversation that lasted the entire two-hour trip. They discussed their mutual love of reading, then talked about food, travel, and writing, as Luc was a travel writer.

'That's fascinating. What a wonderful job,' Sylvie said. 'What do you like most about it?'

Luc thought for a moment. 'Well... this, actually. Meeting new people, seeing places that I've never been to before, eating food I never would have had... it makes life a bit more interesting.'

'And the hardest thing?'

'Living out of my suitcase gets a bit old after a while. And deadlines can be a nightmare. And, frankly, there are places that I've been to that I would have preferred to stay away from. But I've been doing it for thirty years, so I'd have to say the positives have far outweighed the negatives.'

Sylvie nodded. 'You're lucky then. I don't think many people can say that about their careers. I was a teacher for twenty years and, toward the end, it was difficult. Too many tests, too much red tape. So, I took redundancy last year. And now I get to travel. I never imagined that this would be my first trip. I don't know anything about Tallinn, but my daughter Lizzie planned it, so there wasn't much I could do. But I'm enjoying myself now.'

'It's been a while since I've been, but I'm sure you'll love it,' he said.

He excused himself to use the bathroom, so she put her sunglasses back on and looked out the window. *Is that a pier?* she wondered as she squinted against the glare of the sun.

Moments later, an announcement stated that they had arrived in Tallinn.

Sylvie was unsure of what to do; should she disembark or wait for Luc? There were scores of people moving toward the lines, but Luc was nowhere to be seen. He had taken his belongings, joking that he always carried them after an unfortunate incident in Budapest, so it was possible he wasn't coming back.

'Such a shame. He was so nice,' she mumbled as she gathered her bags and walked to the stairwell. She stood there for a while until, finally, the lines began to move, and the passengers disembarked in one large rush.

As she left the ship, she looked back, trying to find one face in a sea of unfamiliar ones. But it was impossible.

'Oh well, guess I'll never see him again.'

Walking along the waterway, she took out her map and focused on getting to her hotel. Lizzie had booked her into the Schlössle Hotel, a stunning place located in the Old Town. She crossed several large roads, her compact luggage rolling alongside her with a pleasant *thumpity-thump* until she approached the wall that enclosed the town. She stopped for a moment to catch her breath, admiring the unique buildings, their tall, lean frames casting shadows in the late afternoon sun. She marveled at the structures' various colors: greens nestling next to yellows, creams, and peaches. As she walked along, her luggage occasionally snagging on the cobblestones underfoot, she felt a pang that her husband wasn't there to enjoy this with her.

Following her map, she finally reached the Schlössle Hotel and checked into her room. It was a delightful space, decorated in subtle tones and lush fabrics. She sat on the bed, which was the perfect height and softness. Getting up, she perched on the window seat that overlooked the courtyard and watched as people drank and talked. After a few minutes, she began feeling restless and left her hotel to wander. She went through Town Hall Square, stopping to admire the stately town hall that loomed over the others, its pale brick blazing in the sun. She stood there, eyes closed, listening to tourists voicing their appreciation of the city and smelling something that had a delicious smokiness about it.

She smiled and opened her eyes. This was exactly what she had needed.

She walked around, eyeballing shops of all kinds – boutique shoe shops, perfumeries, decadent chocolate shops, and woolen goods stores. Entering the latter, she was struck by an immediate temptation to buy everything. From the handmade felted slippers to the wooden utensils, everything had been crafted to an impeccable standard. She ran her hand over a leather notebook, wondering if Luc used something like this for his work.

Leaving the shop, she made her way to Toompea Hill, which she had read about in her guidebook. It was a long walk up the cobblestoned street, but the book described a number of churches and statues as must-see sights. When she reached the top however, all thoughts of statues fled her mind upon seeing the view that lay before her. Red roofs glimmered in the sun, their uniformity broken with the occasional majestic towers, which created a sense of historical drama.

Sylvie's mouth dropped open at the stunning scene before her eyes. She took a few pictures but knew there was no way she could do the views any justice. She walked around, making her way to the castle and marveling at the blush-pink Baroque additions. It was beautiful but, as she looked, her eyes began to close, and she knew it was time for some rest.

She ended up in bed, the glorious mattress sucking her into its delightfully soft embrace. She fell into a deep, dreamless sleep, which was disturbed too soon by the sound of pealing bells. From her window, she could see the sun beginning its descent, so she left the comfort of her bed in search of a restaurant. Heels clicking on the cobblestones, she walked down a laneway and found a small place tucked away in a cozy nook. She sat and ordered a glass of wine and something called sprat off the menu. The food arrived quickly – a small plate that held dark rye bread and fish. Normally, she didn't eat fish, but this dish was exceptional, and she ate with gusto. As she did, a guitarist began playing, his gentle strumming the perfect background music for the night.

How Jack would have loved this, she thought, taking a long, appreciative sip of her wine. *Although he wouldn't have discovered this place, he always liked everything planned out. In fact, dying was the most spontaneous thing he'd ever done. Sad, really.*

Leaving the restaurant, her stomach full, she walked around the areas she had seen earlier. With the sun now gone, they were even more beautiful in the moonlight.

By the time she returned to the hotel, her feet were aching everywhere, the dull throb reminding her of how far she had walked. She threw some bath salts into the tub and rested her feet in the soothing water before staggering to bed. She fell asleep quickly, the grief that usually haunted her dreams diminished for once.

The next morning, she rose early and left Old Town. Stopping frequently to admire the many buskers, the strains of violin and cello kept her company as she continued her journey. She thought she saw Luc once but, as she got closer to the man, she realized that it was not him. She wondered if he was enjoying himself and concluded that he most certainly was. Tallinn was a delightful place; it was inconceivable that someone would have a bad time here.

She crossed a major road and found herself in a large open marketplace. She stopped at a nearby bakery stall, choosing a donut whose decadence was clear from the moment she put it into her mouth. Raspberry and white chocolate created the most delightful taste sensation she had ever experienced. She went back and bought another one, then walked around the market, tasting whatever took her fancy.

Leaving the market, she walked through a neighborhood and admired the timber houses that contrasted so greatly with the buildings from the Old Town. She zigzagged through, her curiosity leading her to a local grocery store to see what kinds of food they had. She bought a few snacks before walking back to her hotel. She went up to her room to grab one of the few books she had packed and went to the Town Hall Square to do some reading.

Truthfully, she spent more time watching people than reading. Watching the huge variety of tourists flooding the area, glued to their phones and cameras was fascinating. Everyone seemed so happy. Including her. She was happy, happier than she had been in a long time. She didn't want this feeling to go away and was fearful that it would end the moment she left Tallinn tomorrow.

The following morning, bags already packed from the night before, she got out of bed slowly, trying to savor every minute. The ferry was due to leave at noon, so she decided to have some tea at a charming tea shop she had seen on her walk the previous day. It didn't take long to find, and soon she was looking at the colorful array of teas, trying to select one. Finally, she chose an oolong and sat at her table with her cup, its fragrance delicately scenting the air. She was about to drop her bag onto the adjacent chair when she saw a notebook on the wooden seat. Picking it up, she turned it around in her hand when she heard 'Sylvie?!'

Looking up, she saw Luc in the doorway, an expression of delight on his face.

***

'Happy anniversary,' his voice brought her back to the present day, nearly fifteen years later.

'You too,' she said. 'I can't believe it's been so long.'

'Me neither. You know, I'm always grateful that I went back for my notebook. Not only did you treat me to the best cup of tea I've ever had, but that meeting was the beginning of us. I wouldn't have changed a thing, even if I did miss my ferry.'

She laughed. 'Me too.'

The Americas

10

I Opened an Oyster and the World Came Tumbling Out

No. 4 Acorn Lane was the kind of unobtrusive building that was frequently overlooked by the ubiquitous tourists who flooded into Boston like a swarm of gnats, bags clutched aggressively and suspiciously in one hand while the other hand took as many pictures as possible with their high-tech phones. These photographs captured every cobblestone, every building in sight… except for No. 4.

It stood somewhat crooked, its brick façade contrasting with the elegant Neoclassical edifices of its neighbors, whose impeccable proportions and sophisticated lines all stood perfectly straight. A small building, it gave no indication as to what it was, and few people entered… until a clear February day when it received two visitors.

Temperatures had plummeted well below zero the night before; the weather forecasts were predicting blizzards, but since the forecasters had been making all sorts of erroneous predictions over the last twelve months, no one took them seriously.

But still, there was something in the air, a hint of unfulfilled drama, that made anything possible.

And so it was, on that sunny February day, a couple, who carried with them the appearance of a recent union, stopped in front of the building and walked up the four steps leading to the warped wooden door.

The man, Hugo, opened the door and held it open for Gabby, his wife – a title she had held for exactly eighteen hours and thirty-six minutes – as she stepped gingerly through the entrance.

'Thanks,' she said, planting a light kiss on his mouth.

'No problem,' he replied as he stepped in behind her.

The door creaked closed, denying entry to the brightness from outside and sending the interior into a murky gloom.

They stood still for a moment as their eyes adjusted. Once they could see, they noticed the feeling of old age and neglect, particularly when Gabby began sneezing.

'Christ, of all the days to forget my allergy medication,' she said.

'Here,' he said, handing her a tissue. She wiped her watery eyes and blew her nose heartily.

'Better?' he asked.

'Oh God, yes. Thanks.'

Gabby shoved the tissue into her bag and walked over to a small door. Like everything else in the entryway, it was aged, but this had been maintained. Even in the dim light, it gleamed subtly, the polished wood's luster illustrating the owner's dedication. Next to the door was a plaque, a small ruby-colored square that read 'Mr. Smythe's Antique Emporium, Est. 1828.'

She pointed. 'This is definitely it.'

'So it seems.'

'That'll be ten dollars,' she said, her hand outstretched toward him.

He took out a twenty-dollar bill. 'Do you have change?'

She laughed and tucked it into her wallet. 'Nope. But, if you're lucky, I'll treat you to lunch.'

She turned the polished brass doorknob and pushed the door open. As they stepped inside, their mouths gaped open at the lushness within.

The walls were lined in a light château-green wallpaper, the silky material shimmering under the light of the vintage chandelier that hung in the center of the room. Rococo paintings, in both style and subject matter, dotted the walls, their indulgent irrelevance complementing the delicate tables scattered throughout, their surfaces full of sparkling trinkets and curiosities. Lamps stood around, the golden orbs sending a sepia-tinged hue that infused the room and heightened the aura of antiquity.

'I'll be with you in a second,' a voice called out.

Gabby circled the room decisively. Hugo followed behind, a near-silent shadow.

'You know exactly what it looks like?' he asked, his voice a faint murmur breaching the museum-like silence.

She sighed. 'Yes, of course. I played with it a lot as a child... and it's only been a few months since I last saw it, so of course I'll know it when I see it.'

'But do you think it's still here? I mean, he could have sold it right after he took it.'

She looked at him and shook her head. 'No, it's here. He hasn't had it long and something tells me that he hasn't figured out the internal puzzle yet. If he had, he would've splashed it all over his fancy website.'

'Hmm... wait, puzzle, what puzzle?'

She frowned. 'I told you about the puzzle last night; weren't you listening?'

A choked-back laugh was the only response she received. Before she could elaborate, the voice from before spoke again, louder this time, as he emerged from behind a curtain.

'Sorry for the delay, I've just had a new shipment come in. Can I help you with something?'

Gabby caught Hugo's eye, her signal that she was going to handle this.

'I'm looking for a box,' she said, her voice mysteriously lacking the confidence it had possessed only moments before.

'Any kind of box in particular?' the owner asked.

'Not really, I just want something big enough to hold a few trinkets. And walnut, it must be walnut. I've always loved that kind of wood, ever since I was little. But don't worry yourself, I'll take a look around to see if there's anything that draws my attention.'

The owner shrugged. 'As you wish. I can show you some now if you like.'

'Maybe later,' Gabby said.

'Of course. Let me know if you need any help.' He sat down at the counter and began typing methodically in front of a large desktop computer.

Gabby scanned the room, her eyes landing on a corner display case that housed a jumble of chests and boxes. She walked over and began looking through them. There were boxes of all types – wooden, silver, large and small. Some were engraved, most not. Some were well maintained – their surfaces gleaming with recently applied polish, their hinges moving with sensuous smoothness – whereas others had not fared so well, their physical defects indicative of the interesting lives they'd had. A rogue splinter here, the tell-tale tracks of a woodworm there and, as she held one up to the light, she thought she detected a hoof print embedded in its surface. She put it down and pursed her lips. So many boxes, but none of them was the right one. Was it possible that she was too late? She had only found out about the box's disappearance a couple of days ago, but what if he already had a buyer lined up?

She felt a pain in her neck. She groaned inwardly; the pain was usually a sign of an impending headache. The last thing she needed. Where was the box? There was no way in hell she was going to see her Gran empty-handed... after all, she had a promise to keep.

She glanced around, contemplating where he would hide it. It didn't look like there were too many nooks and crannies. She strolled around the shop, eyeballing everything and stopping every so often to look at something innocuous, but by the end, she could tell that Gran's box was not there.

'What kind of delivery was it?' Hugo asked in that jovial, matey tone he adapted so easily around a certain type of man.

The proprietor was only too happy to respond. 'Oh, just some bits and pieces from an estate sale I attended last week. But they're nice, quality pieces, not like some of that junk you see. Too many people watch those shows, you know what shows I'm talking about, then go rummaging through their attics looking for anything old. They somehow think old means valuable. It doesn't work like that, unfortunately for me. I'm the one who has to sift through everything, trying to separate the trash from the treasures…. and I've seen a few of those! And inheritances, don't even get me started. Some people are completely delusional. "This clock belonged to my dear Great Aunt M; she got it from her grandfather who bought it in 1815 so it must be worth a fortune." Well, no, actually it's not worth a damn cent. Those blasted shows have so much to answer for! Always giving people false hopes, especially the oldies. I do feel for them… they must not have much going on in their lives so they fill up the emptiness with TV. I just wish they'd watch something different, because now they all think they've got a masterpiece tucked away in their homes.'

As he spoke, Gabby's face reddened until she was the shade of a sun-ripened tomato. How dare this smarmy bastard be so condescending toward the elderly? His livelihood depended on them, how was he capable of speaking this way?

She dug her fingernails into her palms and counted down from ten. She had reached four when she had a thought. Perhaps the box wasn't out on the floor yet, perhaps it was still with the rest of the inventory. She needed to get behind that curtain.

The owner was standing with his back facing her. She gestured toward her husband to keep talking. He nodded discreetly and cracked a joke that had the owner laughing within seconds.

She backed up against the curtain, brushing aside the golden velour to reveal a small room. It was dimly lit, its diminutive size made even smaller by a large hulking cabinet that encompassed most of the room. The cabinet was full of beautiful objects, some sitting haphazardly on the shelves, others placed with great care. She searched quickly and there, on the fourth shelf, she found a small collection of boxes, one of which drew her attention immediately. She reached up and took it off the shelf, using her phone as a light to examine it. The box was small, made of walnut and ebony, with the letters 'BM' embossed on the lid. She traced the letters gently, as she had done since she was a little girl. Closing her eyes, she could almost smell the freshly baked bread in Gran's house and the ever-present scent of her potpourri: a comforting mixture of cloves, orange, and vanilla.

'Sorry, this area is for staff only.' The owner's voice broke through her reverie and abruptly returned her to reality.

'Oops,' she said, her face turning a bright shade of red once again. 'I'm so sorry. I fell against the curtain and saw this wonderful cabinet... it's really quite amazing.'

'Yes,' he said, plucking the box from her hands. The moment the box left her grasp, her fingers twitched, itching to snatch it back. 'But this area is strictly off-limits to customers.'

'Oh, what a shame, I was interested in some of the boxes you have here, including that one,' she replied, gesturing toward the little walnut box.

'You were? Well, you have excellent taste, but I'm afraid these items are spoken for. I already have buyers lined up for them. Collectors, what can I say? They know what they want and are quick to act. They are a seller's dream, if I'm honest with you... but if you're a fan of these boxes, I have a couple in the display room that are similar, if you'd like to see those.'

'Hmmm,' Gabby mumbled noncommittally as she allowed him to escort her back into the main room. He showed her several boxes, all of which were hugely overpriced and underwhelming. She decided it was time to go.

Before leaving, she faked enthusiasm for one specimen, gushing effusively over its delicate proportions and luminescent wood. The owner fell for her act, and negotiations for the box began. It didn't take them long to settle at a reasonable price.

As the couple left the store, she tossed the box casually into her bag.

'That isn't it, is it?' he asked.

She rolled her eyes. 'What do you think? No, of course not. I'd never treat Gran's box like that.'

'Then why did you buy this one?' he asked.

'I had to make him think I was satisfied... because he definitely has the box, and there's no way I'm going to get it. Not legally, at least.'

Her mind was already plotting the best way to steal Gran's box.

His next question was apprehensive. 'I'm not going to like this, am I?'

She stopped walking and looked at him. 'Nope, probably not.'

'And you're sure your Gran can't buy it?' he asked.

It was a stupid question, they both knew it, but she answered anyway.

'Are you kidding me? First off, where'd she find that kind of money? I can only imagine how much he's charging for it. Secondly, and more importantly, why would she buy something that is legally hers? He's the bad guy. He was supposed to appraise some of her things before she moved to the care home, not steal them. Not that anyone listened to her when she said her prized possessions were gone... they all thought she was just being "forgetful." No one cares about the elderly. Well, I do, so I'm going to steal it back for her.'

He spluttered. 'That's your big solution? Stealing it back... Are you crazy? There are so many things that could go wrong... why don't you just go to the police? I know she didn't have any luck, but they might listen to you. Please... let them handle this... they have the resources, after all.'

She laughed. 'You are joking. He's the owner of some fancy antique shop, why are they going to listen to me? Besides, even if they did listen, what the hell would they actually do? At best, they *might* go round and ask a few questions, but he'll have a perfectly legit story all ready for them. He is, unfortunately, related to us, so I'm sure he'll have contingency plans. The whole thing would go nowhere. No, the police can't help, I'll have to take care of this myself.'

'But you'll get caught. There's no way you can do this undetected, they all have security cameras these days. Do you really want to spend what would be our honeymoon in jail?'

She turned and looked at him. 'Look, I know you're worried, but it'll be fine. What do you think I did the first ten minutes we were there? I was casing out the place. Yes, I saw the cameras, but when I went out back, I checked and saw that they weren't connected. They're just for show. As for any security systems, not a chance. And as I said, I know him. Not very well, obviously I'd be screwed if he recognized me, but he's my... second cousin... something removed? Which isn't terribly important, but what *is* important is that I know how tight-fisted his side of the family is. Do you know that when my great-grandfather died, he sent my great-grandmother a reused sympathy card? He covered up some poor person's name and put hers there instead... and flowers... he gave her some half-dead poinsettias that still had their Christmas wrappings. My great-grandfather died in May. And they still had their price tag on – $19.99 reduced to $2.99. But do you know the saddest thing? He didn't give her anything until *after* the will had been read and he found out that he had inherited the shop and a tidy sum of money. So, based on that, I'm betting he does not have a security system. After all,' she paused, looking around, 'this place is pretty much under the radar. It's a quiet area, and his store is underwhelming from the outside. So, there you have it. But... if I do get caught somehow, I can't really see him calling the cops. He's the type who flies under the radar for a reason.'

Hugo nodded slowly. 'Points taken... but still...'

'Look, I'm not asking you to come with me. I can do this myself.'

But he was already shaking his head. 'Nope, still don't agree with it entirely, but I'm not letting you do this on your own.'

She smiled. 'Well, you can be on the lookout then.'

They walked around the block, Gabby muttering to herself as they moved to the back of the building.

She looked at the deserted alley and said, 'Right, this is our entry point.'

'Here?' He couldn't stop the note of apprehension that entered his voice. He had never liked alleys: they were too secluded, too unpredictable, and too many bad things happened in them. 'You know nothing good happens in an alley, right?'

'Relax. Everything will be fine,' she said as she looked around, analyzing the logistics and typing notes into her phone. She leaned against an old oak tree whose roots had long ago disturbed the cobblestones adjacent to the door, which now lurched around drunkenly.

'Relax, she says,' he muttered. It was mildly disturbing how quickly and easily his new wife was embracing illegal activities; one would think that she was the one with familial connections to organized crime, not him.

'Well?' he asked.

'All good, I won't need much tonight.'

She tapped away at her phone for a few minutes longer before turning away and walking down the street. He hurried after her.

***

It was a stormy night, the perfect setting for room service and hours of binging TV with your new wife. It was not, however, an ideal night for breaking and entering.

The sleet was pelting down in a mad frenzy, the sound of it hitting the windshield blocked all other noises.

'Well, this is unfortunate,' she said, gazing out the window in dismay. 'Where was this earlier? They didn't say anything about sleet on the forecast... I'd almost rather have a blizzard.'

'We can always cancel,' Hugo mumbled.

'No... it has to be tonight. I think he has a buyer coming in tomorrow. Can we park a bit closer?'

He nodded and pulled the car over a block from the shop. Before leaving the car, Gabby zipped up her coat and lamented the lack of waterproof material.

'Here,' Hugo said, handing her a large garbage bag.

'What am I supposed to do with this?'

'Really? Did you never do this for Halloween? You make a hole and put it on... it's like a ready-made poncho.'

'You wore a garbage bag for Halloween? Were you going as Oscar the Grouch or something?' she asked, laughing.

He sighed. 'Laugh all you want, but it was a simple solution.'

'Yeah, but then they wouldn't have been able to see your costume. Didn't people wonder what you were?'

'Not really. It was always raining on Halloween; we weren't the only ones wearing garbage bag ponchos.'

She looked at him sideways. 'Well, weren't you the trendsetters.'

'I know... that's why you married me, for my excellent fashion taste.'

She laughed again and they tore a hole in the bag. He placed it over her head.

'You look wonderful,' he said.

'Aren't you going to wear one?' she asked.

'God no, I wouldn't be caught dead wearing the damn thing. It's all yours. Besides, you can use it to protect the box once you've found it.'

They left the car and walked silently to the entry point. The sleet had eased somewhat, but the precipitation made everything slow going.

Once they had reached the door, she pulled out a small wallet from her pocket.

'Is that what I think it is?' he asked.

'Yup, got it off Amazon. Only $30 for the whole kit.' She removed several tools and began laboring over the old lock as he kept the flashlight positioned above. Her fingers moved nimbly until the cold began to set in.

'Damn,' she said as her finger slipped for the third time. 'They always make this look so easy on TV.'

'Do you want me to try?' he asked.

'Sure,' she said. She reached out to hand him the kit, but he had already stepped forward with another kit in hand. He took out several tools and, with a few artful movements, the door was unlocked and open.

'Amazing... and actually quite attractive,' she breathed.

'You're really into the whole criminal thing, aren't you? My parents will love you... it was my dad who gave me this set. I was three. Apparently, I was a whiz at it even then.'

'A lockpicking kit for a toddler? Your dad had some interesting parenting ideas... Well, it's comforting to know that if we ever get locked out of our house, you can get us back in. Alright, I guess I'm going in now. You stay here. Send me a text if anyone's coming.'

With that, she crept into the darkness and was soon out of sight.

Gabby had no clue where the inventory room was. Once she entered the building, she discovered that it was deceptively large; all appearances from earlier were wrong. It may have seemed small, but there were a multitude of rooms zigzagging from the hallway. She jumped when she heard a tapping sound, but it was only the oak tree from outside, its jagged branches rattling against the windowpanes.

'Hurry, you have to hurry,' she chided herself.

Opening a door, she let out a stifled scream when she walked into something big and furry. She pushed away from it and stepped back abruptly, her shoe catching on a crooked floorboard and sending her to the floor. She landed on her knee, an old nail scratching into her skin.

'Fffffffuck!' she hissed, biting her lip.

It was time to use her flashlight. She hadn't wanted to use it in case someone saw... but now she was in danger of hurting herself further or falling down some stairs.

Gabby turned on the light and discovered that the bushy thing was in fact an old fur coat. It was a peculiar place to store a coat, so she moved it aside and gasped. There, behind the coat, was a nook full of treasures – paintings, jewelry, clothing, objects of great beauty and quality. She gasped again, but this time there was a tone of indignation within. There were objects she recognized. Wasn't that Gran's blue topaz and diamond art deco necklace? And that painting of the shepherdess, surely that had been in Gran's drawing room. She looked around, horrified then angry. She was about to let loose with some choice curses but, before she could let a word out, her phone vibrated and she looked down to see a text: 'Car coming, get out.'

'Shit,' she muttered. She walked through the room, fighting the temptation to grab everything and go. She tapped on her phone, writing, 'Distribute him.'

'???' came in response.

'For fuck's sake,' she growled as she bared her teeth at the phone.

'Damn predictive text! Distract him... if you can. Just for a little while,' she texted back.

A thumbs-up emoji popped up on her screen and she slid her phone back into her pocket and continued with her mission. She opened a few more doors before she finally came upon the little inventory room she had been in earlier.

It took a few minutes to locate the box, which for some reason had been placed hazardously on top of the cabinet, right near the edge.

Once she found it, she put it carefully into her poncho and opened the door. She began walking down the hallway, trying to remember the way back, when she heard footsteps at the front of the building coming toward her.

'Shit!' she whispered. She crept to a nearby door, hoping that something useful was on the other side. The door opened noisily but, much to her chagrin, before her was a crooked staircase. She hurried up the stairs, not even bothering to stifle the sound of her ascent as the footsteps obviously followed her. She had just finished the third flight of steps when she spied a window overlooking the alley with the shadowy figure of the oak tree just outside. She raced to it, fought against the lock for several seconds before it gave in, then threw all her weight against the sash. It groaned against the attack but did not move.

After several tries, the painted-over window was still jammed, so she counted to three, wrapped her lockpicking kit around her elbow, and smashed the window open.

'Garrr!' she screamed as the pain from the impact traveled from her funny bone to the rest of her arm. Shards of glass flew in a crystalline shower before landing in the alley below. She reached out for the big tree branch, its rough surface scratching her hands, and launched her upper body out of the window. The footsteps were getting louder. She scrambled to get a grip on the tree and had just pulled one leg outside when a hand grabbed her other foot and a voice shouted, 'Get back here, you bastard!'

She kicked back at him, all anger and rage unleashed. Within seconds, her foot was free, but her balance was off, so she plummeted from the tree, her fall luckily broken by the sole prickly bush in the alley.

'Umph,' she grunted as she tried unsuccessfully to stand up. Her ankle rolled painfully, and she began toppling over until a strong arm supported her.

'An interesting exit,' Hugo said. 'Somewhat lacking your usual grace. You okay?'

'Yes... not an experience I'd like to repeat. God, my ankle is killing me. I need your help, but we should get out of here now...'

They scrambled to the car, slipping on the occasional icy spot, all the while expecting to hear police sirens; fortunately, all was still.

'Guess he won't be calling the police then. Didn't think he would... but you can never be one hundred percent sure,' she said.

'Oh well, lucky for us. How are you? How's the ankle?'

She shrugged. 'I need a steaming hot bath. I imagine the ankle will be fine as long as I don't fall out of any more windows.'

***

The care home had begun life as a grand manor house; its symmetry and grandeur were still evident in its lines and layout, although other parts, including the furnishings and gardens, had been overlooked for decades. Gabby stared at the overgrown greenery, her fingers tightening on the package in her hands.

'Ready?' Hugo asked as they exited the car.

'Yup,' she said, patting the package. 'I'm glad it's going back to its rightful owner. Don't be surprised if she tells you the story of how she was given this... it is very sweet. I don't think I've ever listened to it without tearing up. I can understand why she was so heartbroken when she discovered that *he'd* taken it. She had a hard enough time leaving her home and moving here, only to be robbed of her prized possession... well, all I can say is, I hope this cheers her up.'

They entered the building and walked through a long corridor until they reached the conservatory that overlooked the back of the estate. And there, sitting in a small, padded chair, was Gran. It had only been a few weeks since Gabby had seen her, but she seemed smaller, more fragile.

Gabby greeted her with a hug, then stepped back and placed the box in Gran's lap.

A sharp intake of breath was the only sound in the room. Gran reached down, her hands touching the wood reverently.

'You got it... how?' she asked, her voice tremulous.

'A bit of negotiating,' Gabby said, winking at Hugo.

'I always knew you were a resourceful one. I never should have trusted him in the first place, he was always a cunning child. And to think, I never would have seen it again if it weren't for you! Thank you, Gabriella. And you too, Hugo. It's nice to know there's someone looking out for us oldies.'

'You're not that old, Gran.'

'I am, but that's not a bad thing.' She looked down at the box. 'Hah, well he certainly didn't open it, but that's no big surprise. He never did have the patience for this kind of thing.'

Her hands wrapped around the perimeter of the box. 'Now, did I ever tell you the story of how I got this?' Gabby, who had heard the story dozens of times before, shook her head.

'Well, it all began after the war,' she said as she moved her hands, swiftly pressing and pushing until the box opened.

***

The war had been dragging on for what seemed an eternity. Brigitte's three brothers had gone away to fight, taking with them Noel, Brigitte's fiancé. Their spirits had been buoyant, the desire to prove themselves and protect their own outweighing any potential fears. Brigitte waited... what else could she do? When at last it was over, only two came back alive out of the four – Noel and her youngest brother, Fen. Both had changed; her brother, who had been so garrulous and playful before, was now aloof and reticent, and Noel's easy-going and adventurous nature had gone, replaced by something more serious and cautious.

Brigitte adapted to these changes, knowing that she should be grateful because hundreds of thousands of husbands, brothers, and sons did not come back, and would never come back, but it was difficult. She missed her other brothers, the carefree way they all used to interact. Now, everyone was on edge, and she felt like she was constantly walking on eggshells.

One day, she awoke to find Fen gone. He had left a note on her door, explaining his need for a new start.

Brigitte was devastated. Noel comforted her, and with that comfort came a rediscovery of each other, which in turn led to marriage.

They had their first argument the day after they married; she wanted to go to Paris for the honeymoon, he wanted to stay local. In the end, he conceded after she pointed out there would be plenty of time to explore local areas.

Paris was a romantic whirlwind of adventurous excursions and late nights. In some ways, it was quieter than they were expecting, but that was the war – change was to be expected. Brigette and Noel ate and drank and walked the streets, the cobblestones leading to aching feet and broken blisters.

One day they wandered into an antique store, a dusty, timid place full of unusual objects.

'I'll pick something out for you,' Noel said as they entered.

'Only if I can get something for you,' Brigitte replied.

She perused the shop, her eyes flitting side to side, desperate to find something that he would like. She had been searching for a few moments when she spotted the perfect gift – a silver fly-fishing reel.

She bought it quickly, hiding the small box in her bag.

'Find anything?' Noel said, his voice right behind her.

'No,' she replied, before picking up a wooden box. 'This is interesting,' she said as she tried to open it. 'What do you suppose it is?'

'No idea. Do you want to go now?'

That night, as they sat in a stylish art nouveau café, Noel presented her with a large box. It was wrapped in fabric and topped with a shimmery bow, which flickered in the candlelight.

She unwrapped the package and found the box they had seen at the shop.

She pulled the box out and tried to open it. It did not open. She shook it, then tried opening it again. Nothing.

'It's a puzzle box,' he said.

'I hate puzzles, I'm never good at them,' she complained.

'I think you might feel differently about this one,' he said. 'Here, I'll help you.'

They moved the box around, pushing buttons and sliding panels until a small hidden drawer revealed itself. There, set against a velvet cloth, was an oyster. She removed it carefully. It was a delicate thing, lined in gold with a tiny latch at the front. She undid the latch and opened the oyster. There, encapsulated within, was a pair of pearls, one of which had been painted to resemble the globe.

'I don't have much,' he said. 'But everything I have in the world is yours.'

Tears sprang from her eyes, and she held the spheres tightly.

'It's beautiful… thank you.'

***

'In the end, we didn't have long to enjoy the simplicities of married life. A few months after we returned from our honeymoon, he was hit by a car on his way to the grocery store. He never recovered. But, by then, he had given me your mother so, in a way, he did give me the world.'

'That's so sad, Gran.'

'By the time you've reached my age, you'll realize that most things in life are bittersweet. But I've always loved this box, and I'll always remember the moment when I opened an oyster and the world came tumbling out.'

11

Death and Vanilla

The smell of rotting seaweed hung through the air like a wet curtain. It lurked like a malodorous guest, sending all the tourists scuttling back to their hotel rooms and the comforting hum of their air conditioners, leaving the beaches of Playa del Carmen completely empty for once.

It was the perfect time to bury a body.

Shovels at the ready, two men dug a hole deep in the murky depths of the damp sand, their noses pressed tightly against the bandanas that engulfed the lower half of their faces.

'The smell,' breathed one, his distinctly American accent not at all surprising to hear in this part of Mexico.

His co-conspirator grunted, which was generally how he communicated.

The American pressed his bandana closer to his nose to no avail; the smell was overwhelming. The seaweed, not content with assaulting their noses, also made their digging more difficult. Every shovelful had to be fought; the cloying strands of the slimy green stuff wrapped its way around the clammy sand, weighing it down and causing every muscle of their backs to strain.

At last, after the longest twenty minutes of their lives, they had created a huge hole.

'Finally!' the American said as he pulled down his bandana and stretched his arms, then bent forward to relieve the burn in his lower back. He shrugged one shoulder then the other before putting his shovel down. 'Do you think this is big enough?' He gestured to the hole.

His partner grunted in affirmation.

'It would be a lot easier if you actually spoke once in a while,' the American grumbled under his breath. He looked at the tightly wrapped package that rested at his feet. If he was honest with himself, it made him a little nervous being this close to a dead body, particularly one whose death he had witnessed just a short while ago. As if witnessing the death wasn't bad enough, he then had to worry about the practicalities of disposing a body. Who knew there were so many things to consider? For instance, size. The body had been large; it had been a huge ordeal to wrap it up in the rug and tape it shut. His body ached. He sighed, the sound echoed by his companion who looked at him, an inscrutable expression in his eyes.

The American hit the body with his foot. 'Well, I guess we better get this in.'

Both men crouched down and pushed the taped rug. It rolled slightly, then paused on the edge of the hole. The American heaved toward it, his push sending the body flying into the hole and then his own.

'Oomph,' he grunted as he landed on his face, the gritty sand making its way into his mouth. He spat it out before yelling, 'A little help, please?'

Silence from above. The American gagged as the smell of rotten seaweed mixed with the decaying scent of the corpse underneath him. He reached up, trying to grasp something, anything, to pull himself out of the mess, but the only thing that surrounded him was sand, the fluidity of it now sending a shiver of panic through him.

Above ground, the silent man looked down, his grasp on his shovel uncertain. He knew the American was a problem for them, but he didn't know if his boss had other plans for him. So, he vacillated –

save the man or leave him? For once, he wished his boss was here. He knew that whatever he did, it was going to be the wrong thing.

Unless he let the American sort it out himself. He would give the American a tool to escape; if he made it, the boss would take care of him, if not, he would be dealt with by someone other than him.

Turning away, he picked up the shovel the American had been using, dusted off some of the sand, and let out a brief whistle to alert the American that help was on its way as he threw the shovel downward.

Sadly, the American wasn't well versed in his colleague's whistles, so he was completely unaware of his supposed help. His introduction to it was both brief and severe, a loud thunk as the shovel landed on his head. Within seconds, he was as dead as the body beneath him.

The man above grimaced at the sound of the shovel cracking the man's skull. He waited to see if the American was still alive. After a few minutes passed with no indication of life below, he turned away and began the laborious task of filling in the hole. It was backbreaking work, the likes of which he hadn't experienced since he stopped working on the infamous vanilla farms. He had promised his wife he would never lift another shovel... but here he was.

He stopped shoveling for a second, thinking for a minute that he had heard something below. But as the silence lengthened, he shrugged his shoulders and kept pushing the sand in, wishing that the American was still alive to help him. Then again, maybe it was better this way – the American talked too much.

As the night grew darker still, the humidity began to ease, causing the smell to dissipate. The waves moved back and forth, their movement the only other life on the beach, their sound drowning out anything else.

The man threw in his last shovelful and removed his bandana, using it to wipe his forehead and neck. His body depleted of energy, he carried the shovel back to the truck, its low bulk hidden among the dense growth of the trees and shrubs.

It was time to report to his boss.

***

The discovery of two bodies made national news; as a tourist destination, Playa del Carmen wasn't immune to crime. However, unlike Cancún, where lawlessness was rife, Playa del Carmen was known for minor offenses. This double murder was something else altogether. First off, it was suspected that one of the victims was American – the abnormally white teeth, the presence of American flags on his clothing, and the recently acquired tan were all strong indicators that he had come from the north. This came with complications – it was an unspoken rule among the locals that tourists were off-limits, no matter how obnoxious or entitled they were. The other, more baffling, part of the case was how these killings had occurred without witnesses. It was a mystery that no one could fathom, not even the police.

The bodies weren't found right away. For a time, the pungent seaweed and stormy weather kept all but the most obstinate tourists away from the beach. The few that ventured out stayed within the confines of their resorts, feeling safe and content as they downed endless cocktails and took artfully posed selfies that never captured the barbed-wire fences that separated them from the rest of Playa del Carmen.

However, over time, the sun emerged, and the smell began to clear, causing the people to gradually return to the temperate waters. Beach chairs were set up, towels were laid out, and life returned to normal. Which is when, inevitably, the pull of the tides eroded the sand and a finger emerged. It was a small thing but disgusting enough that the child who saw it ran screaming back to his mother. She went with him to investigate and crossed herself when she saw the digit pointing upward at the sky. With shaky hands, she called the police.

The inspector had just bought a concha and café con late when he was called in the next morning. He walked quickly; his grizzled head bowed as he approached the crime scene. He looked for the officer who had called it in and took a bite of the perfectly baked sweetbread before taking a sip of his drink.

'It's a bit early for this,' the officer said, gesturing toward the bodies and taking out his notebook. 'We have two bodies, one wrapped in what looks like a rug, the other one exposed. Next to the bodies, we found a plastic bag, so it could've been a deal gone bad.' At this, the inspector sighed. Drugs... so obvious, but it would make his job easier.

'Well, we'll keep our options open... after all, if that was the case, you'd expect one body, not two,' he said. 'Anything else?'

'We've just unwrapped the other body. The rug looks pretty generic to me, but my wife says I don't know anything about interior design, so maybe it's something special. As to the body, it's in better shape than the other one, but I have a feeling it'll be hard to identify.'

The inspector scooted closer to the bodies and looked down. He glanced briefly at the heavily bloated body before turning to the other one. The second victim had one of those faces; he was the kind of person who looked like everyone and no one at the same time. The inspector studied him. He didn't look like anyone he knew from the local cartel, but then again, you never could tell.

'Anything else on the bodies?' he asked, stepping back.

The officer pulled out a bag containing a card. 'This. It was in the first man's pocket.'

'Which one is the first man?' the inspector asked.

'You know, the one not wrapped up. I just thought it would be easier to call them first man, second man... or we could say man one, man two if you want...'

The inspector shook his head and took the bag. He looked closely at the slim business card. It was cream colored with an artistic spray of flowers on one side. Scrawled across the middle were the words 'La Reina de Vanilla' with a phone number listed below.

'You call yet?' he asked the officer.

'No, thought I'd wait for you,' he replied. 'But that name sounds familiar... food related? She might be one of those celebrity chefs... I think my wife knows about her. She might have written a cookbook, chefs always do.'

The inspector shrugged. While he loved eating, he was not particularly interested in chefs or cookbooks. He much preferred reading classics like Fuentes. He flipped the card around in his hand while pressing the numbers on his phone. It rang.

'Bueno.'

The voice was deep and rich. It enticed him to move the phone closer to his ear.

'Good morning. I'm the inspector in charge of an investigation near the beach. I have some questions to ask you. Will you be home today?'

He went silent as she spoke, jotting down notes in his notebook. After a minute, he said 'Hasta pronto' before hanging up the phone.

'What do you think?' the officer asked him.

'Interesting. She's not from here, her Spanish was heavily accented. Regarding the case... well, she's a potential suspect... but then again, you'd have to be stupid to leave your business card on the body.' He looked at his watch. 'I better get to her place soon.'

'You need me to come with?'

'No, you finish up here.'

The inspector finished his lukewarm drink and typed the address into his phone. It seemed familiar; he was confident he knew the area it was in. Close to the beach, it was one of those prestigious communities filled with sparkling condos and people. Checking the directions on his phone, he put it back into his pocket and started walking.

As he moved further away from the crime scene and toward 5th Avenue, the usual chatter and shouts from street vendors gradually faded and he was soon left with an eerie quiet broken only by the sounds of fluttering parrots as they flew from tree to tree. On his right was a continuous line of barbed-wire fencing, giving pedestrians the impression that the community within was impervious to crime. He assessed the surroundings as he drew closer to the gate. It was a strange place. He had never understood gated communities – what was the point of setting yourself apart from the town or city you lived in?

He showed his badge to the security guard on duty, who buzzed him through. His eyebrows raised when he glanced around the complex. It was surreal. What had been an untamed wilderness was now a domesticated oasis of perfection; condos lined the streets, each one gleaming like a newly minted peso. The only things that differentiated them were the numbers and the color of stucco. He looked for number twelve and soon found it. It was bigger than the others, and its brilliant white exterior made his eyes strain behind his sunglasses.

'Great, just what I need,' he muttered, thinking of all the rich assholes he dealt with daily. His job, his life, consisted of tourists who thought that money negated any misdemeanors, or thugs working in cartels who tried to solve every problem with significant bribes. He had always dealt with those people decisively and consistently yet, somehow, they always thought they deserved special treatment.

He pressed the bell and waited as the sound of footsteps approached. He was taken aback by the woman who greeted him. She was dressed casually in a white linen sundress, her brown limbs contrasting with the brightness of the fabric. His first impressions of her were favorable – she didn't look difficult; in truth, she seemed rather down to earth. As he stood there, he felt the warmth that exuded from her so naturally that it had to be authentic.

'You're the inspector,' she said, her hand tapping against the door frame.

'Yes, I'm the inspector,' he replied as he showed her his badge.

She nodded. 'This way.' She stepped back to let him through the doorway. He entered the cool oasis of her hallway, the stark walls punctuated by several large paintings whose rich colors leached into the area, making him pause. He gazed at them, the dramatic landscapes which consisted of storms and desolation, all containing a single figure who faced away from the viewer.

'These are good,' he said, without any real clue whether they were. 'Relics from my previous life,' was the only response he received.

He looked at the paintings again, then at her. Her status as a suspect notwithstanding, he could feel his fascination with this woman growing by the second. Not only was she beautiful and cultured, but she seemed like a nice person. He peeked around the classy interior of her home but saw no indication that she had a husband or family.

'You live here alone?' he asked, following her into a brightly decorated kitchen.

'Yes. Sadly, my marriage ended sooner than I anticipated. My husband died of a heart attack seven years ago. One of those tragic things that happens all too frequently. Life had been so stressful for us in the US, that's part of the reason why we moved down here... then a few months after we finalized everything, he was gone.' She grabbed an apron that had been hanging on the wall opposite them. 'Do you mind if I bake while we talk?' she asked, gesturing toward the counter that had several canisters and boxes laid out.

'No, not at all. What are you making?' he asked as she began measuring ingredients and mixing them together in a bowl.

'A raspberry vanilla birthday cake for my friend's daughter. It's her favorite, and I said I'd have it ready for her party tomorrow. So, what can I do for you?'

'Like I said before on the phone, we found some bodies on the beach, and we're trying to identify them and figure out how they died.'

'How awful,' she said as she added some eggs into the bowl and gently folded them into the mixture.

'Yes, well, these things tend to be unpleasant. But the reason why I'm here is that your card was found on one of them, so we thought you might know who he is.'

'And you believe I might have killed this person,' she stated. 'I've watched enough crime shows to know that I'd be a suspect in your eyes.'

'At this point, we need to find out who he is and how you know him. I don't like speculating.'

'Do you have a picture? I meet a lot of people with my catering business... clients and new employees, so it can be difficult to remember everyone. But if you have a visual, it might jog my memory... if I've met him.'

The inspector pulled out the picture of the deceased that his photographer had taken earlier and handed it to her. She looked at it, the blonde hair curling gently at the forehead, that sloping nose that ended just before narrow lips, and sighed. 'Yes, I know him. He was my nephew. At least, that's what he said. I'd never actually met him before. My brother and I are not on speaking terms – we haven't seen each other for... twenty-six, twenty-seven years? We didn't have a happy childhood... he was a bit of an asshole, if I'm honest. Once our parents died, there wasn't any reason for us to stay in touch. I'd heard he had a son, but I'd never met him until he showed up on my doorstep about two weeks ago wanting a job. At the time, I was short of staff, so I hired him to help me with an event, but he never showed up.'

'Weren't you worried?'

'No... I just thought he'd found something else. I work with a lot of young people. Trust me, there's no such thing as employee loyalty. If there's a hint of a better job elsewhere, they'll go.'

'Except he didn't.'

'No, I guess not.' She shook her head. 'It's sad, a young life, just gone like that. I feel guilty, I should have reported him missing... I just didn't know.'

'Well, if you could give me his information so we can get in touch with his parents... and it would be good to know more about him. Is there anything else you can tell me?'

'Yes, we talked a bit. He was quite chatty about some things... I guess that since we were technically related, he wanted to catch up. He was twenty-four, had just graduated with his masters in biochemistry, and had decided to take some time off to see the world. He seemed nice. Maybe he took after his mother – he sure wasn't like his father. I made us dinner and he helped with the clean-up – that's rare with boys. He was a bit fidgety, but some people are like that, aren't they?'

As she spoke, the inspector wrote hurriedly in his notebook. He paused, then asked, 'If he had a master's degree, why do you think he applied for the job? He would have been overqualified for it, yes?'

She shrugged, her shoulders moving in one fluid, expressive line. 'I don't know. Perhaps he liked the idea of working with family, or maybe I was the first one to offer him a job. If you're traveling, you're not always going to be picky. I did ask him a few questions about his family, but he didn't seem that inclined to talk about them. If he hadn't shown me the picture of my brother and I when we were younger, I wouldn't have believed he was my nephew.'

'How come he didn't want to talk about his family? You *were* family, after all.'

'I got the impression that he and my brother did not get on... he said something about not being allowed to have fun and making up for it now, but beyond that, he just clammed up.'

'Do you know where he was staying?' the inspector asked.

'Somewhere near the beach? He said he wanted to hear the waves while he slept. I'm sorry, I know I haven't given you much information, but I only met him once. He may have been my nephew, but he was a complete stranger to me. It's sad, I would have liked to have had a relationship with him. Yet another thing my brother has denied me.'

'Hmph,' the inspector said, taking the picture from her hands. 'Did he seem frightened of anyone?'

'No, just jittery.' She finished mixing and handed him a spoon. 'What do you think?'

He took the spoon and put it into his mouth. An explosion of raspberries combined with a delicate hint of vanilla danced across his taste buds.

'Incredible,' he said, when he was finally able to speak.

She beamed, the smile lighting up her face.

'Good. Kids these days... they're hard to please.'

'That tastes amazing, how do you do it?'

She winked at him. 'It's easy. Baking comes down to two things – good recipes and good ingredients. You have those, you can make anything... but I'm sure that applies to most endeavors, good or bad.'

'Well, I can see why you're so busy. And...' he looked down at his watch. 'I've probably taken enough of your time, so I should get going.'

'Thank you, yes, I do have a lot that needs to be done. It was very nice meeting you. I'm sorry I couldn't help you more, but I do hope you find out who killed my nephew. He seemed like a good kid.'

The inspector sighed. 'Yes, thank you for taking the time to talk with me. I hope the party goes well.'

She smiled again as she escorted him to the front door.

As he walked back to the scene, he frowned and took out his notebook again. Below the information she had provided, he had written a column for suspects. She was the only one. He stared at her name. No, there was no way in hell she could kill anyone, and definitely not her own nephew. A person who made such delectable creations was altogether incapable of doing something so base as murdering someone. He was certain there would be more names on the list soon.

Once he left, she closed the door, whipped her brand-new iPhone out of her pocket, and quickly dialed a number.

'My place, now.' Her voice, which before had been as silky as the flans she made, was now sharp, the tone bordering on menacing. There was a brief pause as the person spoke, then she said, 'Ten minutes then. You'd better not be late,' before hanging up and setting the phone down on the hallway table.

Nine minutes later, the bell rang, and she walked to the door. She greeted the man standing there before walking with him back to the kitchen. He had barely entered the room before she turned to him and said, 'The police were here asking about the American... apparently, he's dead. Is there a reason I didn't know about this?'

The man nodded hesitantly, wondering what kind of shit he was in. He should have told her about the kid earlier, but he thought he had gotten away with it.

'What happened?'

The man shrugged.

'You said everything had been taken care of... you didn't say you killed him, for Christ's sake. I thought you sent him away. Do you know the shit pile you've just landed me in? He's my nephew, for fuck's sake, the police are going to be all over me, which is not good for you. I swear, you better hope this goes away, because if not, well... you're a good manager, but I can and will replace you.'

A familiar icy sensation streamed through him when he heard that. He had seen the bodies and knew that his boss was not one to make idle threats. There was no doubt in his mind that he had to avoid any problems in the future. That he was alive now meant that she was in a forgiving mood.

She sighed heavily, wearily. 'I just wish people would stop interfering with my business. I was the one who discovered the potential of a vanilla monopoly. While all the cartel thugs were concentrating on their drugs, I was selling my art collection to buy vanilla farms. You know what they were like.'

He nodded. He did remember them. His life had revolved around those damn orchids: the monotony of pollinating them by hand, then waiting for the pods to appear months later... and, worst of all, the harvesting. It was mind-numbing, backbreaking work. He was glad to be done with it. She had rescued him from that life, though there were times when he wondered if this one was going to be shorter.

She was still talking.

'I was the one who saw how much tourists love vanilla. They'd buy it in barrels if they could. And "Mexican" vanilla? Even better! They're willing to pay top dollar, no matter how much it's diluted. So, is it a crime that I've made a fortune using my own ingenuity? No! But now I've got people from everywhere trying to get in... it's so rude! My own damn nephew too. I never wanted my family to find me, especially anyone related to my brother. You met my nephew... he was trouble, wasn't he?'

He nodded.

'Exactly like his father. Always wanted what wasn't his. The moment he stepped in here, he wanted everything I had... everything *I* had built up. I wish I'd been going through the catering books instead of the vanilla finances, he saw them and was smart enough to see what was going on. He should have taken the money I offered him. Greedy bastard. He would have found a way to destroy me... God, kids these days. So obnoxious. And rude. No wonder Americans have such a bad reputation. Ah well, I guess I should be grateful. You took care of him, and my business is safe from yet another greedy parasite. I just have to figure out a way to get this inspector off my back.' She walked over to a cabinet and took out a Tupperware container. 'Would you like some sopaipillas?'

She pushed the container of fluffy pastries toward him. He shrugged and sat down, eating the sweets like he hadn't eaten all day.

'When you've finished with those, we'll get to work. I have another order that just came in.'

He left soon after, his hands full of delightfully scented boxes destined for a large corporate event.

***

A week later, her phone pinged with a text message from an unknown sender. It showed a picture of her nephew and a man, whose back was to the camera, kicking a large, wrapped object into a hole.

'What the?' she asked incredulously.

'I have more.' The next message said.

'What do you want?' she typed.

'50% of your profits.'

'Over my dead body, you son of a bitch,' she said, her fingers hovering over the keys before texting. 'Let's meet so we can negotiate.'

'Son of a bitch!' she seethed, punching her fist into a ball of dough.

'Inti Beach Club, 10pm.'

'You are so dead,' she muttered to her phone as she threw the dough into the garbage can and walked away.

She pondered her next step; this threat had to be handled with speed and permanence. She picked up the phone again and made several calls. When she hung up an hour later, she smiled. It was so easy to get a phone traced when you employed the right people. She looked down at the image on her phone. This particular cartel boss was going to realize it was a mistake trying to intrude on her business.

The sun had long since set, its departure bringing a cool wind that provided relief to the crowd gathered at the beach. A man dressed in a linen suit stood at the bar, his foot tapping in time to the music as he casually looked around the club. He did business everywhere, so he knew all the clubs in town – this wasn't one of his, but it was still nice. He spoke with the bartender, their conversation drowned out by the arrival of a bachelorette party who squealed and yelled as they entered the room. While everyone watched the women, the cartel boss handed the bartender a large envelope before taking his drink and moving to a small table. He watched as the bartender placed the envelope behind a bottle on the top shelf; once the envelope had been hidden, the man in the linen suit glanced down at his watch. She had thirty minutes to get there.

He watched as the participants in the bachelorette party, all in their thirties, began dancing, their bodies moving languidly to the sound of the solo guitarist. He tsked. These foreigners had no sense of rhythm – their inability to move in time with the music was embarrassing. And alcohol never helped. He didn't know why they bothered. He moved back as one woman came veering toward his table, sending his drink scuttling across the surface. A hand from behind her righted it, and she giggled drunkenly.

'Bottoms up!' she yelled, thrusting the drink into his hand.

He drank, just wanting her gone.

It took less than two minutes of excruciating pain for the potassium cyanide to complete its job, but his wish was granted. She was gone. Everyone was gone, including the man who had righted his drink and upended the cyanide capsule into it.

With a dead body in their midst, the revelers soon became hysterical, and chaos ensued. People shoved their way out, crying and screaming, and the bartender, paranoid that he would be blamed for everything, ducked out the back entrance without telling anyone. In his haste to leave, he forgot about the envelope, tucked away behind an old dusty bottle of sherry. Its contents, which could explain so much and cause so much damage were quiet... for now.

***

'You've redeemed yourself,' she said, handing the man a piece of flan. 'You managed that very well. I didn't even see you put the cyanide in.'

He demurred, his mouth full of food. He wondered why his wife never made anything this tasty.

'Amazing that he never recognized me, not even when I bumped into his table. You'd think he'd remember the person who catered his Christmas party. Oh well, it worked out in the end, I have a handy little souvenir from our encounter.' She rummaged through her bag for a minute before producing a severed finger covered in plastic wrap. She waved it around while he blanched... the flan's color was awfully similar to the digit. 'I plan on putting this to good use.'

It was easy to alter the picture she had been sent on her phone. She deleted her man and filled the empty space with an image of the cartel boss she found online. After some advanced editing, it was ready to go. She printed the photograph and attached it to the package containing the finger. She had her man drop it off at a courier service, who delivered it to the main police station.

***

8 months later

In the end, the finger was the catalyst for solving the homicides. Before its arrival, the inspector and the officer had worked tirelessly on the case with little progress. It had been a journey fraught with tension and disagreements; the officer was convinced that the La Reina de Vanilla was behind the deaths, even after several names had been added to the list of suspects. The inspector tore this theory into shreds, pointing out that their main piece of evidence was purely circumstantial.

'But she was related to the American, what more do you want?' the officer yelled, pounding his fist on a table.

'Motive? Opportunity? I don't know what you have against her, but I don't think she's our killer. We've examined the evidence; we've spoken with her countless times... other than the family ties, there's nothing connecting her to the victims. Besides, I've met a lot of criminals in my time, and trust me, she is not one. But I think we're missing something... there will be something connecting the two murders. We just have to be patient.'

The finger's arrival was their big break. Once they sent it to forensics and discovered who it belonged to, everything changed. It wasn't every day they had an appendage belonging to Quintana Roo's most sinister businessman and the reputed mastermind behind the Tres Cartel, one of the most brutal organizations in the region. The cartel boss had been universally hated, so it made sense that the finger belonged to him. As the inspector studied the picture, he felt the puzzle pieces slotting in... except for one thing that bothered him – the presence of the cartel boss in the picture. It was commonly known that he usually hired someone else to deal with any unpleasantness.

'Well, a picture doesn't lie,' he said while clicking his pen.

'Actually, that's not really true anymore. Have you seen what people can do with Photoshop?' the officer asked as he sat down next to his boss. 'But this is authentic, I'd stake my career on it. God, he was a nasty piece of work. We never would have nailed him for this, you know? In a way, his death was the best possible outcome. Bet he never saw it coming too... dying in a club, of all places.'

***

The whispers on the street began shortly thereafter; they started as the slightest of breaths, vague inferences that found their way into everyone's ears. Tales of rivalries between cartels, of power struggles that dragged on and led to the deaths of members and nonmembers alike. Everywhere, there was talk... and 'el invierno' was at the center of it.

The inspector knew who 'el invierno' was. Everyone on the force did. He was at the very top, even higher than the cartel bosses. It was a known fact that he'd had a strong dislike toward the dead cartel boss. No one had gotten close to him. As the inspector sat at his desk, he wondered if the death of the cartel boss was enough to bring 'el invierno' down. He suspected it was not.

At least he had justice for the two men. The American's father was flying down soon, and the inspector had promised to give him the news of his son's killer in person.

Notwithstanding his upcoming ordeal with 'el invierno,' the inspector was feeling content, so much so that he took a long break, soaking in the feelings of righteousness and the conviction of a job well done. The birds were singing, their songs a pleasant background, when his phone rang.

'Yes?'

'Where are you?' the officer asked.

'Walking, why?'

A sigh. 'Someone just arrived from Inti Beach Club. A new bartender. He found a package addressed to you. What do you want me to do with it?'

The inspector frowned. 'Just leave it on my desk. I'll look at it when I come back.'

He thought about returning to the station, but his desire to see her again propelled him forward. The vanilla queen. In the last eight months, he had thought about her constantly, had actually read her cookbook, and concluded that she was his ideal woman. There was something special about her. She was truly amazing... and, over time, he had seen for himself how kind she was. She never had a harsh word to say about anyone. And her food... well, it was breathtaking. He licked his lips, thinking about her tres leches cakes, flans, and, best of all, her vanilla cake.

Yes, a proper woman, that's what she was. She was exactly what he needed.

So, he turned the corner and began walking in the direction of her house, his mind consumed with visions of her and the cake, all thoughts of mysterious packages left behind.

12

What Tears Us Apart

It was a languid summer day in Schenectady, New York. The air had a dense humidity that frizzed hair and rattled tempers, the occasional breeze doing nothing to alleviate the heat and everything to spread those familiar smells of summer – grass that had been obsessively cut to an eighth of an inch, the tiny shards standing to attention, waiting for their next clipping; barbecues sending their smoky aromas into the air; and, underlying them all, the fragrant wildflowers that crept up to the porches. The sounds of children playing, their voices weaving in and out of homes, their feet beating on the sidewalks, provided constant background noise.

A girl watched a group of kids running, their attention on a soccer ball that went flying through the air. For a moment, she contemplated joining in before realizing that, at eighteen, she was too old to play with kids. She sat back in her hammock, picked up the book she had set aside earlier, and began reading once more. Things would have been different if her friend Jake was still there; he would've taken the book out of her hands and talked her into playing. But that was Jake; for someone who had left only last week for college, he still acted like a child most of the time. His levity balanced out her seriousness, which was why their friendship worked.

She sighed and stretched, the book slipping from her grasp and falling onto the dusty wooden floor. Sweeping was one of her chores, but somehow she always forgot to do the porch. A small line of sunlight filtered through the huge tree in her front yard and illuminated the dust motes as they danced in the aftermath of the book's landing.

As she picked up the book, she glanced at her watch and jumped. How had it gotten so late?

She ran inside and grabbed the keys to her clunker, a 1985 Yugo. Given the number of breakdowns that had prevented her from going anywhere, she always found its name ironic. She had been hoping to get something a bit more reliable, but money was tight and, for now, her dad's mechanic lessons were enough to keep it going.

The stores were mostly shut as she drove down Union Street, but she was relieved to find that the bagel shop was still open. She pulled into the parking lot, the car barely making it over the bump. After parking, she ran to the door, which opened as she touched the handle. A teenager was standing there, a bag of bagels in hand.

'Lottie... you're always late. I should be closing now,' he said.

'I know, I know. I do try, really. I just get so distracted. But thanks for this,' she said, taking the bag.

'No problem... Jake told me to take care of you once he'd gone.'

'How much do I owe you?' she asked, taking a small white package out of the bag. The paper crinkled as she unwrapped an egg bagel with veggie cream cheese.

'Eh, we'll sort it out tomorrow.'

'Sooo good,' she said as she bit into the bagel. 'How was it today?'

'Pretty crappy now that Jake's at college. It used to be fun... now everyone's serious. I mean, we're selling bagels. It's not rocket science. Anyways... why don't you work here? You clearly have a thing for them.'

'I know...' she said sadly through a mouthful of bagel. 'I'm obsessed with bagels. But my first love was the library, so I'm stuck there. It's a hard life, but someone's gotta do it. Besides, Jake and I had the perfect arrangement: he fed my bagel obsession, I fed his book and movie obsession. Win-win.'

'Well, try to get here earlier tomorrow, yeah?'

'Will do,' she said, saluting him before running back to her car.

She took the long way home past the library, a brick building dating back to the mid-1960s. She remembered a conversation she'd had with Jake about working there.

'You know it's the perfect place for you,' he had said, laughing. 'You barely talk and you can hide among the books.'

This was true; the library was ideal for a lifelong introvert. For the most part, it was peaceful; she spent her days shelving books and finding book series for little kids. But then you had the moments that few people knew about – arguments between old ladies about who was using the microfilm machine and frustrations when favorite books were out on loan.

'Well, you sometimes *ssh* people, how many did you do today?' Jake asked, breaking the silence.

'Five... not like it mattered. No one listens to me. It's not like I'm an actual librarian. I'm just a clerk, very low on the library career ladder.'

She sighed. It wasn't the same without Jake around.

She pulled up to her house and ran to the door, calling out 'Lila!' A geriatric beagle came padding out of her room.

'Walkies?' she asked.

Lila stared at her before slowly walking to the front door.

'Okay, let's go pick up Dad.'

They began walking, Lottie's attempts at a brisk pace thwarted by Lila, whose idea of exercise was a slow amble. She stopped to sniff every flower on the way, her nails clicking against the sidewalk.

'Really? Another flower?' Lottie asked quietly, looking down at the sluggish dog. 'I swear you smell them just so we can stop.'

Hearing Lottie's voice, Lila glanced up at her, her plaintive expression causing a sense of guilt to pierce through Lottie. 'I know, you're old... you used to be so energetic. You'd run all over the place. What happened to you, huh?' She knelt and patted the dog.

'I hope Dad's okay... I heard him talking to his friend about some obnoxious students. They've been acting up, doing stupid things, but the dean's office is putting pressure on the staff to keep everything under wraps. Just because the students come from wealthy families. Crazy, isn't it?' She stopped and looked down at Lila. 'Then again, I am talking to a dog. But you'll have to do now that Jake's out in California.'

There had been a moment of sadness when they discovered how far away from each other they would be. Jake had been offered a place at UCLA where he could pursue his love of movies and a degree in filmmaking. Lottie was staying relatively close by; she was going to Endicott in Maine. She wasn't sure how this was going to work; Jake's departure symbolized the end of everything she had known. She wasn't particularly fond of change, and this was huge. Not only would she be away from her dad, but she would be apart from Jake for the first time in thirteen years.

She and Lila continued their walk, climbing the hill filled with trees that stretched out and cast shadows on the large Colonial Revivals, Dutch Colonials, and Queen Anne houses that lined the street.

As they went down the hill, Lottie puffing from coercing Lila to move, she thought about how easy these walks were during winter when Lila would slide down the hill on the ice that inevitably formed on the sidewalks. Granted, it was much nicer weather now – not freezing your butt off and the flowers were beautiful – but everything was so much slower.

They approached the college campus, which was empty at this time of the year. Most of the students had gone home for the long summer break, and school wasn't scheduled to start for a few more weeks. Lottie and Lila passed several buildings before reaching the ice rink, a cavernous brown-and-white building that had been Lottie's sanctuary for as long as she could remember. Skating was a hobby her dad had introduced her to at an early age, probably something he did to keep her mom's memory alive as it had been one of her passions.

Once they passed the rink, they encountered the 'Idol,' a strange sculpture covered in layers of paint. Every year, the graduating class would decorate it with buckets of paint. She had often wondered what its original color was, but it seemed unlikely that anyone would ever know.

They zigzagged through the campus until they arrived at the library where Lottie's dad was the head librarian.

Jake had asked her once if he had ever worked anywhere else. She had thought for a second, standing in front of the Neoclassical building, its white columns bright against the sun, before shaking her head. 'I don't think so. Dad loves this place. Not just the building, although it's nice, but he's got a connection to it. After all, he went to school here, and the library's where he met my mom. There's so much of his history here.'

'Too much?'

'I don't know... maybe. But he loves it, and it makes him happy, so I can't imagine us going anywhere else. And don't forget, he gets really good perks. I mean, if I wasn't going to Endicott, I'd totally be tempted to go here.'

'Really? I wouldn't. I can't wait to finally escape this place.'

Lottie remembered her surprise at his statement – at the time, it had rendered her speechless. She had looked at him, then down at Lila, who had been sniffling enthusiastically around a wet spot on the pavement – a spilt drink? Melted ice cream? Who knew, but Lila obviously liked the smell of it.

'Yeah, I guess we're both ready for something new,' Lottie had said, eventually.

'Wow, I'm not hearing a lot of excitement,' Jake had replied.

As she opened the door, Lottie's thoughts moved to her main worry – with her gone, how would her dad cope? It had been the two of them for so long, ever since she could remember, and it worked so well. Her mom had died when Lottie was only three years old, so it was difficult to think of him alone. And she knew she was going to miss him – the times he would come home from work enthusing about some recent acquisition, or their weekend hikes in the Adirondacks, enjoying the peace of the mountain ranges when no one else was around, stopping to pick wild blackberries. Or the countless road trips to some random monument that most people didn't care about. She sighed. Deep down, she knew her dad could cope, she just didn't know if she could.

She blinked back the tears that were threatening to spill over and walked into the library. She smiled as they strolled through, looking around the stacks for her dad who, in all honesty, looked more like a football player than a librarian.

Lila was the first to spot him tucked away in a sea of old books and maps. Although they usually didn't allow animals in the library, they had made special allowances for Lila. Over the years, she had become a well-known figure in the building. Students loved Lila. The minute they saw her, her placid and friendly demeanor drew them toward her.

'I could go for a walk, you interested?' Her dad asked after he had given Lila a doggy treat from his pocket.

Lottie nodded and they left the library. They walked along a colonnade before wandering over to a sixteen-sided memorial building, its grandness emphasized by its isolation on the expansive lawn.

'What are they planning?' Her dad muttered as they approached the distinctive Victorian building, its dome casting a long shadow on the grass.

'What are who planning?' Lottie asked him.

He shook his head. 'Oh, just some students... don't mind me, it's something I thought I heard in the stacks. It's nothing, I'm sure.'

'Are they the ones causing all the problems?' she asked.

'How do you know about that?' he asked. 'I didn't think I told you about them.' He stared at her. She looked away.

'I might have heard you talking to someone... but that's beside the point. You seemed worried. You can talk to me, you know.'

He placed a hand on her shoulder. 'I know. But there are some things that even I don't know how to handle. Up to now, they've been doing stupid pranks, but I'm always worried that someone will take it a step too far. Frats... they have a lot to answer for.' He looked at the building before turning away and throwing a stick for Lila, who had become miraculously re-energized after eating her treat.

The day passed, then another and another. As much as she wanted it to stop, time flew by, and Lottie had to begin packing her things. On the days she wasn't working, she was walking, trying to fill her mind with memories of all the places and people she loved.

Toward the middle of August, she became listless and uneasy; she was due to leave at the end of the month. She didn't talk about it with her dad much; they had taken an unofficial stance to avoid the topic completely, leaving all emotion lurking below the surface. There were moments when she could detect sadness and fear in his eyes, but she knew there was nothing either of them could do about the situation.

Before she knew it, she was hugging him goodbye and driving away, watching the long road ahead and the image of her father growing smaller and smaller in the rear-view mirror until she couldn't see him anymore.

Once she reached Endicott, all thoughts of loneliness and homesickness faded. She became consumed with registering for classes and making friends. Her schedule was soon packed; she had crew practice early in the morning and classes most days, which didn't leave much time for anything else. But she was content – she enjoyed her lectures, meeting interesting people, and trying new things like rock climbing and printmaking.

Halloween came and went, celebrated by parties and little kids trick-or-treating at the dorms. Fall decorations were removed, soon replaced with turkeys as November arrived. She commenced packing again when Thanksgiving was a week away, ready to go home for some rest.

The Yugo decided to behave for once, and she drove home in record time, her stomach anticipating a giant turkey and her dad's famous stuffing. As she pulled in, she looked over at Jake's house. She couldn't believe she wasn't going to see him; he had called Lottie a few days before to tell her he was staying in LA over Thanksgiving break to work on a movie.

Lottie's dad was at the door, the joy of her being home practically emanating from him. The next few days were peaceful and comforting... the warmth of the fire as the temperature dropped, eating too much food on Thanksgiving Day, and watching the NHL on TV with her dad. One night, she gazed at him thoughtfully as he watched the TV, his eyes darting continuously to follow the puck, its minuscule shape barely discernible on the screen. She frowned. There was something different about him. It was hard to put her finger on it, but there was a subdued, almost defeatist air about him that usually wasn't there.

'Dad, is everything okay?' she asked, her voice sounding a hundred times louder than the ones coming from the TV.

Her father glanced at her, then looked away. 'Yeah, why would you ask that?'

'You seem a little off. Like something's bothering you.'

After a minute of silence, her dad picked up the remote and turned off the TV. He looked down at his hands, then at her.

'I always forget how perceptive you can be. I didn't want to bother you with this, but you're right. Something happened. There was an incident involving those students... the ones we talked about back in August. They climbed up onto the roof of the library on Halloween, drank a ton of wine... then tried to climb down.' His voice broke. 'And one kid fell.' Lottie shook her head. There were always incidents like this, they were to be expected on a college campus, especially when frats were involved, but this sounded particularly bad.

'Did he die or something?' she asked bluntly.

Her dad shook his head. 'No, he's in a coma. But the doctors say he probably won't make it.'

'That's so sad,' Lottie cried out. 'His poor parents.'

Her dad nodded. 'Yes, the college president spoke to them, and they are completely devastated. He was their only child. I can't imagine what they must be feeling right now.'

'Me either. Wait, since it happened at the library, you aren't in trouble, are you?'

'I don't know. The thing is... I'm the one who found him. I've been working a lot since you've been gone, and I was in the basement when I heard the commotion. I ran upstairs and found him. I also saw the other students... but I was too late. If only I'd gone up there sooner, maybe I could have prevented it from happening... stopped them all somehow. And then there's a part of me that wonders that if I'd reported them back in August, maybe this wouldn't have happened. I did try talking to the dean, but there wasn't much to go on, just hearing "tallest building" and "climb". It wasn't really clear.'

'Are the other boys talking? You know, the ones who made it down okay?'

'Well, they ran away... but I spoke with the dean and identified them, so he's been talking to them. You know these frat boys, they tend to stick together... although one has been open about his role in this whole business, which is unusual. The other one hasn't said a word. The dean's been trying to figure out what to do. Of course, it doesn't help that the boys' parents are applying pressure on the college... so I guess the dean has that to consider,' he said dryly. 'Heaven forbid the college lose any money.'

'Yes, well they better take some kind of action, otherwise the hurt boy's parents could sue them.'

'I'm not sure they would. I met them. They didn't seem the type.'

'I'm so sorry, Dad. When does the dean have to decide?'

He shrugged. 'In the next couple of weeks, I think. I just hope justice is done; they've already destroyed one boy's life.'

The rest of the break passed quickly and quietly. Her dad was preoccupied with the student in the hospital, and Lottie found herself thinking about him too. They visited and brought flowers but saw no change in his condition.

Lottie returned to college emotionally drained. Once again, she was consumed with schoolwork, which she appreciated as it gave her something else to focus on. Winter arrived in Maine, the snow burying everything in heavy white mounds. Classes began winding down as everyone started preparing for final exams. When she wasn't in class, Lottie escaped to the library, the hours drifting away as she studied furiously. She reached a point of fatigue where her eyes began stinging. She closed them briefly only to open them hours later, a small drop of drool on her sleeve.

Packing up, she headed back to her dorm building, the cold air waking her up even more.

When she returned to her room, she was surprised to see a missed call from her dad. She decided to risk calling him back.

'Are you okay? You're not usually up this late,' she said the second he picked up.

'Yeah, I'm sorry... I didn't realize what time it was. I just found out that the boy passed away. His parents are devastated and angry. They're pressing charges against the other boys. And, because of that, the president had to expel them.'

'Oh Dad, I'm so sorry to hear that. I was hoping that he'd pull through somehow. I hope his parents will be okay.'

'I don't think they'll ever recover. Losing your child... it's something every parent fears. But I'm happy about the dean's decision; it was the right thing to do. Hopefully it'll deter other students from trying similar things.'

'Yeah. Did they ever find out what it was? Hazing? Bullying? Or a stupid prank gone wrong?'

'I don't know... the boys have been very quiet about that. All I can say is that the right thing has been done. But anyways, you sound tired, you should go to bed.'

'Thanks Dad, but I'm glad you called. And I'm really happy that justice has been done.'

'Me too. Good luck with your exams.'

'Thanks. Night.'

Over the next five days, sleep and study were the only two things that mattered. She barely ate, and the most exercise she did was trudging to and from the library.

Then finally, finally, she was finished.

The day she was due to leave, she packed up her car, excited to go home and get some rest. She inserted the key in the ignition... and nothing happened. Again and again, she tried and, again and again, it failed to start.

'No!' she yelled. She tried tinkering with the car, but she was too damn tired, and it was too damn cold, so she called up a mechanic who arranged to pick it up the following day.

She called her dad to explain the change in plans, then fell asleep, completely exhausted.

The next morning, she woke to the persistent sound of her phone ringing. Bleary eyed, she scrambled to find it underneath the pile of clothes she had thrown on her desk chair and answered it. Her car was ready.

'Yes, yes!' she screamed before jumping into the shower and racing to the mechanic where her tiny car waited in all its glory. The second that Lottie placed the key in, the car sprang to life, and she began driving home. Once she hit the road, she called her dad to let him know she was coming. She left a voicemail and placed her phone on the passenger side, only noticing as she did that the tiny screen was black. She pressed a button. Nothing.

'What the hell, you were fully charged this morning,' she muttered as she searched for her charger. She found an old one that barely worked and plugged it in.

The drive home was treacherous. The roads were slippery, and parts were completely submerged under snowdrifts. She slowed down until she was going 20 mph/h in a 50 zone.

She had just pulled into Schenectady and switched her phone on when she noticed numerous missed calls from an unknown caller, but none from her dad.

'Strange,' she muttered to herself as she kept driving, eventually turning onto their street.

While she crept forward, the snow making a constant crunching sound under her tires, she became aware of a smell wafting into her car. Smoke. She glanced out the window and saw large plumes of it floating up into the sky. She automatically slowed down even more, one hand going up to cover her nose. Just as she had taken her hand from the steering wheel, she saw it.

Police tape.

Surrounding her home.

Her home, smoldering.

Braking hard, she flung open the door and ran...

'Dad?!' she screamed.

A man stepped forward, his skin gray from the smoke, his uniform covered in soot. His face, somber and compassionate, gave her the answer she needed to the question she didn't want to ask.

The inquest confirmed that it had been arson, and, within days, the police had a suspect in custody. It was one of the expelled students, the one who hadn't co-operated.

She saw him from a distance. He was standing in court, his face completely blank. It didn't seem to bother him that he had destroyed her life. He received a sentence, but Lottie didn't care. His being in prison wasn't going to change anything – it wasn't going to bring her dad back. Nothing could. The funeral, a small and dignified affair, brought home the fact that she was now completely alone. She knew Jake was there, he had flown back from California to see her, but it wasn't the same. As much as he wanted to, he couldn't help her; no one could help her now.

She stayed with Jake's family, trying to be normal, act normal. For a time, it seemed to work a little... until she started receiving letters.

When the first letter arrived in the mailbox, she thought it was a sympathy card. Then she opened it.

'Your father killed that boy... and now you've ruined another. You should be ashamed of yourself.'

It was crudely written with no signature.

A week later, another one arrived:

'You should have died with your father.'

Again, no indication as to who had sent it.

Every week, another letter would arrive. Little by little, Lottie felt herself closing up, her despair of being in this place, around these people, eating away at her. That someone, anyone, should have these beliefs about her father was crazy. She just wanted to be left alone.

The day she received a letter saying, 'You're next,' she decided it was time to go.

She packed her few possessions then asked Jake to go for a drive with her.

They drove to their favorite place, Lake Moreau, where Lottie's father used to take them hiking.

'What's going on?' he asked. 'Don't tell me nothing. I know something's happening.'

Silently, she handed him the letters. He took out his glasses and began reading. His face darkened when he read the accusations and became further enraged once he read the threats.

'This is bullshit, these should be with the police!' he said. 'Someone is threatening you!'

'Yes,' she said quietly.

'Do you know who it is?'

'I have an idea... it could be one of his frat brothers... or someone in his family. I do remember them giving me death stares at the trial. I don't think they were happy about him going to jail. A strange viewpoint, given what he did.'

'So, are you going to do something about it?' he asked.

'I'm leaving,' she said.

'What? Why?' he asked.

She glared at him. 'Seriously? Because these people,' she gestured toward the letters, 'are crazy. And I don't want to deal with it.'

'But they should be held accountable.'

'Should, but won't... I really think it's best that I go.'

'Well, are you at least going back to college?' he asked.

She shook her head. 'No, I can't... it'll just bring up memories I'd like to forget. I think I need a new start. Somewhere else... somewhere far away.'

'You should come to LA!' he said. 'You could live with me.'

'That's really nice of you... but I need somewhere quiet. LA is your kind of place, not mine. I think I'd go crazy if I moved there. Besides, you have your own life and career to lead. I have to figure out mine, and it's going to take time. And honestly, it's something I need to do on my own.'

'You're sure? It's no big deal for you to live with me.'

'No, really... you're so nice Jake, but I have to help myself.' She sighed. 'But I do want to thank you for everything. You've been so lovely since Dad died...'

'Lottie, you're my best friend. Of course I'll do anything possible to help you.'

'Well, I do need your help with something. Two things, actually. One is easy, the other... not so easy. The easy thing is dropping me off at a bus station. Is that okay?'

'Yeah, no problem. What's the other thing?'

'It's kind of weird, but I want you to have my car.'

'The Yugo?' he yelped. 'But that's your car... and, frankly, we all know it's a heap of crap.'

'I know, I know... but I don't want to get rid of it, and at the same time I can't have it anymore... it's the reason I wasn't with Dad. I just can't keep it, it's too painful. But if you kept it, well, that would mean something to me. So will you?'

'Yeah, I suppose... I promise I'll take care of it. But if you ever change your mind, just let me know and it's yours.' His face softened as he looked at her. 'So, when did you want to go to the station?'

She looked at her watch. 'Probably now, if that's okay with you.'

They drove to a nearby bus station and parked, their headlights beaming on a sign that read 'Wait here for bus.' They sat, staring at the sign, waiting for the dingy gray bus to arrive.

'Where are you going?' he asked.

'Colorado for now, then who knows.'

'Will you call me? I just want to know you're okay,' he said.

'Yeah, once I've settled in.' She looked down. 'I don't know if or when we'll see each other again, but thank you for everything.'

Their conversation was broken by the sound of the bus hitting the curb as it arrived at the bus stop.

'Goodbye Lottie,' Jake said, reaching out to pull her into a hug.

'Goodbye Jake,' she said, choking back tears.

'Let me know if you need anything. But just take care of yourself, you promise?'

'I will. I won't give them the pleasure of letting something happen to me.'

She got on the bus and sat at the back, her desire to watch him greater than her dislike of the back seat. As they pulled away, she waved to him and stayed sitting backward, her eyes filling with tears as he grew smaller.

***

Thirty years later, she was in Seattle waiting for a coffee when she saw a familiar car parked on the opposite side of the street. It was a classic car in some ways, one she had not seen for decades. She crossed the road and walked around the car, trying to figure out if it was, in fact, her old car.

'Can I help you?' a voice asked.

She turned.

It was Jake. But not Jake. He was much too young.

'Is this your Yugo?' she asked him.

'Yes,' he replied, a question in his tone.

'It looks exactly like the one I used to have a long time ago,' she said.

'Yeah, it's pretty old. It used to be my dad's. His best friend gave it to him when they were young... it's been through a lot, but he tried to keep it in good shape. Didn't help when we were born.' He laughed. 'I've always liked it though, used to hide in it when I was little. Supposedly it's a bit of a joke, not the best car in the world... but there's something about it. Anyways, I thought I'd try and restore it to surprise him. He was definitely surprised. But then he decided to give it to me when I got into college, so here I am. I just hope we make it to campus alright.'

She smiled. 'Well, if it breaks, all you need to fix it is some duct tape and a screwdriver. It's nice to see that it's being looked after so well. I'm sure you'll have some great memories with it.'

'You should hear some of my dad's stories,' he said.

She laughed. 'I bet! If cars could talk, I'm sure that one would tell some shockers.'

'Yeah, too bad it couldn't tell my dad what happened to his friend... I think he was always waiting for her to turn up, but she never did.'

'I'm sure she wanted to... but like most things, life probably got in the way. But he had a good life?'

He shrugged, 'Yeah, of course.'

She smiled. 'Well, I'm sure hers was good too. And you can tell him that one day.'

He looked down at his feet. 'I better get going. It was nice meeting you...'

'Charlotte,' she said.

'I'm Charlie,' he said.

'Nice to meet you. Enjoy the car.'

13

The Grave Robber

In Montreal, so the legend goes, there is a special graveyard; it is difficult to find and not visited frequently. It sits in the middle of the city, a labyrinth of stones and trees –the dead dwelling next to the living. It is the Cemetery of Forgotten Stories, and it is only open to a select few. Most of its visitors have used it as a source of inspiration or to reflect on stories long lost, but a handful have used it for their own selfish purposes. This is the tale of one such man.

It was created in the late-19th century by one of Canada's most infamous writers, a man known only as Monsieur S. That Monsieur S was known at all indicated a noticeable lack of quality writers in the first place as most of his published works had been deemed mediocre by the literary world. One newspaper reviewer aptly described his prose: 'Monsieur S's books were regrettably long, and best read when one could neither see nor hear the words.' This scathing commentary succeeded where others had failed; Monsieur S's publishers finally dropped him, and his books were relegated to the ash carts.

Monsieur S was inconsolable. For decades, he had defined himself by his writing; his words were as much a part of him as his hands or feet. It was inconceivable that one miserly review had been the catalyst for destroying his life's work. Monsieur S hid away in his home, his frustrations and fury threatening to overpower him. He sat in his hunter green armchair and ranted against the reviewer until his mouth ran dry. As he poured himself a drink one day, he had an idea.

He would create a cemetery for all the stories he would never publish or complete. It would be his way of commemorating his work.

One night, Monsieur S gathered his money and set off in search of a plot of land worthy of this momentous endeavor. He stalked through the streets of Old Montreal, the flickering gas lights sending shadows scattering before his feet and making the nearby buildings seem larger than they were. As he walked, he maintained his own excellent company by murmuring excerpts from his books, causing him to remember just how talented he was. Where else could one find such creative and innovative storylines? And one could not find a more lyrical prose than his own. He paused to reflect on the ingenious ending of his last novel when he recognized a familiar and repugnant figure standing across the street. Monsieur S's eyes narrowed as he focused on the face, one he had seen too frequently in the newspaper. It was the reviewer, that repellent dullard who had written so disparagingly of his novel. Before Monsieur S could say a word to the man, the reviewer disappeared into a house, the door shut firmly behind him.

Monsieur S cursed. Then he saw something that made his mouth snap shut. Adjacent to the reviewer's house was a block of land, unusual in this part of Montreal. A majestic maple fronted the street, its autumnal foliage muted by the deepening darkness of the sky. He traversed the road, taking measure of the block's size. As he approached, he could have sworn the tree shifted, welcoming him. Ensconced high above in the tree's branches, an owl hooted, creating an aura of gravitas that only Monsieur S could appreciate. He stared, elation moving through his body, and knew with absolute certainty that this was going to be the haven for all the stories he would never complete. That it was next to the reviewer's house was completely circumstantial. Monsieur S resolved not to waste another thought on the man.

But, of course, he did. At night, visions of the reviewer flooded in, causing him to awake with feelings of anger and frustration. He was able to suppress these feelings during the day when his mind was fully consumed with his project. This obsession proved beneficial; after only a matter of months, and the depletion of most of his savings, he was the proud owner of the Cemetery of Forgotten Stories, a landmark known only to himself. At first, his visits were infrequent; he was simply too busy writing. The few times he ventured out, he spent most of his time glowering at the reviewer's home, inwardly daring the man to come out. The reviewer never did, which fueled Monsieur S's fury even more.

Gradually, his visits increased as his writing proliferated. He wrote constantly, finishing some pieces, casting others aside. Every few months, he would go through the papers until he had accumulated enough to go into a special metal box he had purchased earlier. He commissioned a stonemason to create a gravestone for the box, with the words 'For too many, there was so little' etched in a highly stylized script.

As time passed, the number of boxes buried grew, and the gravestones multiplied. Five years after he had first laid eyes on his cemetery, Monsieur S returned one warm spring day to appreciate everything he had achieved. He sat contentedly on a bench in the middle of his cemetery, surrounded by words that had never been published nor appreciated by the public, and he knew that someday, somehow, they would be known. When he finally left, he was so focused on his own thoughts that he failed to notice the reviewer's front door opening.

The full moon dominated the sky that night, its luminosity filtering through Monsieur S's drapes, sending beams of light onto the writer's face. His head twitched and his eyelids fluttered before one eye opened unexpectedly, and he sighed, 'Best idea yet.' Then, and only then, did Monsieur S breathe his last breath.

***

It had been another listless night preceded by a frustrating day spent sitting in front of the computer. His fingers had been poised, ready to type, but his brain had been unable to overcome the block which was preventing the words from coming out.

No, it wasn't going to happen. Boulanger shook his head. He had been trying to write for so long that he couldn't even remember what it felt like to write effortlessly. He had done it in the past – his first three books had come to him with an almost supernatural ease. But that had been a while ago, and he had been blocked since. He had tried everything... meditation, reading – Christ, he had read so many uninspired books this past year alone. He had even tried writing prompts, something he had always scorned in the past, to no avail; nothing worked. It was all her fault – his agent. She was the one always putting pressure on him. How in God's name was he supposed to write when she was continuously emailing him? She was constantly barraging him with information about book sales, deadlines for his first draft and, most annoyingly, updates about other writers who were producing works at an alarming pace. He had, of course, changed his settings so her emails went straight to his junk folder. Unfortunately, he couldn't stop himself from reading them, particularly when he was supposed to be working.

He knew of at least five authors who were publishing books at lightning speed – how was he meant to compete with that? Was it any wonder he couldn't find the words and didn't even know where to start?

Boulanger punched his cushion, the only thing that would submit to him at this point.

That night, his restless mind working overtime, he decided to go for a walk. As if in a dream, he reached for his coat and ambled through the city, its features hazy from the light mist that engulfed it. Strains of a jazz quartet were swallowed up by the night. He walked and walked until he arrived at a house that looked familiar. He frowned, wondering how he knew the house when he didn't recognize the area. He shook his head, perplexed, and strolled past the house slowly before stopping at an astonishing sight. It was land, a rarity in Old Montreal, with an unkempt appearance that bordered on wild. An imposing maple tree guarded what Boulanger assumed was an entrance. As he approached, he saw a small sign next to the tree that read 'The Cemetery of Forgotten Stories.' Squinting, he searched for more information, but though there were characters engraved below, it was hard to decipher them. Drawn to the mysterious nature of the place, he entered, looking around to ensure that no one saw him trespassing on private property.

Inside the cemetery, he was met with more untamed greenery. Ivy created a dense carpet, its tendrils creeping upward, threatening to engulf everything in view, particularly the tiny gravestones that dotted the ground. He bent down to read one and was astonished to read the inscription, 'He was born with too little imagination to understand what was happening.'

'What is this?' Boulanger asked himself as he came to the next one, which stated, 'It was the smallest twig that decided the fate of Adalie.' He shook his head and walked to a stone set back from the others. It was fancier than its neighbors, and its engraving took up the entire stone: 'For too many, there was so little.' Intrigued, Boulanger did something he would normally have never dreamed of doing – he picked up a large stick nearby and began digging. A compulsion within him demanded that he find out what this all meant. The ground resisted at first, but his determination brought a strength of its own, and soon he was pulling a small box from deep underground. It was an ordinary-looking metal box, locked with a key that he did not have. He solved this problem by hitting it with a rock. Its lid flew open, presenting him with a sheaf of papers. In the hazy light of the moon, he read the contents, his heart pounding madly.

Sunlight flickered through his curtains the following morning, the warm rays pressing down on Boulanger's eyelids. The second his eyes opened, Boulanger had the most brilliant idea for a new book. He jumped out of bed, ran to his desk, and began typing furiously, the keys barely managing to keep up with his fingers. For weeks, he was consumed; all he did was type, sleep, and revisit the cemetery. With every trip, he felt his story progressing more and more until one rainy Thursday when he typed the last word.

He sent it off to his agent, who called him later that day, gushing over the sheer brilliance of his prose, the ingenuity of his plot. He smiled and said the usual platitudes about his stories being ninety-five percent hard work and five percent inspiration.

'Well, I don't know where you got your inspiration for this one, but keep it up,' she said.

It didn't take long for the book to be published, and it became an instant success, rising through the ranks like a geyser. There was talk of awards, critics and readers alike agreeing that nothing of this caliber had been written in over a decade.

Boulanger, it must be confessed, soaked up these accolades like the middle-aged sponge he was. Fortunately, the kudos were constant and gushing, the kind he liked best. More importantly, it showed no signs of abating; everyone in Canada was reading and talking about his latest book.

During the day, he was surrounded by fans and publishers who wanted to be part of his genius. At night, he continued his visits to the cemetery. He had been there so often that it felt like an old friend. As he wandered through, always with the sense that he was somehow being guided, he would inevitably end up in front of a stone that contained the smallest stirrings of a story. In this way, he continued writing, and writing more than he had ever written before.

It didn't take long for the media to notice him.

'How does it feel to be one of Canada's most successful and beloved authors?' a morning TV host asked, his body leaning toward Boulanger as if to gain a better understanding of him through osmosis.

'Well, if I'm honest, it's wonderful. I love what I do, and I've always tried to write books that would make people think, so it's gratifying that it's all going so well.'

'It must be a relief. I'm sure we all remember that five-year period after your third novel, which won several awards, when there was silence. No books, nothing. There was talk of you being done.'

Boulanger fought the temptation to roll his eyes. 'Yes, well, fortunately that was all that it was – talk. As you can see, I've come back with more books, and one can say that the last two have been better than anything else I've ever written.' Boulanger flicked at a minuscule piece of lint on his pants.

'Hmm... yes. That would be *The True Story of Adalie Beaufort* and *The Division*, the latter of which won the prestigious Enlightened Prize. As you might have guessed, I've read both books and enjoyed them tremendously...'

Boulanger preened momentarily before remembering where he was and attempting to adopt a humbler demeanor.

'... but I was surprised with how different they are from your previous works. I mean, they are literally night and day. There's something about these latest books that the others lacked... a certain creative flair that makes them so imaginative and unusual. I have to ask: Where did you get your ideas? Because I've never read anything like these books before and, frankly, there's a lot of rumors racing around... some say drugs, others say you've matured, and then there's the more sinister speculation that you pilfered the material from another writer – a Monsieur S in particular. So, which one is it? I must admit, I find the plagiarism accusation most compelling.' The host's voice trailed off as he put down his card, took a sip of water, and stared at Boulanger.

Boulanger's heart, which had been lub-dubbing at a respectable pace, abruptly stepped up to a slightly more frantic speed. 'What?' Boulanger spluttered. 'What are you even talking about?'

'Am I to understand you deny these allegations?'

'Absolutely! These books were the result of my own imagination, creativity, and hard work, and I resent this very much. Whoever came up with these wild allegations is clearly a disturbed individual who needs to stop spreading slanderous accusations. I mean really! The whole thing is preposterous!'

'Is it?' the host asked, a cunning expression in his eyes. 'Well, on the table in front of you is a copy of a letter we've received that accuses you of stealing material. How would you respond to that?'

'I've never heard of this Monsieur S, let alone stolen his ideas,' Boulanger expounded, pounding emphatically on the stack of books that sat on the coffee table in front of him. 'Over the years, my writing style has changed, and these books are the result of that.'

'Well, it just so happens that we have Monsieur S's descendent with us today. Please welcome Stéphanie to the show.'

He gestured, and a woman walked on set, her face wearing the resigned expression of one who has faced too many of life's no's and simply wants to hear a yes. She sat down in the chair offered by the host, barely seeming to notice where she was. She gave a brief nod to Boulanger, her eyes narrowed slightly, before turning to face the presenter.

'You are related to Monsieur S,' he started, staring earnestly into the woman's eyes.

The woman nodded. 'Yes, I am. He was my great-great-great-grandfather.'

'And you believe that Monsieur Boulanger has stolen some of his work?'

'Yes, absolutely. In fact, I have the proof right here.' She fumbled with a leather case, its clasps making a clinking sound as they snapped shut and she brought several pieces of paper to her lap with a flourish.

As she began reading one of them out loud, Boulanger rolled his eyes. It was the opening for his first book. He scoffed. 'I'm sorry, but this is absurd. It's obvious you just copied what I wrote...'

She handed him the paper. 'Does it look like I copied you? It's not even my handwriting,' she said. 'Besides, I'm not done.'

She read another; this one damning because it was the original beginning for *The Division* before he had modified it. His chest tightened. He did a few breathing exercises, trying to settle himself, but it was no use – he could feel the panic creeping in.

'Well, it sounds familiar, I can't deny that. But it's still a ridiculous idea. Besides, there are ways to forge documents and make them seem old, so how do I know you didn't do that?'

'Because they've been locked up in my parents' house for the last seventy years,' she said. 'And they've been authenticated.'

How is this happening? I thought I was the only person with those manuscripts! Boulanger thought to himself as he tried to stay calm. There was no way she was lying, no one knew the original beginning for *The Beginning*, not even his editor.

'So, what do you have to say?' The host turned toward Boulanger once again. 'You seem to be rather quiet now.'

'I'm... I'm speechless. But I will say this. I wrote these books from beginning to end. I have no idea who this Monsieur S is, and I don't know what you're trying to achieve by coming here and besmirching my name, but I can assure you once more that these are my books and no one else's. That is all.' He stared at her, daring her to contradict him. Strangely, she didn't; she just looked at him and tilted her head.

'Well, this has been lively,' the host stated, a smarmy smile plastered on his face.

'That's one way to describe it. Is this how you normally treat your guests? Attacking their talents, their life's work? It's scandalous, and I, for one, will not stand for it.' Boulanger glanced at his watch, a limited-edition Blancpain he had treated himself to when he won the Enlightened Prize, and said, 'As it happens, I must leave you both. I have an important meeting with my publisher that I must attend.' He rose from his chair, nodded abruptly at the host, and left the room, his mind in a whirl from what had just occurred.

He hurried back home to the safety of his peaceful surroundings, the Prussian blue wallpaper in his study working to ease the anxiety that was threatening to overwhelm him.

He sat in his chair, staring helplessly at his computer screen. The cursor blinked at the end of the sentence – the twenty words forming the prologue for his next novel. Unfortunately, he had seen the same sentence earlier that day, the elegant penmanship on the paper in Stéphanie's hand contrasting greatly with the sterile typed version before him. It had been this, more so than anything else, that had sent him fleeing. Rubbing his head, he stood up and got a bottle of wine. He figured if ever there was a time to drink, this was it.

He downed one glass, barely tasting it as he considered his dilemma. Somehow Stéphanie had acquired these manuscripts and was trying to discredit all his hard work. Yes, that was the line he would use. Oh God, that was rubbish. Who would believe that? But then again, who was she? And why would they believe her over him? Maybe he could say she had stolen the originals from him? But no, that wouldn't work... the originals were locked up and his house was burglarproof, he had seen to that. But what did she know about him? She couldn't know about the cemetery visits as he had never seen anyone there, ever.

Maybe he should reach out to her, get some more information and, of course, find out what she wanted. There was no doubt in his mind that she wanted something, most likely money.

He continued mulling and drinking, the bottle replaced by another until two wine bottles sat on a table, their emptiness offsetting the heaviness of his mind and eyes. He closed his aching lids for a moment, knowing that he would have to go back to the cemetery.

He was there again. He could sense it before he even opened his eyes. There was a solemnity in the air, a stillness that heightened his senses. He was standing there, his jacket on somehow, standing in front of a stone he had never seen. As he moved nearer, he could hear footsteps behind him and knew that someone was coming closer.

'I thought I'd find you here,' a familiar voice said.

He turned around slowly, wondering how she had found him.

She smiled at him with pity before speaking again. 'You're wondering how I know about this place. Yes, it's obvious from the look on your face. My ancestor created it, so it's only right that I know where it is and how to get here. You, on the other hand, are the intruder. You have no right to be here, just like you have no right to steal his words.'

'How can I be a thief of words that have never been completed, nor seen?' His voice rose in volume as he became more righteous. 'In fact, you should be thanking me; without me, these words, these ideas, would have never seen life, they would have stayed buried forever... just like your ancestor.'

'Well, I'm glad you think that,' she said, holding her phone up into the air, its screen showing that the recording had been paused. 'Now I have it on record that you admit to taking his work.'

For the second time in twenty-four hours, he was at a momentary loss for words. He glared before rushing to contradict her claim. 'I did no such thing. Did his words serve as a source of inspiration? Perhaps... but it never went beyond that. Those books were my own. Since you're obviously not a writer, you don't know the difference between inspiration and plagiarism.'

'You are so deluded,' she said. 'Do you actually believe what you say?'

'Of course,' he said without hesitation. 'It's the truth.'

She laughed at that. 'If there's one thing I've learned in my life, it's the relativity of truth.' She looked at his thoughtful expression. 'Go ahead, you can take that for the title of your next book. My gift to you.'

He rolled his eyes. 'I don't think you could inspire anyone, let alone me. Speaking of which, what are you doing here now? Are you following me? I've never seen you here before.'

'I've only just inherited this,' she said, gesturing toward the cemetery, the wintry scene a smaller, less-formalized version of Mount

Royal. Her voice hardened as she stared at him. 'And I don't aim to have anyone profit from it. Especially you.'

'Do you have a problem with me?'

She laughed, the sound devoid of mirth. 'Actually yes, I do.' She removed a paper from her purse and handed it to him. He unfolded an ancient-looking newspaper to a page with a marked article.

'What is it?' he asked.

'Read it.'

He leaned against a tree and read what was a scathing review of a book entitled 'The Lost One.' The reviewer attacked the whole premise of the book, the characters, and the writing style.

'Brutal,' he said, folding it into a neat rectangle when he was finished. 'Then again, as a writer, you have to expect that.'

'Look at it again,' she said. 'Particularly the name of the reviewer.'

He flipped it open and read the name – Pierre Boulanger – and looked at her.

'I did some research into your family. Turns out your ancestors were just as despicable as you.'

'So, you're angry at something that happened over a hundred years ago? Are you really going to hold me responsible for my ancestor's actions? Are you insane? Christ, I barely knew my father's side of the family in the first place... I must have visited their house when I was young, but that was the only interaction I had with them. I can't believe you're holding on to this grudge. It's crazy – you're crazy. You need to leave me alone – you are clearly obsessed with this so-called "connection." Here, let me make this very simple for you. You are a sad woman whose ancestor was obviously an unsuccessful writer – I am an award-winning novelist with the kind of prestige that someone like you can only ever dream of. No one will care about your damned family history, your recordings, your silly lawsuit, or you. Those words were lost until I breathed life into them – they are mine!'

'We'll see about that.' Her final words were muffled and, as he watched, she began walking away, the trees shielding her from his sight.

Good riddance, he thought as he turned back toward the gravestone. He peered closer at its inscription: 'He who had it, lost it all.' Hmm. Not the most original starting point, but one he could work with. Especially once he dug up the box. He stood and rubbed his hands together. If only this tiresome woman would go away, everything would be perfect. He shrugged. He was sure it would work out in the end, stuff like that usually did. He smiled gleefully at the thought of another prize-winning book on the not-so-distant horizon. Who knew, maybe they would want to do film adaptations? His lip curled at the thought of a pleasantly plump bank account. He would show all those people who had written him off during his quiet years.

He left the cemetery, moving past his ancestor's house and down the street. A pebble found its way into his shoe, and he stopped and dumped it out before yawning and rubbing his eyes, only to find himself back in his study, sitting in his blue velvet writing chair, a wine glass perched precariously on the armrest.

Another day, another book, he thought as he walked over to his coffee machine. The espresso came out perfectly extra hot and strong, just the way he liked it.

Holding it in one hand, he walked to the front door to pick up his daily newspaper. He was just bending down to retrieve it when he saw the headlines.

'A Grave Matter for Montreal's Most Beloved Writer: Plagiarizing the Dead?' with a portrait of himself underneath.

'Shit!' he yelled, grabbing the paper, but losing his cup. The hot liquid splashed onto his hand and soaked the headline, its essence moving closer to his black-and-white face until he was a featureless brown blob, wiped out for all eternity by a woman and an extra-strong espresso.

14

The Lucky Bean

March 2010

The river had been dyed an emerald green, or so the organizers said. This opinion was not widely shared by the people on the street, whose verdicts ranged from 'Kelly green' to 'swamp-water green' and everything in between. No matter what the shade, one could not debate the fact that the Chicago River was indeed green, its vivid hues contrasting with the rusted industrial canal that encompassed it.

As was to be expected, it was a cold day, the temperature barely reaching sixteen degrees Fahrenheit, the sky a murky gray that held no promise or pleasure for those brave enough to venture outside. The winds, which had the unpleasant habit of cutting through multiple layers of clothing to freeze any flesh within, were temperamental today – at times mild, other times almost fierce.

The bagpipes could be heard from miles away as the St Patrick's Day parade made its way south through the city. The stomping feet of the marchers were in time with the tapping feet of the viewers, who had hoped that, for once, their extremities would not freeze. Necks were craned, straining right and left to see flashes of drummers and Irish step dancers. Moving spryly, the dancers went by quickly, their corkscrew curls bouncing impishly in the air. The melodious sounds of 'Danny Boy' and 'Molly Malone' stirred the bystanders, who nodded appreciatively in time to the music, taking the occasional swig from their coffee cups.

Gradually, the crowds began to disperse, a slow yet steady exodus to the bars and restaurants that lined the streets of downtown Chicago. Beers were drunk, and TVs were turned on. It was hockey season and, for once, the Chicago Blackhawks were doing well, much to the shock of the team's supporters. Deep down, they knew there was no hope for their team to reach the Stanley Cup playoffs; it was inconceivable. As the fans watched the tiny figures skating furiously, they wondered when their team was going to fizzle out.

Amidst the chaos and mess, two young women walked along West Wacker Drive on their way to Millennium Park. Both women were tall, giving credence to the belief that Midwestern children grow as tall as the cornstalks.

'I can't believe you're making us do this,' the brunette, Suzanne, said. 'You do realize this is completely ridiculous.'

Her friend Molly rolled her eyes. 'Yeah, so you keep saying. But Liza went there last St Patrick's Day and made a wish, and now she's engaged to the hottest and nicest guy in her company. He'd never even noticed her before.'

Suzanne shook her head and sighed. 'Are you serious? What worked for her was getting a nose and boob job. Even I noticed her after that, it's no wonder he did too.'

'You keep saying that she had work done, but I don't think she looks any different,' Molly said.

Suzanne looked at her friend in exasperation, a hint of a smile forming on her lips. 'You don't notice anything different about her? Are you sure about that?'

'Yeah, she looks the same. I must say, she does her makeup beautifully. I wish I could contour like that.'

Suzanne sighed. 'I can't believe how naïve you are sometimes. Like this plan of yours. I don't think it's going to work. Contrary to what Liza told you, it is not magic.'

'You never know,' Molly said. 'There's so much out there that's unexplainable.'

'Yes, yes... I know, you've already told me. I just choose to be more logical.' Suzanne looked down at her watch and lengthened her already long stride. 'But since I've been roped into coming, we had better pick up our pace. I'd actually like to watch part of the game before it ends.'

They passed the House of Blues, the gray, whale-shaped music hall flanked by the Marina City complex, two buildings known throughout the city for their resemblance to corn cobs.

'Those buildings look so strange; I wonder what they were thinking when they designed them,' Suzanne said as they walked by. 'Ugh, I really wish I had worn thicker socks – my feet are cold.'

Molly nodded. 'I'm sorry, they said it was going to be mid-thirties.'

As they approached Clark Street, a large gust of wind came sweeping through, causing the two women to tighten their grips on their coats and scurry along at a faster pace. When they drew closer to Michigan Ave, their eyes moved upward as they both silently appreciated the beauty of the buildings, the architectural styles showing when they had been constructed.

Once they hit Michigan Ave, traffic increased. Taxis wove in and out of lanes while horns blared continuously. As they crossed Washington Street, Molly yanked Suzanne back before a taxi almost plowed into her.

'Oof, that was a close one,' Suzanne said, her voice a touch shaky. 'Thanks.'

'No problem, that's what friends are for.'

They crossed Michigan Ave and walked up the steps to McCormick Place, looking at the ice-skating rink's lustrous surface, which for now was empty.

Nearer to their target, they sprinted up the multiple flights of steps leading to their ultimate destination – *Cloud Gate*.

Made from stainless-steel plates shaped into the form that had given it its nickname, 'The Bean,' it had a fluidity that was unusual in a sculpture of its size. It draped heavily, its curved and sinuous shape isolated from, yet connected to, the surroundings. As they moved around the piece, they saw Chicago's cityscape reflected on its surface.

'Wow,' said Suzanne. 'I didn't realize it was so big.'

'It's amazing,' breathed Molly as she reached out to touch the mirror-like surface. 'You can see everything so clearly.'

'It's pretty amazing how you can see the cityscape, but it's still just a sculpture,' Suzanne reminded her.

'No, it's more than that, I can tell. And now that we're here, I know that Liza's experience was real. I mean, can't you feel it? There's something special about it.' Molly's hand trembled as she gently stroked the metal.

Suzanne tutted, her disbelief evident in the left eyebrow that arched high on her forehead. 'Do you even hear yourself? You're talking nonsense.'

'Well, we'll see who's right, won't we? Now, do you remember what Liza said? I want to make sure I do this right.'

Suzanne rolled her eyes.

'Something about standing underneath it, touching it, then stating her wish out loud,' she said, then mumbled under her breath, 'It's not going to work no matter what you do.' She shook her head and stepped away to give Molly some space.

Suzanne watched as Molly stood underneath 'The Bean,' reached up to touch it and closed her eyes. Molly had been standing there for a minute before Suzanne called out, 'I hope your wish doesn't include a certain person at work. You do realize he's gay, right?'

Silence.

Suzanne tapped her foot, waiting for a sliver of warmth to make its way to her toes. Nothing.

'I imagine you're talking about Sam.' Molly's voice echoed as she emerged from under 'The Bean.' 'I've seen enough of him to know that he's as straight as they come. Well, I'm done, so now it's your turn.' Molly walked over to where Suzanne had been standing. 'Make sure you wish for something good!'

I can't believe I'm doing this, Suzanne thought as she walked over to 'The Bean,' staring at the silver cloud as it rose majestically above her. *Ugh, I wish my feet weren't so damn cold.*

She sighed, then reached out to touch the cold metal and muttered something under her breath, something that she knew was impossible. When she finished, she stood there and, for a brief moment, she thought she heard the faintest of whispers saying 'Granted.' She looked around, but Molly was far away, preoccupied with something. Suzanne shook her head. Surely it had only been an echo?

She walked away from 'The Bean' and to Molly, her mind completely discarding what had happened.

As they left, Suzanne almost bumped into a tall man who was talking quickly into his cell phone, the name 'Rescculp' prominent on his hunter green jacket. She huffed as he kept talking without noticing or apologizing to her. 'Some people,' she muttered before Molly, who had run ahead, called back to tell her to hurry up.

The two young women exited the park and approached the intersection where Michigan Ave meets Monroe Street. While she listened to Molly talk about something that had happened at work the previous day, Suzanne could see a young man approaching them with something in his hands. Molly stopped chatting as the man came up and gave each of them a free pair of 'EAZE FOOFREEZE,' a new product on the market. According to his spiel, it was a revolutionary pad that attached to the outside of the shoe to warm the foot. They thanked him before he walked off.

Molly put the sample in her bag, but Suzanne was desperate, so she opened the packet and slapped the pads onto her shoes. Miracle of miracles, the things actually worked, and her feet were infused with a pleasant warming sensation. The fact that her first wish for warm feet had been granted did not immediately cross her mind. She and

Molly walked south on Michigan Ave to the Art Institute of Chicago. By the time they reached the stately bronze lions that guarded the entrance to the museum and the glorious Caravaggio exhibition within, all thoughts of 'The Bean' were gone.

***

Suzanne was walking to work on a particularly warm day in June, the thrill of the previous night lingering like a hangover. Not only had the Blackhawks made it to the playoffs, but they had won the Stanley Cup! Who would have ever guessed it?

At that thought, her wave of euphoria ebbed, and she stopped abruptly in front of the Chicago Theatre on State Street.

Someone plowed into her from behind, but she was oblivious to everything and everyone as she stood there remembering her trip to 'The Bean' three months earlier and what she had wished for.

'No fucking way,' she said.

It had worked.

While Suzanne was contemplating the impossible, two men were crossing Millennium Park, on their way to 'The Bean,' their uniforms bearing the name 'Rescculp.'

'Well, looks like you were right, here's that twenty dollars I owe you,' the taller man said, handing his partner a crisp new bill.

'I should feel bad for this – it was almost too easy in the end,' the shorter man said, pocketing the money.

'Who would have thought that they'd win? Never in a million years.'

'Really? I mean, in the beginning it was pretty surprising, but then it was like they could do no wrong. And what an ending! Did you see the last play? It was fucking amazing, never seen anything like it. Doubt I ever will again, that was a once-in-a-lifetime opportunity. Well, thanks for the money, maybe I'll buy you a beer later on.'

'Thanks. So, what's on for the day?' the taller man asked.

'I don't know, don't you have the schedule?'

The taller man pursed his lips and reached into the backpack that was hanging over his right shoulder. He pulled out a piece of paper and smiled sheepishly.

'Whoops, my bad. Looks like one of the panels is loose, so we'll have to fix it.'

'We will, or I will?' the shorter man said, staring intently at the other man.

'Well, you will.' The taller man laughed, then walked off while the shorter man unscrewed one of the lower panels and pulled himself up into 'The Bean.'

As he set out his tools, he heard footsteps approaching then stopping underneath him.

'Mayday! You've got a hopeful looking young 'un about to reach up to 'The Bean.' You gonna pull your genie act, today?' the man's voice crackled over his radio.

'Crap!' the shorter man exclaimed before turning down his radio. His voice muffled, he responded. 'Nah, that's only something I do for St Patrick's Day. And, by the by, I prefer "leprechaun" – I am Irish, after all. The City of Chicago should pay me double for what I do on March 17th.'

'I don't think they know you exist,' the other man laughed into the radio.

'They should. I can see it now, they can totally redesign their brochures to read, "Luck of the Irish, Luck of 'The Bean,' come to Chicago on St Patrick's Day".'

'You're delusional.'

'Yeah, but at least I'm twenty dollars richer today. Guess that makes me lucky after all.'

Australia

15

Icarus

I sit in isolation. My eyes gaze wearily at the lights, those yellow-tinged bulbs flickering sporadically, casting a jaundiced hue on everything. Not that there's much in the room. A bed and chair are the only furniture, and my personal effects are scattered about, the only items that were deemed 'safe.' A few books, a notebook, some pictures... that is all I have left of my former life. Then again, it was greed, pure and simple, that got me here, so maybe my lack of possessions is one of those ironic moments that the universe adores.

But I guess that's the beauty of my current position – it gives me the opportunity to think about philosophical stuff.

I would trade that opportunity to have my old life back in a heartbeat. But unfortunately, that's not going to happen. I'm just an ordinary guy whose brilliant idea didn't quite work out the way it was supposed to...

It all started with abseiling. My job. Rather, it was my job until I got thrown in here. I worked for a rope access company, one of the good ones in Melbourne. It was the kind of work a person sometimes falls into. I liked climbing and had some trade experience. Once I got my IRATA certification, it wasn't long before I found this maintenance job. It was perfect for me: easy work, yet a lot of variety. One day we might be fixing sprinklers, another day we would be hanging a painting in the foyer of an office building. We also did a lot of caulking, there were lots of mistakes to fix, tons of leaks to mend. I did it all while dangling from industrial ropes, enjoying the birds-eye view of the city. When working on a building in Southbank, I would sit in my seat two hundred and fifty meters in the air, watching as the sun came up beyond the Botanical Gardens, the calls of the birds competing with the noise of the traffic below. The week I spent painting a building in Little Bourke Street, I listened to the cafés as they opened for business: the sound of chairs scraping the pavement as they were set down, the flap of umbrellas as they were opened and encountered their first gust of wind. These were the sounds of my mornings.

As fun as the job was, it did have its moments. I'll never forget the time I was caulking some windows on the side of a newly built building in Docklands when a giant gush of wind came tunneling through and knocked me flat against the building. Thankfully, my helmet received the brunt of it, but it did leave me a bit jittery.

Then, one day, I got the call that changed my life.

The work was due to take place on a building in Little Collins Street. It was a small job, rendering a tiny patch of retaining wall and caulking around a window just below. About as simple as they come, it would only take a day to do.

I drove to site, weaving through traffic that was intense, even this early in the day. *When are they going to do something about this?* I wondered as I dodged a potential crash. I had been complaining about the traffic for years but, if anything, it had gotten worse. A lot worse. It was still dark when I parked in the loading zone, just a few meters from the building itself. I unpacked my equipment, making sure that my caulking gun had a full battery. I walked over to the building, noticing a massive, suited man standing near the entrance. His suit strained to contain the bulky muscles within, and he kept sliding a finger underneath the collar of his shirt in an attempt to loosen it.

I looked up at the building. It was old and narrow, one of those places that's been built around instead of being torn down. It was also small, only about forty meters high, which would make my job easier.

I entered it and approached the reception desk. Upon getting my information, she directed me toward the stairwell. I was surprised that I didn't need a fob or key to gain access to the roof, but these small places can be like that. I began my ascent, grateful that there weren't too many stairs. Some of the taller buildings can be awful. You think you're going to have a heart attack when you're halfway up.

By the tenth floor, I had slowed down, pacing myself. Once I made it to the roof, I dropped my bag onto the floor, rubbing my sore shoulder.

I had just found the anchor point and tied the ropes to it when my partner Matty finally arrived.

'Let me guess, traffic was shit?'

He laughed. 'Mate, you have no idea. Cheltenham may as well be on the other side of the planet... it takes fucking ages to get anywhere. I tried leaving earlier, but it doesn't seem to make any difference. And there are accidents everywhere.'

I shrugged. 'Oh well, I guess that's what happens when you live in the "World's Most Livable City".'

He rolled his eyes. 'Yeah, no. I bet the people giving the awards don't have to drive here. Well, having survived, I need a coffee. You want one?'

'Sure.'

I watched as he crossed the road to the nearest café, which was now open. After he placed his order, he stood there for a while, talking to the barista like he had all the time in the world. I sighed. That's what happens when you work with Mr. Extrovert. Finally, I saw him laugh and start to walk back, his hands balancing two drinks and a pink donut.

By the time he was on the roof, the donut was gone and one of the drinks was considerably lighter. I took mine, grateful for the warmth and the caffeine as I gulped it down. We stood there, watching the street below as the city came alive. The early morning uniform of fluro was quickly replaced by the Melbourne office uniform —

black, black, and more black. I looked down as hordes of city workers flooded the streets, their walk to the office only interrupted by stops at local cafés from which they emerged triumphantly, coffee cups and little bags in their clutches.

What would we do without coffee? I thought as I drank the last of my latte. I tried not to spend too much as I was saving for a house, but my daily coffee was a necessity, and it seemed like most people felt the same.

Matty and I stood in silence, watching all the movement below, counting the near misses as pedestrians, cyclists, and drivers all battled to get to their destinations quickly. *Quick quick quick* tapped the heels of a lady walking by, her phone clenched in one hand as she gestured angrily in the air.

'Who do you think she's talking to? Looks like she's giving someone a mouthful.'

I shrugged. 'Who knows. The person at the other end probably deserves it. There's a lot of dickheads around here.'

Matty didn't look entirely convinced. 'Or she loves drama.'

We continued watching as she finished her call and jammed her phone into the bag that hung off her shoulder. She quickened her pace and was soon out of sight.

We got to work, quickly rendering the patch, which was small indeed, then set our sights on the window. As I revved up my caulking gun, I saw the big guy near the entrance walk away, only to be replaced by another one who looked identical- same build, suit, everything. I shook my head, then looked around the roof, where I noticed that there were several CCTV cameras, all looking in the same direction – the entrance.

'What kind of place is this?' I asked Matty, pointing out the cameras.

He shook his head. 'No idea. That's a lot of security though.'

Once we finished the window, I made my way down slowly, trying to peer unobtrusively into the windows to find out what was going on. Finally, I was rewarded by my patience. I watched from a window – which must have been situated high in the room – as a man walked in. He was the kind of person who exuded class, perfect hair, perfect suit, perfect everything. An annoying kind of man. I looked on as he went over to a counter, pulled open a drawer, and took out a small tray on which a dozen small shiny objects lay. My eyes almost popped out of my head – even I could recognize diamonds. I had never really thought about diamonds and diamond dealers; they always seemed to have that distant, removed-from-real-life feeling, much like I would imagine arms dealers. But here they were; apparently, I had been working on a building where a diamond dealer plied his trade.

Just think, a couple of those stones could make a huge difference to your savings. This was the first thought that sprang to my mind.

No, no... I couldn't. Could I?

I don't see why not.

But it's risky.

So's everything in life. And most of the time, risk pays off.

Over and over, the argument played in my head, the possible rewards and the potential risks. I couldn't sleep... I couldn't think about anything but those diamonds. My decision, when it came, was sudden and resolute. It was the result of external forces, which made me believe the universe was trying to tell me something. My unit flooded, creating mess and mayhem... expensive mayhem, particularly since I hadn't gotten around to renewing my contents insurance.

That was the day I cracked and decided to go for it.

One Sunday, when most businesses were closed, I planned a reconnoiter to see what I needed for my plan to work. I already knew that the diamond dealership was open, so I drove into the city and parked a few blocks away.

A security guard was there, lounging against the wall on the far side, staring down at his phone with earbuds securely in his ears. As I'd had the foresight to leave my gear in the equipment box on site, it was easy to duck inside the building unseen. Moving along the narrow passageway, I stopped at an innocuous back door and propped it slightly open with a tiny wedge I had brought with me. Then, I moved back to the stairwell and began climbing. As I moved up the stairs, my heart began pounding fast, the adrenalin moving through my body, urging me to move faster.

Once I was on the roof, I checked my kit, making sure there weren't any frays in the ropes and that all my carabiners were working properly. Then I began setting up, securing my ropes to the anchor point with a figure-eight knot. I stretched, loosening up the muscles that I was going to need for this drop.

I began my descent, using my phone to take pictures and notes of everything that I encountered. As I had noticed before, there were several security cameras, but these were all focused on the main entrance on Little Collins Street. As they were stationary, they presented no problems for me. I searched for an entry point and eventually found it – a small, old window that clearly hadn't been maintained for years. Its glass looked brittle, and the frame seemed just as fragile, which was good, because I was going to destroy it with a chisel.

Satisfied, I continued descending until I reached the bottom. Once I hit the ground, I followed the laneway until I came across the back door, then re-entered the building and went back up to the roof. I packed away my kit and hurried down the steps and out of the building. My job was done.

The next few days were spent analyzing my pictures and notes while I brainstormed potential plans. I had dozens, ranging from simple to stupid. I had just discarded yet another one when my eye spotted a commercial for footy, and then everything fell into place. It was going to be simple, and the date that I would begin my operations was the following Friday – the start of a long weekend and, more importantly, the opening week of footy.

The rest of my week was consumed with work and ironing out my plan. By Friday, I was feeling good, confident.

That Friday, after a long day of doing fuck all, I drove to Little Collins Street, which was a dead zone. The office buildings were all closed, most of the workers either at home with their loved ones or getting smashed at the closest pub serving chili chocolate martinis. A group of women, their shrill voices echoing down the street as they walked by, took up all the space on the footpath, leaving me to step into the street. I wasn't the only one distracted by them – the security guard turned to watch them, their presence undoubtedly breaking the monotony of his watch.

When he turned away, I entered the building and began my stopwatch. It took me five minutes to get to the top. I quickly prepared my gear and had just finished securing the ropes to the anchor point when I looked down over the edge and frowned. Weird. There was a line of people, a line that had not been there ten minutes ago. It started in the distance, snaking its way back toward my building.

I paused, debating for a moment about what to do. The thought of going ahead with the plan won. Whatever store or event they were lining up for would open soon and then all these people would go away.

Mind made up, I settled into my seat and slowly made my way to the window. I took out my chisel and set to work, quietly chipping away the caulk that held the frame in place. It was slow going, but eventually the window was free, and I slid in, carefully making my way into the room. It didn't take long to realize that this room didn't have anything of value in it, so I went to the next one.

Jackpot.

There were trays upon trays of diamonds.

I had decided to take a few stones from each tray so there was less chance of the robbery being discovered. After selecting a couple, I carefully placed them into a small bag and put the bag into my pocket. I slid the trays back into their drawers and crept back to the other room. The window was a tight fit, but I maneuvered my way out. I had just begun chiseling the rest of the old silicone out of the frame when a loud noise sounded below. Startled, the chisel dropped out of my hand and fell with horrifying speed to the pavement below.

And so I sit here, staring at the four sterile walls that have been my companions for the last year. I stare and I think.

If only I had been happy with what I had.

If only I hadn't been so greedy. My plan to achieve the Australian dream backfired and left me here to rot.

If only the chisel hadn't dropped.

If only that girl hadn't been standing in line for a free ice cream.

If only she hadn't died from her head wound.

If only, if only...

United Kingdom

16

A Jane Affair

The Americans had landed. Their crusade of being more British than the British was well underway, the journey from Heathrow to London magically transforming their brash accents into a plummy elocution that was found only in the best BBC adaptations... or the Royal Family.

Disembarking from the black cabs, they inundated the prestigious lobby of Claridges, their voices echoing off the shiny black-and-white tiled floor. Caroline, president of the British-based Austen Regency Society – aptly known as ARS – cringed when she heard their running commentaries.

'Will you look at this place?'

'You've gotta hand it to the Brits, they certainly know how to make hotels properly.'

Do the inanities ever end? Caroline thought as she searched for her counterpart, the president of the North American Regency Society (commonly known as NARS), eventually finding her behind an officious older man whose luggage had bumped into a chair.

'Abigail, lovely to meet you,' she said.

'And you must be Caroline. I'm so glad I went with Claridges. I know you recommended Browns due to its history, but everyone knows Claridges. It has more clout with this group,' she said, gesturing around her. 'I must say, it was a good thing I booked so far in advance. It's quite busy.'

Caroline's indifference to this statement was clear to anyone with an understanding of the human psyche. Abigail, who did not and was in a state of oblivion, remained oblivious. Caroline glanced at her watch. It read eleven am. She and Abigail were scheduled to have tea at two pm to finalize the preparations for this, the thirtieth annual gathering of ARS and NARS, a three-day event that culminated in the Regency Soirée. The location for said-soirée had been a hard-fought battle; Abigail had wanted the gardens in Windsor Castle, Caroline had pointed out the logistical impossibilities of this and, after much passive-aggressive bickering, they settled on Hampstead Heath.

At two o'clock, the presidents were seated regally in the foyer, both armed with documents and brochures. The meeting went as expected, given that two personalities, both strong-willed and obstinate, were together with the sole purpose of confirming details for a social event. The tea, beautifully made, went untouched by one, and was diluted by copious amounts of milk and sugar by the other; the cakes, so delightfully presented, were admired briefly before a disagreement broke out and turned all attention elsewhere. By the time Caroline left, she was annoyed and hungry, bemoaning the fact that she had to deal with someone as unaccommodating as Abigail. After all, Caroline knew what she was doing.

Notwithstanding her irritation with Abigail, Caroline kept a close tab on her American guests over the next two days. They certainly made effective use of their time; much like vampires, they descended upon London with the sole purpose of sucking it dry. Everything had to be visited, experienced, and photographed, from the most mundane street sign to the pigeons perched on statues. Caroline was simultaneously fascinated and horrified by their need to document everything... all while continuing an endless commentary.

The day of the soirée finally arrived, a surprisingly nice day in terms of English weather. It was neither too hot nor too cold, but the Americans excelled in finding something to complain about.

'The humidity is killing me,' one woman huffed as she patted her hair, which had admittedly frizzed up in the two minutes she had been outside. 'My hair would not be doing this if we were in California.'

Caroline grimaced. Why did Americans persist in comparing everywhere to America? It was never a favorable comparison, and it defeated the purpose of going anywhere new.

She and Abigail counted heads – twenty-four, all sporting various Regency hairstyles – then herded everyone into the black cabs assembled at the front of Claridges.

As they drove, Caroline glanced at her phone to check that her ARS members were enroute. She was pleased to see that most had already arrived and had, in fact, sent her pictures of the elegantly decorated marquee on the lawn at Kenwood House.

'Fantastic,' she said, snapping her phone shut.

'What?' Abigail asked. 'How soon will we be there?'

'Not long; we'll be at the West Lodge within a few minutes if traffic stays like this,' she said, staring out of the window as a few cars passed by.

Like usual, Caroline was proven right. Five minutes later, they were parked at the West Lodge, carefully removing themselves from the cabs, their Regency-era slippers resting hesitantly on the gravel. It was a short walk, but one that had to be endured rather than enjoyed. Abigail was, once again, bringing up Windsor Gardens. It was clearly her Waterloo.

'I just don't see why we couldn't have had it there... I mean, who knows Hampstead Heath? No one. It's not going to do our society any good if we don't have the proper settings for our soirées.'

Caroline rolled her eyes. Abigail was making Hampstead Heath sound like a slum instead of one of the most desirable places in London. She couldn't wait to reach their destination so that these ridiculous complaints would stop.

She closed her eyes briefly, her feet moving softly over the gravel. Then, she sensed it – the moment she had been waiting for; a sudden silence as the endless stream of talking ceased and the grandeur of Kenwood House stopped everyone in their tracks.

'Stunning!' Abigail said, her face a caricature as her mouth gaped and her eyebrows skyrocketed.

Caroline smiled. She had been here often, but even she was struck by the house's beauty, particularly when the afternoon sunlight caressed the stones. At that moment, the house was transformed into a celestial sight – a Neoclassical building with a glowing cream façade, the stuff of dreams or weddings.

They walked around to the other side, spotting the marquee that stood in front of the lakes. Tourists dotted the landscape, attempting to take a unique picture of the view. As they approached the marquee, a lady came rushing out, her mouth puckered in disdain.

'What should we do with them?' she asked, gesturing toward a couple who were stretching their arms out for a selfie. 'I mean, what is the point of them?'

Her questions, asked to no one in particular, went unanswered. Margery, the lady in question, was known to be dull and self-absorbed, a person that one should stay away from if one did not want to be trapped into listening to mundane monologues.

Caroline shrugged her shoulders elegantly. She had been caught one too many times by Margery and was determined that it would not happen again. There was only so much nonsense a person like her could handle. Abigail, on the other hand, would be a perfect match for Margery... they both saw themselves as the epitome of the modern Regency society. Laughable, but there it was. She turned around to find Abigail and saw something that brought an abrupt end to all thoughts. There, beyond the ridge, was an altogether unfamiliar yet most welcoming sight. Standing there, near the house was an unaccompanied male, attired in standard Regency clothing: a captain's uniform. True, it looked like something from a costume shop, it lacked the truly authentic feel that Caroline's had, but she was willing to overlook that, for he was very attractive, similar in build to Rupert what's his name, but far more honorable looking. A single man attending these soirées was rare; a gorgeous one was unheard of.

Caroline smiled at him; her face showing its perfect mix of elegance and condescension, a look she had appropriated from Jane Austen's portrait and had perfected, time after time, in her hallway mirror.

He caught sight of her, which was to be expected, and seemed completely overtaken by her poise.

'You're here!' A woman squealed as she ran up to him.

Caroline's smooth brow furrowed briefly as she tried to think of the girl's name. Flora? Poesy? Something connected to flowers, surely. A twinge of disappointment went through her as she realized that, of course, he wasn't single.

But then the girl spoke again, her words causing a tsunami of joy in Caroline.

'Where in God's name did you get that costume, Hugh? It's looking a bit worn out... did you hire it from a costume shop? I was hoping you'd look better; you are my brother, after all. Now, some of the members have been asking about you. I told them I finally persuaded you to join after years of nagging. Honestly Hugh, I can't figure out why it took you so long. You love history, and your understanding of Austen's novels is incredible. And we both know you'd have much better luck finding your special someone here rather than wherever you've been searching... at least we know they'll be intelligent.'

Good Lord, let the man speak. Then again, what could he say after this considerable overshare? thought Caroline as she shamelessly eavesdropped. She felt for him. It was hard finding the right person – she knew. She had been trying for a solid decade. At least she didn't have a sister telling everyone everything about her, though she couldn't deny that she had gained some valuable information. First off, she knew his name. Tick. He was single. Tick. He appreciated Jane. Tick. And finally, he was looking for an intelligent mate. Tick. What else was there to know? She knew less about her fellow members who waffled on endlessly to her; she had long perfected the art of appearing to listen without hearing a single word. It was better that way – they were, for the most part, a rather uninteresting bunch, and she did not have the energy to deal with them. That she was president made it worse, because they were always seeking her out.

But this man, Hugh, was a far more tantalizing character.

Caroline decided to play the enigmatic card. She glided to the marquee, admiring the elegant decorations that covered the tables. Twilight was approaching and the caterers arrived while she circulated throughout the marquee, gracing little groups with her presence and legendary wit. A few seemed surprised by her interest, but most were overwhelmingly grateful.

Finally, it was time for dinner. Candles flickered, creating soft orbs of light that wove their way around the guests, who were now seating themselves. Caroline was pleased to see that the presidential table was perfectly situated to enjoy the scenic vista of the lakes. If she had not left her phone in the coat check, she might have been tempted to take a picture; however, she had decided early on that while memories were important, authenticity took precedence.

Caroline was pleasantly surprised to see Hugh, looking quite dapper, taking the seat next to hers. She smiled while slowly reclining in her chair.

'Hello, I don't think we've met. I'm Hugh,' he said, turning to face her.

'Lovely to meet you. I'm Caroline,' she said, picking up her wineglass. 'Have you been enjoying yourself?'

'Yes, it's been interesting. My sister Poesy has been urging me to join the society for a while now, but I've only recently succumbed. Poesy was saying you're the president. I take it then you've been a member for a long time.' He paused, taking a sip of his wine, and staring appreciatively at Caroline's delicate figure, so delightfully enhanced by her Regency dress and the flattering candlelight.

'Yes, I've been a member for ten years and the president for three. It comes with a great deal of responsibility, but I love it. For some people, it's just a hobby, but for me, it's a way of life – the way life should be, the importance of family, one's standing in society... and a certain gentility... these are all so important now, especially with the crudeness you see today.'

An hour passed. The first course had just been brought out, and Caroline was still espousing the benefits of Regency life and ideals. She noticed that Hugh's eyes had glazed over but attributed that to the considerable amount of wine that he had consumed.

'So, what's the story with the two societies?' he asked, his rather abrupt intrusion into Caroline's monologue bringing her to a standstill. 'There seems to be this peculiar feeling between them, and I can't figure it out.'

Caroline sighed. 'Really? Well, ours is older – it was set up more than one hundred years ago as a homage to Jane Austen and Regency life. Then the Americans cottoned on... you know how they are. Once they grab onto something, they claim it as their own. They even tried to take our name. But we put an end to that, so we have ARS and they have NARS. Truth be told, ours is much more respected. Theirs is mostly for amateurs, you know, people who read Austen for school and like the TV adaptations but are still very much engaged in the modern world.'

'And you aren't?'

'Well, we have more of a balance. But I'd say that we have a more authentic understanding of Jane in our daily life. And I think the Americans have a difficult time comprehending that.'

'I see. Well, thank you for clearing that up,' he said, a note of sarcasm in his voice.

'You're welcome. It's all about creating a more genteel and refined way of life for our members. If you're interested in joining, you are more than welcome to apply. But I should warn you, it's an arduous process. I created the current application questions, and they are quite exacting. I feel they're relatively easy if you've completely immersed yourself in Jane's world, but they can be difficult if you haven't. I can assist you if you like. I have been known to give private tutorials for a very few select people.' She looked at him coyly, her eyelashes fluttering down.

'That's very kind, but I really should go now and find my sister. I've barely seen her since the beginning of this event.' He stood, made his excuses to the rest of the table, and walked away. Caroline's eyes followed his figure as it wandered over to another table, one that lacked his sister.

'What is he doing?' she murmured to herself as he stopped and began speaking with someone, their body hidden behind an elaborate floral arrangement. All she could see was a flash of blonde hair. She adjusted her seat and caught a glimpse of someone... was that Abigail? Yes, it was. Why was he talking to her? Caroline's eyes narrowed as the conversation continued. She talked half-heartedly to Michael, a civil servant with a passion for motorbikes and Jane Austen, then heaved a sigh when the dinner plates were carted away.

The lights dimmed and a band emerged. It was time for the dancing to begin. The dance floor had been laid earlier in the day, its wooden surface gleaming under the twinkling lights that entwined the posts and rafters of the marquee.

Once the first notes played, society members gathered and began pairing up. Caroline looked around for Hugh, but he was nowhere to be seen. This was unfortunate; she felt his presence would have brought the right kind of attention to her exceptional dance skills. She sighed, dancing a bit, but her heart wasn't in it. As she walked away from her last partner, who had been disastrous to her feet, she found herself hidden behind one of the Regency planters, which held a beautifully trimmed orange tree. As she bent down to rub her toe through her slipper, she heard a familiar voice, Hugh's sister, say, 'There you are, I was wondering where you'd gone.'

'Just taking a breather. It's been quite an evening so far...' Hugh's rich voice sent thrills down Caroline's spine. He really was a most delightful man.

'Who are you running from?' his sister asked with a note of amusement evident in her voice.

He sighed. 'No one, really... well, let's just say I'm keeping a low profile. I suffered through a long monologue by your president. God, what a frightful woman, she was so incredibly boring, so full of herself that I could barely finish my dinner. Thank God I managed to escape and meet a few normal people, which is a good thing. I was a bit worried that they'd all be like her.'

She laughed. 'Hah, poor you. I must admit, I've heard Caroline's pretty uppity, but I've barely spoken to her myself. And don't judge all of us on her behavior, most of us are a good bunch. After all, this is supposed to be fun.'

'Huh. Fun. I don't think that woman knows the meaning of the word. I might spend some more time with the Americans. At least they know how to unwind.'

'Well, as long as you enjoy yourself, that's the main thing.' Her voice drifted off as they walked away from the corner, moving toward the dance floor.

Caroline blinked. For a second, she felt like crying. This is what people thought of her? And said about her? She couldn't believe it. Not only was it incredibly rude... but it was so callous. No consideration of her thoughts or feelings, just unkind words and blatant dismissals. She pressed her hand against her chest, her heart-beating so strongly that the delicate fabric of her dress seemed like it might rip at any time. What should she do? What would Jane do? She was passionate about Jane, but maybe not everyone shared that enthusiasm.

She didn't know what to do anymore, but she knew that she couldn't stay here. She breathed in slowly for a moment, the tears winding their way down her cheek, then walked, ever so calmly, down to the boating lake where she encountered Hugh locked in an embrace with Abigail. She froze as the American broke free, laughing, before pushing a fully clothed Hugh into the water.

As he emerged, a laugh sprang from his lips and Abigail soon joined him in the water, her dress becoming more and more transparent.

From her position near the water, Caroline watched the escapades, her eyebrows slowly raising at their antics. She looked at Hugh, this time, her emotions completely detached.

He isn't that good-looking after all. And he didn't act with honor, which one could say is the most important thing of all.

Nodding her head, Caroline turned and walked back to the party. She knew she had come close to making a big mistake. Thank God she'd had enough intelligence to see Hugh for who he was. In the end, it came down to one thing – if she were here, Jane would not have approved of Hugh. Of that, Caroline, as president of The Austen Regency Society, was certain.

As she stepped back into the marquee, Caroline reflected on Abigail's behavior, both at the lake and the constant demands from before. Perhaps it was time for the alliance between NARS and ARS to come to an end. After all, it was crucial to uphold standards, and this kind of behavior was in clear breach of both societies' standards. These Americans... they said one thing, then did something completely different. Perhaps she would reach out to the French. They had been very eager to make an alliance... and say what you will about the French, at least they knew how to behave.

17

The Golden Touch

Before the installation, they had been advised to wear gloves.

'They care that much about smudge marks?' one of the handlers scoffed, whipping a pair out of his pants pocket. He was a large man, his physique made all the bigger by his uniform, which stretched over the lumps and bumps of his muscles. The name 'John' was displayed on his shirt, the stiff embroidery sitting flush against his chest.

'What do you expect? It's a gold toilet, for Christ's sake,' his colleague Bart growled, cramming his meaty fingers into the only gloves he had on hand, a pair of rarely used gardening gloves that were a size too small.

John shook his head, amazed at what constituted art these days. When he first started this job, he had mostly been dealing with paintings, maybe a few sculptures. Nowadays, it seemed like anything qualified as art, especially if the artist included a long-winded description of their piece. Recently, he had helped with the installation of one of these postmodern artist's exhibitions. One of her pieces had been a plate with the remnants of her dinner from the previous night.

They approached the large crate, which sat smugly in the middle of the room. When they opened the box and sorted through the protective covering, they hesitated a moment before unveiling the golden throne. At first, it seemed deceptively simple. Then, under the bright lights, it came to life. The toilet seemed to absorb the light, soaking it in like a malnourished plant. It glowed provocatively, enticing those around to draw nearer. The two men leaned in, hands outstretched...

'What are you two doing? You're supposed to be unpacking it, not ogling the bloody thing,' their supervisor snapped as he stepped into the room. 'Come on, things are on a tight schedule. This isn't the time to play around. This has to be installed within an hour.'

The handlers looked at each other and rolled their eyes. Their boss was known to be a difficult man on the best of days; on the worst, he was a pain in the arse.

'It'll get done,' John said.

'We've never been late before,' Bart confirmed.

The supervisor checked his watch. 'Yes well, we've never handled such an expensive piece before, so it's imperative that it's done right and done quickly.' He gave them one last death stare before flouncing away, his hands waving around dramatically.

'What's his deal? Why does he always have to get so worked up? You'd think he'd know by now that we always get the job done. It doesn't make any sense,' John said, a peevish look on his face.

Bart shook his head. 'Who knows? Maybe he's one of those guys who likes drama. Gives him some kind of edge or something.'

They went back to work, carefully following the detailed instructions for the removal and installation of the piece.

'Do you think this'll be popular?' John asked.

Bart laughed. 'Yeah, of course. It's a gold toilet. People will want to see it, but more than that, they'll want to use it.'

'Would you use it?'

'As long as it does its job, I don't care what it's made of. When it comes down to it, it's a toilet. If it works, great, if it doesn't, well, that's not so good.'

John looked at it, 'I kind of want to sit on it.'

'Don't. They probably have some kind of device on it, keeping track of all unauthorized arses.'

John gazed at it longingly. 'But it's here. I'm here. It's right in front of me, just waiting for me to sit on it.'

Bart sighed heavily, knowing that this was one of those arguments that would go nowhere. He didn't know what he had done in a previous life to deserve a work colleague like John, but it must have been something bad. *Why do I bother*, he asked himself. *It's the same thing every bloody time and I get tired of always being the voice of reason.*

'Do what you want, but if you get into trouble, don't come to me for help. You get yourself into a mess, you can bloody well get yourself out of it.'

'It must be so hard to be so perfect,' John sniped back.

'Not perfect, just a person with some common sense. I'm hoping you'll get some of that one day.'

John rolled his eyes.

'What's taking the two of you so long?' The supervisor had re-entered the room again during their circular discussion.

'Almost done,' said Bart.

'Nearly there,' said John.

They both rolled their eyes as the boss looked at their work and walked away in a huff.

'He seems a bit more on edge than usual,' Bart commented.

John shrugged. 'Maybe all that gold makes him nervous.'

Bart snorted. 'Why would this thing make anyone nervous? It's just a toilet made of gold... it can't do anything.'

'Unlike those voodoo dolls we had to arrange last month. God, those things gave me the creeps. I swear they were looking at me... probably cursing me too.' John shuddered.

'Yeah, they weren't pleasant. I'd rather set up another exhibit on torture devices than deal with those little things again. Then again, I don't think we'll have to worry about that, they weren't overly popular. Numbers were abysmal for that show,' Bart pointed out.

'Don't think they'll have that problem with this one,' John said, looking at the toilet, which was now fully installed. 'I better take my chance now,' he added, beginning to undo his belt.

'No, no, no... if you want to sit on it, fine. But you're keeping your bloody pants on, I refuse to be exposed to your naked arse.' Bart stepped back and folded his arms.

John paused, the belt partially off. 'But how am I supposed to have the full experience if my pants are still on?'

'I don't know or care. What I do know is that if you take them off, I'm getting the supervisor in.'

John sighed. 'Fine, be like that.' He huffed as he put his belt back on. 'I hope you're happy now, destroying my one chance of sitting on a gold toilet with my bare arse.'

'I'm sure you'll survive. So, you going to sit on it or what?'

John approached the toilet and slowly sat down.

'This is very anticlimactic,' he said. 'Thank you for ruining the experience for me.'

Bart shook his head. 'Whatever. Do you want a picture?'

'Yep.' John took his phone out of his vest pocket and handed it to Bart. 'Make sure you get the whole thing in there.'

'Yeah, yeah, I know. There, it's done. May the picture live on forever.'

'Hey, when's the last time you saw someone sitting on a gold toilet? I will annihilate the internet with this thing.'

Bart laughed. 'Good luck with that. You know this toilet's been making the rounds, right? There's probably thousands of people with pictures of themselves sitting on it... you're just one of many.'

'Yeah, but mine was the best. Don't worry, when I'm rich and famous, I'll still remember the little people like you,' John said, admiring the photograph.

'Bloody hell, I'm leaving now before this goes any further.'

The two left, and the room was empty once again. Day passed into night, and not a sound was heard until the lights were switched off and the security alarm was set.

In the darkness of the room, the toilet sat, a tantalizing presence. Even in the absence of light, its own luminosity made it stand out. And then, it was reflecting a light as it moved toward the sculpture.

'Jesus, will you put that thing away?' The masked man said, his voice raspy and fatigued.

'I can't help it, I can't see a damn thing,' the other man said, adjusting his mask for what felt like the five-millionth time. 'Why do we have to wear these things? It's so hard to breathe with them on.'

'Do I really need to point out the necessity of wearing masks when one is committing a robbery?' asked Raspy. 'Christ, I swear you're going to kill me one of these days with your stupid questions.'

'Well, the mask is killing me as we speak. So, where's the gold?'

Raspy looked at him. 'You're kidding, right? Your light was just on it.'

'Nah, that was a toilet.'

'Exactly. It's a toilet made of gold.'

'What?! You're kidding me.'

Raspy sighed and looked at the ceiling. 'No, I'm not kidding. It's right there in front of you.'

'Oh, right. I see it now. Wow, I thought your cousin was pulling your leg.'

'Bart doesn't joke. Ever.'

'Look at it, isn't there something comforting about the color of gold? It just says to me... I will take care of you.'

The two men stood there for a moment, admiring the rich gleam of the metal. Then they began thinking of all the wonderful things they would do with the money they were getting for this job.

Raspy was contemplating where he should go for his first vacation in years. He couldn't remember the last day he had off from work, let alone his last vacation, so he wanted it to be a good one. Preferably somewhere exotic. Morocco? Yeah, that'd be nice.

The other man was making plans. With the money, he would finally be able to buy that apartment he had been eyeballing for months. And, if he had anything left over, he would buy that ring for his girlfriend and finally propose to her.

They snapped out of their reverie, realizing that if they didn't get going, there would be no money at all.

Raspy kept watch while the other man set to work dismantling the piping and preparing the toilet for removal. They weren't overly concerned about security as Raspy had switched the security alarm off, but they were erring on the side of caution.

Time passed slowly, Raspy checking the news on his phone while his accomplice continued with his work. Finally, he stepped back and said, 'All done.'

'Excellent,' Raspy said. He opened an app on his phone and pressed a button. He went and opened the door they had come through, and a large robot swept into the room.

The other man looked at it skeptically. 'Really? That thing is going to handle this? It's heavy as hell.'

Raspy nodded emphatically. 'It'll be fine. The payload is something like 200 kg. It looks small, but it's powerful.'

'I guess I'll have to take your word.'

They hitched the toilet up to the robot, which lifted it onto a wheeled platform. Everything ready, they cleaned up the mess from removing the toilet and turned the security alarm back on as they left the room.

They escorted the robot out of the building and to their van, which was parked in a forest up the road.

'Well, that was easy,' Raspy said as he started the engine.

'Yeah, surprisingly so,' the other one agreed. 'Almost makes me think it was too easy. I feel like something has to happen to stuff everything up.'

Raspy laughed. 'I think we're okay. We just have to get it to the buyer, and he'll take it from there.'

He took out his phone and called his contact, confirming the meeting place.

They began driving, following the instructions on the other man's phone. For hours they drove, going from highways to long winding roads.

'We almost there yet? I'm getting tired and my arse is sore,' the passenger complained.

Raspy shook his head in frustration. 'Just a bit longer. If your phone hadn't taken us the long way, we would be there by now.'

Finally, they reached their destination, a modern monolithic home set in the middle of a large field. The house was massive, its concrete façade only broken by the line of large windows that marched across its surface.

'Well, here we go,' Raspy said, turning off the engine.

They got out of the van and opened the back as a group of guys came out of the house.

The robot lowered the toilet to the ground, and Raspy and his colleague undid the straps.

As Raspy unbuckled the last strap, he reached out and touched the toilet. He was amazed at how cold it was; his fingers caressed the smooth surface, trying to instill some warmth into the metal. It resisted, its coldness sinking into his fingertips. After a few seconds, he took his hand away.

Money was transferred using their online banking apps, and the buyer graciously gave them a cash tip of five thousand dollars each. Within minutes, the two men set off again, this time, each person one million dollars richer.

'Turn the heat up?' Raspy asked.

The other man looked at him, incredulous. 'You kidding? I'm roasting in here, it's so bloody hot.'

'I'm just cold, that's all.'

He took his hand out from his pocket and looked at it, the hand that had touched a 24-karat gold toilet. It was still icy cold. He blew on it, trying to warm it up without taking his eyes off the road.

Ten minutes later, his hand was still bitterly cold. He looked at it and was shocked to see that it was turning a delicate shade of yellow and gaining a metallic sheen. It was also becoming incredibly heavy.

'Oh shit,' he said, just before he swerved off the road and crashed into a tree.

Russia

18

A New Future

Slivers of arctic air seeped through gaps in Anya's window, their icy fingers creeping toward the small bed in the middle of the room. Anya's eyes snapped open as her feet pulled in closer to the warmth of her upper body. She had been dreaming about somewhere warm. In the haziness of her mind, she could almost feel the electrifying rays of the sun on her face and smell the heavenly scent of coconut. A humid breeze swept through her tousled hair and sent windchimes dancing, their gentle tingling interrupted by a wild screech that tore through her body. The wind, taking on a superhuman force, was wailing against her window. All thoughts of hot paradises slid from Anya's mind. There was no escaping the cold. But today, today was the day she had been waiting for. She was going to the market.

She had been wanting to go for ages, ever since she had heard all about it from her friend Alexei. They had been best friends since they were born and would be until they died. That was the way of their world – the unforgiving terrain and permanent isolation banded them together. Everyone worked together, socialized together, and died together. Survival was on their minds constantly – it was the driving force that dictated their daily lives and enabled them to keep going. There were some in the village who questioned the point of their existence, but most just accepted it. Anya, not yet affected by the cynicism rife in her community's elders, had simpler views. Her days were endless and boring, and she wanted to escape and see the world. Understanding this, Alexei filled her days with stories, wonderful stories that made her forget everything, even her dreaded chores.

It was spring when he first mentioned the market. They had been outside, milking the cows and listening to the trills of the chaffinches, watching as they swooped down from the trees.

'Did I tell you about the market?' he asked, stretching his fingers wide.

'No, you know you didn't! What was it like?' Anya's bucket tipped precariously as she jumped up.

He smiled. 'Amazing, I was sad you weren't there with me. You would have loved it. Give me a minute, I'll tell you a story.'

Alexei's stories were well known throughout their village. Anya's grandmother said storytelling ran in his family; Alexei's father and great-grandfather had both been blessed with the gift of the gab, and now it was Alexei's turn.

Alexei played with a piece of hay before starting.

'Long ago, there was so much sadness in the world that the king and queen decided to create a special place at the market, just for children. It was enchanted, somewhere that had never been seen before. Created and governed by magic, adults spent years trying to find and enter it, but never succeeded.

When this place, the Winter Castle, first opened, every child was welcome within its doors, but the king and queen soon realized that not all children were deserving of this great honor, for some were cruel, and others treated this haven with disdain...'

He paused before dipping a cup in the milk bucket and taking a sip.

'And?' Anya asked, her stool tilting awkwardly as she leaned forward.

Alexei wiped his mouth. 'So, the king and queen decided that only the most worthy could enter. They devised a test, which only the kindest, smartest children could pass. And those that did were allowed into the most beautiful, magical place they'd ever seen... a castle within a castle.'

'And those who didn't?' she asked breathily.

'Banished.'

The harshness of that word cracked through the shed, destroying the sense of pleasant escapism and bringing Anya back to reality.

'Have you ever seen it?' she asked.

He shook his head. 'No... we couldn't go to the market when I was younger, and now...well, I looked everywhere, but I couldn't find it.'

Alexei's words stayed in her mind for months, so too did the sad look on his face. When her grandmother told her they were going to the market, Anya promised herself she would find this wonderful castle.

'A castle within a castle,' she murmured, repeating what he had said earlier.

***

The day of their trip had arrived. She jumped out of bed, her stockinged feet hopping nimbly on the cold floor. Her warmest clothes had been laid out the night before, so she dressed in record time. Within minutes, Anya's clothes were on, and her grandmother greeted her by the door with her heaviest coat and mittens.

'I can't believe we're going, grandmother,' she said as she jerked one arm into a sleeve.

Her grandmother smiled, stroking Anya's hair. 'You're a good girl. You've been waiting such a long time for this.'

Both prepared, they left their house and walked to the nearest train station. They trudged through high snow drifts, their footsteps muffled by the sounds of the forest. Anya followed in her grandmother's path, her tiny feet jumping from one footprint to another. With every step, Anya dreamed about the market, her mind creating dazzling scenes of exotic foods and toys.

These fantasies were cut abruptly when they approached the station, their arrival much later than expected due to the snow.

'No!' Anya cried as the train pulled away from the station, its red-and-black body moving slowly at first, then gaining momentum as it powered through the monochromatic landscape.

'We'll get the next one,' her grandmother said. 'This will give us a chance to rest our feet.'

They walked along the platform and sat gingerly on a decrepit old bench, its frame sagging from years of usage and neglect. Anya squirmed as the wooden slats dug into her legs. She looked eagerly for the train before running her fingers along the armrest, her fingers picking at the flaking paint. It came away easily, the black flecks resembling tiny insects underneath her fingernails. As they waited, the pile of paint fragments grew and spilled onto the ground, only to rise once more when the next train arrived, the tiny bits swirling through the air like sooty snowflakes.

Anya and her grandmother boarded the train, moving along the corridor until they found their seats. They stored their bags and sat down, her grandmother taking out a thermos of tea and pouring them both a small cupful. The train pulled away, and Anya stared out the windows, watching as the scenery transformed from dark forests and villages to small cities, their tall gray buildings towering over the train when it stopped. Anya had been chattering the entire journey, her excitement about the market impossible to contain, but as they drew closer to their destination, she grew quieter and cuddled up to her grandmother. Would it really be as wonderful as Alexei had described? What if it wasn't? She hoped they would have animals – she loved animals, especially cats.

She was thinking about her neighbor's cat, which she would usually be playing with at this time of the day, when the train reached its final stop. Her grandmother stood, retrieved their bags, and took hold of Anya's hand. They hurried through the carriage, Anya's heart pounding with every step she took.

As they stepped down from the train, the first thing Anya noticed was the stillness. It was as if the world had stopped for a fleeting moment, just for her. She looked down at her feet, which were sinking into the pillowy depths of some moss. She lifted her foot up and stepped down again, softly this time. The moss sprang up, then lowered again, its dainty tendrils contrasting with the dull solidity of her boots. Her gaze moved upward, past the birches and pines to the colorful peaks and towers of a castle. They crossed a bridge, the heavy structure acting as a boundary between the forest and the market entrance. Anya skipped in excitement as they approached the market's front gate. The tall buildings soared above her, their spires reaching toward the sun and casting intricate shadows on the ground. She swirled around, eager to see everything. Enjoying the feeling of movement, she twirled and swirled, faster and faster, the sunlight casting a gentle warmth on her eyelids, until she stopped. For a moment, she was disorientated, her brain at odds with the rest of her body and trying desperately to keep up. As she stood there, she was swamped by a horrible feeling that she was all alone: that her grandmother, who loved and cared for her, was gone. The sadness swept through her, threatening to undo her... but then she opened her eyes and there was her grandmother, just ahead of her, waiting for her. Anya ran up and hugged her, her eyes brimming with tears at the thought of life without her.

'Hello little one,' her grandmother said, hugging her back. 'Now, remember to stay close to me. And don't talk to strangers.'

As they entered, Anya sighed happily, all thoughts of her earlier distress forgotten. The market was set within the castle's main forecourt. It looked exactly how Alexei had described it: a fairytale brought to life, complete with the surrounding towers and castle buildings that were all the colors of the rainbow – deep blues that shimmered in the afternoon light, their intensity reminding her of pictures of oceans she had seen at home; passionate reds, their beauty matching that of her grandmother's crimson cloak, a special garment only worn on certain occasions; and lastly yellows, their brilliance matching that of the sun overhead.

She didn't know where to look next; the market was a kaleidoscope of vibrant sights, smells, and sounds, all vying for her attention. Amidst the blinding hues of color, she was drawn to one plain wooden building, its lack of color offset by the fanciful carvings that pranced along the windows. She reached out to touch them, almost expecting the little woodland creatures to jump off the ledge into her lap. Stroking them, she was soon distracted by a raucous laugh that echoed throughout the square. She gazed around, her attention fixed on a building with a distinctive zigzag red-and-white tiled roof. She stared at it briefly before looking elsewhere, the design making her dizzy. She spied another window display housing an assortment of candles. The tall spires of wax colored in vibrant shades of blue, purple, and pink contrasted with the stark white background. She longed to run over and explore them more, but her grandmother held her hand in a tight grip and they continued.

Her grandmother led the way past several shops selling woolen goods and military memorabilia, both full of people and both incredibly boring. Anya didn't understand what people could possibly buy in those stores. As they walked, she heard the unexpected sound of water running from a tiny creek with a bridge ahead. They had just approached it when she saw a gray cat, the fluffiest one she had ever seen before, cleaning itself with a tiny pink tongue as it sat on the wooden railing.

'Ooh, look!' she squealed, pointing at the cat. The cat, knowing that it was being admired, preened for a second longer before walking away.

'Oh Anya, you and your animals!' her grandmother said as they walked.

They crossed the bridge, a heavy layer of snow crunching underfoot while a dusting of flakes swirled off the bridge, shimmering in the sunlight before falling, ever so gently, into the water.

As they stepped off the bridge, Anya looked up, gazing at the never-ending row of wooden stalls that lined the pathway, their simple brown structures disguised by the flowing drapery and colorful goods that were displayed. Anya stopped, her eyes overwhelmed by the sheer number of interesting things. And people too... it was teeming with people of all types, from merchants and makers to tourists and children playing hide-and-seek. Anya paused longingly at a stall covered in midnight-blue fabric with delicate dolls all in a row. She reached out, but her grandmother pulled her along.

'Not yet. First, we look at clothes, then toys.' They stopped at a stall further along, its sign proclaiming it to be a purveyor of fine shawls. Her grandmother touched one, her rough finger gently caressing the pale blue wool. She moved that one aside and tried on several while Anya stood there, fidgeting, moving her body this way and that to see the other stalls. Finally, her grandmother decided on a shawl that looked so soft it was as if it had been spun by a cellar spider. The deep blush wool made her grandmother's cheeks even pinker, like a babushka doll.

'Let's look at those dolls now,' her grandmother said. They walked back to the stall, and Anya gazed admiringly at the vast display, their painted eyes watching her. She wasn't sure which one she liked best, the red or the purple one. But then she saw one that had such a funny expression on its face, it made her laugh. She knew this was the doll for her. She looked at her grandmother imploringly. It didn't take long for her grandmother to hand over the money to buy it.

They continued looking at various stalls, one that sold boots, another that sold wooden puzzles, until Anya's stomach began rumbling. Her grandmother looked at her watch. 'It's a bit early, but I think you're hungry, little one. So, time for lunch.'

An intoxicating smell of cinnamon and spices met them as they turned a corner. 'Would you like some sbiten to warm up?' Anya nodded, the thought of the sweet, warm drink making her mouth water. They stopped at a vendor, his samovar gleaming, its surface freshly polished, and bought two cups of sbiten. Finding two seats, they sat, cradling their mugs in their hands. Anya had a small sip of the hot liquid, the comforting taste of honey, fruit, and spices familiar and warming. 'Should we have something with our drinks?' her grandmother asked. 'I see someone selling pirozhki, would you like some?' Anya nodded. It had been a long morning, and the syrniki she'd had for breakfast were long forgotten. 'Just don't move an inch,' her grandmother said as she went to the nearby stall. Anya did as her grandmother said, her eyes following as her grandmother ordered, paid and came back with hot pirozhki. Anya took little bites of the pirozhki, her mouth scorching, until gradually they cooled. She interspersed her bites with big gulps of sbiten and watched as her grandmother ate everything on her plate. They had finished eating and Anya was still drinking her sbiten when her grandmother's eyes started to droop, a sign that she was ready for her afternoon nap. Sometimes, when Anya was tired, she would curl up in her grandmother's expansive lap and fall asleep, surrounded by the warmth of the fire and the ever-present smell of bread.

But today was different. Even with a full stomach, there was no way Anya was going to fall asleep, not while there was so much to see.

For a few minutes she sat in her chair, watching all the surrounding activity – two people dancing in the aisle, their laughter infectious, while one man carrying a tower of fur hats stumbled, sending the hats flying through the air. The fuzzy hats landed all over the place, including one that dropped straight onto a baby's head. Anya giggled as the baby sat up, confused. Anya turned toward her right as a woman scowled at some tourists who had been trying to sneak pictures of her beautiful handmade dolls. An argument ensued, but they finally left, gesturing wildly at the woman, who shrugged and pointed at a sign saying 'No pictures' before turning away. Anya was amazed – she had never been in such a noisy environment before. Everyone was so quiet back home. There were disagreements, but nothing like this.

Then there was a break in the noise, and she saw something that took her breath away: a cat with fur so soft and white that it resembled powdery snow, and eyes so blue they rivaled the sky. It was the most beautiful cat she had ever seen. It sat on a rough wooden floor, its tail twitching, and stared directly at her, almost beckoning her to come closer.

Anya pursed her lips. It was so pretty, she imagined petting it would be like touching a cloud. But her grandmother... she would be angry if Anya left. She eyed her grandmother, who was still sleeping soundly, her mouth slightly open. Anya tapped her foot against the floor. Nothing. She slid off her chair and ran after the cat, which had begun walking away.

The cat moved quickly, running toward the grandest building in the market. Anya paused briefly, looking back at her grandmother, who was still slumped in the hard wooden chair. Anya smiled. Her grandmother's afternoon naps could drag on for hours, so she would have plenty of time to spend with the cat. She imagined her grandmother would still be sleeping by the time she came back. Her mind made up, she ran swiftly after the cat, her small footprints trailing behind.

As they approached the building, Anya gasped. It looked like the sky, except in reverse. It was white, a clear, cottony white with touches of aquamarine that dotted the upper reaches of the building, like clouds guiding one's eyes to the onion domes that rested at the top. They had been painted gold, their brilliance outshining even the sun. In her appreciation for the building, she neglected to notice that it was isolated – people went around it, but no one entered or left it. She followed the cat through the large wooden door and was surprised to find it empty. 'Hello, where are you?' she called out, before spotting a flash of white flying up the stairs. She chased it, her short legs taking longer to scamper up the steps. She reached the first landing, panting heavily, and stopped to look around. In front of her stretched a long corridor, its darkness at odds with the number of windows. It was quiet too, until a low growl echoed down the hallway. She paused. It happened again, followed closely by a hiss. Anya started forward, stopping short when she saw a shadow pass a doorway nearby. She squatted down alongside the architrave and watched as a man, wild in appearance, approach the white cat that crouched in the corner, back arched and tail flicking. He knelt and mumbled something to the cat before rising to his feet. He stood, then took something out of his pocket. He moved closer to the cat and raised his arm. She could see what looked like a big stick in his hand and knew instinctively that he meant to hurt the animal. 'No!' she screamed, flinging her body through the doorway and toward the man. Startled, he dropped the cudgel. Anya descended upon him, hitting and kicking him while yelling, 'Don't hurt it, don't hurt it!' The man tossed her off and picked up the cudgel again, but the cat, sensing a sympathetic being, leapt into Anya's arms.

Anya and the cat took off, their breathing intertwined as they ran down the hallway together.

It happened in an instant. One minute she was running, the cat's tail tickling her ear, the next, something hit her ankles and she went flying. She crashed into a wall, her head smacking into it.

When she came to, it was dark. Her head throbbed, the dull sensation spreading from her forehead to her neck, making it hard to move her upper body. She blinked furiously, trying to see, trying not to cry. It must be late – her grandmother would have woken up from her nap long ago and would be wondering where she was. She was going to be cross when she found Anya. But what if she couldn't find her? Anya's mind raced at all the possibilities, panic starting to build within her. She glanced down and spotted the cudgel on the floor next to her feet. The man must have thrown it at her, causing her to trip. There was no sign of him, or the cat.

Starting down the hallway, she heard the gentle tinkling of a piano; music was being played, music that she recognized. She ran quietly toward it, curious to know what it was and hoping the white cat would be nearby.

She fled, only realizing as she ran that the hallway was becoming brighter, an organic light was infusing the area and dispelling all lingering traces of darkness. The music, which she heard once more, became louder as she reached the last door. She opened it and was greeted immediately by the white cat, who leapt toward her and entwined its body around her legs. Anya automatically bent down to pet it and felt its purr intensify until it was as loud as the music. After a few moments of patting it, she entered the room and was surprised to see an old lady sitting in a majestic chair by the far window. Anya frowned. The lady looked old because she had white hair coiffed above a crown, but, unlike her grandmother, this woman's face was smooth, no lines engraved in her skin.

'You're hurt. Is that what kept you?' the woman asked, her fingers reaching out to touch Anya's forehead. A warm, soothing sensation swept across Anya's skin, removing the last vestiges of the pain she had felt earlier.

'No matter, you're here now. I've been waiting for you to come,' the lady said, looking down at a delicate music box that was playing in her lap.

'But who are you? How did you know I was coming?' Anya asked.

'I'm the Queen of the Winter Castle, of course. Don't you know where you are?' She laughed. 'Although I should say I'm the former queen... now that you're here.'

'Winter Castle? Then I made it! But how? I didn't take any tests...'

The woman smiled. 'Yes, you did. Our test is more practical, but no less effective. You showed your goodness of nature by protecting a defenseless animal.' She gestured toward the cat. 'Not everyone believes that animals are deserving of our protection. But you risked your own life to help him.'

'That was a test? But that was horrible! How could you do that to your cat? I hope it's okay...'

'He's fine. I don't allow anyone to hurt him.'

'Good, he's too beautiful.' Anya looked around. 'I can't believe I'm here... my grandmother will love this castle, it's beautiful. Alexei will too, he couldn't find it last time. Can I bring my grandmother in? I know she'll be wondering where I am.'

The lady shook her head. 'I'm sorry, that's not how this works. Your grandmother will never see or visit the Winter Castle – she's too old. For her, this space will only ever be a market. But you, on the other hand, you'll see everything, the whole domain. From the vineyards in the south to the farming villages in the east and everything beyond... your world is going to open up more than you've ever dreamed possible. You, my dear, are very lucky.'

'Me? How am I lucky?' Anya asked.

'Because you've come at the right time. My reign as the Queen of the Winter Castle is over. It has been a long and peaceful period, but all things come to an end. I have been feeling weary for a long time, but I had to wait until the right successor came along. And, now you're here, I can finally retire knowing that the throne is in good hands.'

'What? Queen, me?'

'Yes, you. It is a very important role. Not only do you have to hide the Castle within the illusion of the market, but you must maintain the market itself... standards are very exacting here. Then, there's everything I mentioned before... the entire realm, which is quite large...160 square kilometers in total... which doesn't mean much to someone your age, but it's farther than your eye can see. And you will rule it all.' She gestured outward, that one movement encapsulating so much.

'You mean I'm staying here?'

The lady nodded. 'Yes, of course.'

Anya's eyebrows furrowed. 'But my grandmother can't stay. And what about Alexei, can he come? He isn't old.'

A sigh escaped the woman's mouth. 'This is the difficult part,' she said softly. 'When you heard about the Castle, was a sacrifice ever mentioned?'

'No... Alexei never said anything about that. He said if you didn't pass the test, you would be banished... but I passed the test, so I can't be banished, right?' Her hands twisted together in growing alarm.

'No, you're fine. But to be queen, you must sacrifice your previous life and devote yourself to this kingdom, which needs you so very much. Do you understand what I'm saying?' she asked.

'No,' Anya said.

The lady stood, her cream velvet gown shimmering in the light as she paced from the throne to the window and back again. 'It means that your grandmother will return home without you and, once you are crowned queen, your memories will be erased. In your mind, your grandmother and Alexei will cease to exist.' She paused, seeing a look of panic on Anya's face. 'It is a big sacrifice, I know... but one that every queen before has made.'

Anya looked down at the floor, tears running down her face. No grandmother, no Alexei? That wasn't possible. They were everything to her. She was about to say this when the lady spoke. 'You're young. I know that what I'm asking you to do seems impossible. But when you take the crown, you will have an amazing life. You will see wondrous sights and do things that you have never even dreamed about. Think carefully. What kind of life would your grandmother want for you?'

The tears eased. Anya thought about life back in the village... how much she hated the monotony and how she knew it was never going to change.

Anya thought about her grandmother and Alexei. They would want a better life for her. Besides, whatever this lady said, there was no way she could forget about them and maybe, once she was queen, she could go and visit them.

With that thought in mind, Anya brightened. She nodded toward the lady, who stepped down from her throne.

'This is an informal ceremony, just between the two of us.'

She guided Anya to a chest and opened it to reveal a luxurious coronation robe. The heavy red velvet flowed in her hands, the bright gold embroidery on it glimmering in the sunlight. The lady placed it gently on Anya's shoulders before leading her back to the throne.

Anya looked at the throne. It seemed even bigger now than when she had first entered the room. She placed a tentative hand on the armrest nearest her. The cool metal underneath her fingertips felt smooth, fluid. She looked at the throne again. It was big, but there was a delicacy about it too, particularly near the top where it twisted and twirled into intricate spires.

'Are you ready?' the lady asked. Anya nodded.

The lady removed her crown then knelt in front of Anya. She held it up, her hands trembling with the effort. Anya took the crown and carefully placed it on her head.

The former queen sat back, tears of happiness falling down her cheeks.

'My queen.'

Anya smiled and looked out the window. She imagined her grandmother and Alexei sharing stories as they sat around the ancient table in their cold, faded kitchen. The image was so vivid, so lifelike, that she raised her hand, expecting to feel the roughness of her grandmother's skin... but even as her hand went up, the image began dissolving, first around the edges, then the figures themselves. Within seconds, the image was gone. Her hand dropped and she turned away from the window. As she did so, the light caressed her, giving her face and blue eyes an ethereal luminescence.

When she sat on the throne moments later, all memories of her past were erased, and she looked to her future as the Queen of the Winter Castle.

19

Plight of the Peacock

Dusk arrived in St Petersburg, the sun's final rays landing on the city's buildings and transforming their stones from cream to dusky rose. The day's noise made by tourists and workers flocking to various parts of the city died away, only to be replaced by the occasional sounds of nighttime buskers, diners, and theater-goers. All was peaceful, particularly around the Hermitage, where a letter was presently being delivered.

It was a special dispatch, one that came annually. The envelope was heavy cream parchment with elaborate gilded script across the front. It was an invitation, albeit one that was not appreciated by its recipient.

The recipient saw the invitation being carried by his favorite staff member, Annika. Her small feet glided across the floor, making no sound as she approached him and placed the envelope on the ledge surrounding the cage. She stepped back and winked at him before leaving the room, disappearing into the labyrinth beyond. Upon her departure, he waited for what would inevitably happen next, all the while gazing at his fellow prisoners who stared at him mutely, their eyes expressing everything their mouths could not.

Beams from the overhead lights touched the cage, casting stark, linear shadows on its inhabitants. The birds drew most of the attention, their bodies frozen high within the trees of the garden setting whereas others, the squirrels and mushrooms, dwelled below. As the sun set and darkness crept into the room, the peacock felt the habitual stiffness that usually encapsulated his body melt away. Warmth inundated him, starting its journey from the top of his head and moving to his talons. At nine in the evening, the clock within the mushroom chimed, setting off a course of autonomous movements that terminated in the grand finale – the lifting of the cage, done so slowly and deliberately that his cohabitants barely noticed.

The peacock shook out his feathers, the lower ones tinkling as they caught on the branches of the gilded tree below. He flicked them aside, the luminescent metal shining under the cage lights from above. He glanced at his companions, the owl and rooster, and gave them a brief look of sympathy before jumping out onto the ledge. He picked up the envelope and opened it, even though he knew what it was going to say.

Dear Sir,
You are cordially invited to an intimate dinner party at the Kremlin tomorrow night from 8-12.
Sincerely yours,
President Galkin

The peacock tilted his head in resignation. This was going to be an unpleasant ordeal. He had dined with the president for years now; while the dinner could never be described as fun, they were generally bearable. However, this year was different. There was a general feeling of discontent and anger in the air, one that had been building for quite some time. When he had first detected it, he'd had the strangest feeling of déjà vu. He remembered the same whispers of unease, the same desires for change, snaking through the museum one hundred years ago. Would there be another revolution? He didn't know, but something was brewing and it made tomorrow's engagement even more disconcerting.

Then again, if chaos was to unfold, perhaps it would mean the end of these dinners. They had weighed on him for almost two hundred years. Surely, if Russia was to fall, then his role too would end? He was so tired of these damn envelopes, so depleted from these dinners. It had to end soon... it had to.

Silently saying goodbye to his friends, he left the room, talons clicking on the parquet floors. The museum was still, its employees long gone, and the night engulfed the building in a silence that suffocated its inhabitants. As he continued through a maze of rooms, each one more elaborate and gilded than the last, he contemplated veering off to explore the rest of the building... but he knew that doing so would put him behind schedule and potentially make him late for the dinner.

He swiftly exited the building, tall lamps casting dark shadows on the wide path as he made his way out of the complex. It was time for his journey to begin.

Out of everything, this was the part he actually enjoyed. His flight from St Petersburg to Moscow took him across an ever-changing panoramic view of Russia – small cities, canals and forests, and woodland towns. His vista from above was vast, but he flew slowly, resting frequently in isolated areas, until finally he arrived in Moscow with the dawn.

As the sun rose, he cruised along the Moscow River and stopped at the statue of Peter the Great, a colossal figure that always filled him with a sense of adventure and freedom. He had witnessed its erection and remembered the controversies surrounding the statue; it was considered hideous by many, and its subject matter, Peter the Great, had despised Moscow so much that he moved the capital to St Petersburg. The peacock couldn't deny the first point, and he found the second point to be a beautiful irony. Perching for a moment on the metal ship, he looked out over the city before flying off to Muzeon Park, gliding from sculpture to sculpture, admiring the peace and quiet of the early morning. He continued onward, circling around the Basmanny District, the fragrance of blooming lilacs enticing him to swoop lower. He passed several bakeries, their windows full of mouthwatering displays of cakes and pastries. He could practically smell the sharlotkas, medoviks, rum babas, and bird's milk cakes, and his stomach rumbled in protest as he went forth. He glided through Krasnoselskiy, enjoying the pastel-hued buildings that lined the wide boulevards. A riot of color and shape caused him to look at a bookstore's window display briefly before he circled back and landed in Red Square.

The power emanating from Red Square was palpable. It infused his talons the moment he stepped on the ground. He had always had this feeling that no matter the location of the capital, whether it was St Petersburg or Moscow, the Kremlin was destined to forever be the seat of authority and influence.

He entered the Kremlin, making his way to the Grand Palace, where he was greeted by several military guards who escorted him to his room. It was the same room, year after year, so he barely glanced around before falling asleep.

When he awoke, the room was swathed in darkness. He pulled aside the curtain, enabling the full moon to reveal glimpses of the red, white, and gold decorations in the room. He stepped in front of a large, gilded mirror and preened his feathers until he heard a distant gong that signaled it was time.

A subtle knock on the door precipitated his accompaniment to Georgievsky Hall, the majestic room making him all too aware of where the real power lay.

He sat, taking care that his plumage draped perfectly over the chair, its golden hue shining under the chandeliers' bright lights.

And then it was time to wait.

In years past, the wait had been vexing. President Galkin's predecessors were rarely punctual, so dinner usually started around half-past nine or ten. This was an improvement on tsarist times, as the tsars had no qualms about letting him wait three or four hours before flouncing in. He had thought it quite insulting but, like so many things, there was nothing he could do about it.

Thankfully, in recent times, there had been some changes. He only had to wait thirty minutes before the door opened and the president entered, his walk brisk and resolute. Galkin sat at the head of the table and, without further ado, the dinner began.

It was rumored that Galkin's family tree was an interesting mix of peasantry and royal bastardy, a belief that his choice of food supported. Solid Russian food had been on the menu since he had come to office, much to the chagrin of the peacock, whose tastes veered toward the more refined and more European. The first course was brought out, the sight of which made the peacock's stomach drop. Kholodets – the most disgusting dish he had ever encountered – cold, gelatinous meat that wobbled as it was set down. Considered by some to be a delightful delicacy, the peacock knew better. No amount of horseradish or hot Russian mustard would ever improve its flavor. He poked it with a knife and watched it quiver, then scrutinized the president as he consumed his with relish, forkful after forkful moving toward his mouth. The next course was marginally better, a salad Olivier, which was in turn followed by the main course, a rustic soup called ukha. The peacock lifted a spoonful and wrinkled its beak at the dominating smell of vodka that emanated from the bowl.

The president was completely immersed in his meal and was oblivious to the peacock's distaste. Time passed, with scarcely two words said until the last course, a heavenly polyot cake, was brought out. The peacock looked at the dessert in confusion – he had been expecting an intricately made korolevskiy cake – the king's cake. The polyot was nice with its meringue and buttercream, but it was much simpler and smaller than the king's cake. He had been looking forward to that towering display of Russian excellence. Cherries, chocolate, sour cream... his salivary glands went into overdrive just thinking about the korolevskiy cake.

He looked down at his plate, and a small puff of discontent escaped his beak. One simply had to be in the mood for meringue, and tonight he was not interested. He pushed the slice around on his plate and watched the president devour his.

Once the president had finished, the plates were cleared and he spoke, his soft voice echoing through the cavernous room.

'This has been an interesting year for Russia... a hard one at times... with difficult decisions being made. These have not always been popular, yes, I will admit that. The people of Russia have been very clear about their unhappiness... but they haven't seen the full picture. They don't understand how these things work. It is my job to see everything and do what I think is best for Russia, whether it's popular or not. We've had testing times, but we persevered... just like we did for hundreds of years.' He shook his head wearily. 'Next year will be better... it must be...'

The peacock was taken aback, this was far from the usual dinner talk. He was accustomed to long, boastful monologues revolving around greatness and strength. In the centuries he had been dining with Russia's rulers, they had always focused on these two main topics. After all, as the ruler of the best country in the world, why wouldn't you brag about your achievements? For years, the peacock had heard it all – proud descriptions of enemy destruction, self-congratulatory speeches after diplomatic successes, malignant diatribes that went on and on... but tonight was something new. He could detect uncertainty in the president's speech. What made this year so different?

But, as always, his question went unasked. The peacock never spoke during these dinners. He had once had a voice; however, it had been snatched from him after his arrival to St Petersburg in 1781. He had been a valued treasure of the Empress, but that was long ago and, since then, he has attended these dinners in silence, his role demoted to observer.

He watched as the president sat, immersed in his chair and his thoughts, eyes fixated on the roaring fire set within the polished marble fireplace. Galkin stared at the flames as though they would offer all the solutions to his problems. Time dragged on, and nothing more was said. The flames hissed and popped, desecrating the stillness that held the hall.

As the candles burned down, the peacock's eyes began to droop, the rich food making its way through his system and sending his body into a catatonic state.

'It's late,' the president said, the words cutting through the silence of the last two hours. He rose from his chair to bid his companion goodnight when his words were swallowed up by a deafening hammering on the doors.

'What...' the president began, only to be cut off again by the renewed sound of pounding.

'Open up!! President Galkin! Open this door!' a loud voice yelled.

The president's security forces hurried into action. They blockaded the door and prepared for the president's departure through a secret panel.

'Galkin! If you don't open this door right now, we're going to torch this entire hall! You, and whoever else is in there with you, will die for what you have done to Russia!' the voice shouted.

'It's time to leave, President Galkin,' the top security man said before guiding Galkin toward the panel. The peacock, not wanting to become a roast delicacy under whatever new regime was about to install itself, scrambled after them, his tail feathers catching in the panel as it shut behind him.

The peacock jerked backward against the panel, tugging at his feathers until they came free, though he was annoyed to see that several had fallen out. He chased after the president, his body unused to such exertion, when they stopped abruptly in front of another panel. The security man opened it cautiously, then indicated for the others to follow him. As they walked, he talked quietly into his radio, shaking his head in frustration. They walked through a maze of rooms before descending a staircase, its dizzying spiral reminding the peacock of a snail. At the bottom landing, they encountered a thick steel door, its silver surface smooth and unmarred except for the presence of a keypad in the middle. The guard pressed several buttons in quick succession before a red light flashed and a beep emanated from the pad.

'You are security and you do not know the code?' the president asked, his tone expressing both contempt and resignation.

'I just started last week,' the guard said, stone-faced.

'All the more reason for it to be fresh in your mind,' the president replied.

'Yes, President Galkin,' the man said, reaching for the keypad again. He pressed different buttons, more slowly this time and, once he finished, a green light flashed. The door slid open silently, welcoming them into the tunnel.

The tunnel was the worst-kept secret in Russia. No one was supposed to know of its existence, but everyone – from small children in school to the elderly – knew of it. Like most things shrouded in mystery, there were countless theories about it circulating through Russia. Most believed it was for the protection of the state, others believed it served as a major spy network. And then there was the size of it – it was supposedly the longest tunnel in the world, a claim that could never be confirmed because no one was ever allowed to enter it.

As they began their journey through it, the peacock decided those claims, true or false, didn't matter. The tunnel was massive. Much to his dismay, it went on and on and on...

'How far does this damn thing go?' he overheard the security guard mutter to himself.

The peacock wondered too. Since entering the tunnel, his energy levels had nosedived. He just wanted to go home to St Petersburg.

They walked on for twenty more minutes, the two men occasionally glancing back, when they came to another door. With another keypad.

'Move, I don't have time for your incompetence,' Galkin said, pushing the security guard out of the way. He entered a code decisively and stepped back as the light flashed green. Once again, the door slid open, and they stepped through into the cool Moscovian air.

The moon was hiding, its glow hidden by the clouds that weighed down the sky. That was the first thing the peacock noticed.

The second thing was the noise.

Everywhere, he could hear shouts and sharp, jarring explosions of gunfire. Flashes of fire lit the sky, and though he couldn't see anyone, he could sense them. Their anger was palpable, their desire for change intense. The peaceful city he had encountered on his arrival was gone; its tranquility replaced with rage.

The peacock, who had seen this all before, was on the verge of crumbling into a mess of nerves for the second time that century when he realized that the others had gone, the president doubtless escorted to a safe zone.

It was time for him to go.

He set off, his desire to stay inconspicuous at odds with his physical appearance. Swooping down low somewhere in Tverskoy to follow the aromatic scent of baking pastries, he was spotted by a group of unruly citizens.

'Late night snack, anyone?' an unimposing but obnoxious man yelled out before launching a stone in the peacock's direction. The peacock dodged it with ease but decided to fly higher.

Moving beyond the central district, the peacock noticed a few tourists, their confusion and alarm visible in the way they scurried back to their hotels. As they ran, the tourists played hide-and-seek with the streetlights, their bodies weaving from light to dark.

The peacock paused, watching as chaos and violence spread their tentacles through the city he loved, before turning his back and departing Moscow. His return took twice as long as usual, the turn of events occupying his mind and making his body seem heavier. He stopped several times to rest before finally reaching the outskirts of St Petersburg, just as the sun was beginning its ascent.

The Hermitage was gleaming in the early morning light, its soft aura welcoming to the exhausted bird. He climbed the steps and made his way to the Pavilion Hall. Once he stepped inside, the cage slid up, startling its inhabitants, who had been sound asleep. Their bleary eyes opened briefly before closing again as he joined their ranks and settled himself on his perch. The cage swiftly descended, leaving the room quiet once more. The peacock sighed. It had been a long and arduous journey, but it was over. The clock was signaling four in the morning when the peacock closed his eyes and fell asleep.

Within minutes of entering deep sleep, his body flinched as a dream began. This was normal – every year he dreamed about her, the Empress Catherine, the way she had sat before him, her face cold and calculating as she determined his fate.

'You have made your position clear; you believe me unfit to rule, even after the enlightened conversation we have had. Even after I gave you your position, your voice.'

The peacock, unaware or uncaring of social niceties, remained oblivious to the menacing gleam in her eyes. He nodded emphatically, confident in his assertion that her character flaws would prove disastrous to Russia.

'Very well,' she said, her tone becoming more glacial. 'Then I have no choice. Your duty, from now until eternity, is to dine with the ruler of Russia once a year. During that meal, you will be incapable of speech. Not one word will slip from your mouth, no matter what is being revealed to you.'

She stood quickly, the gold and silver threads of her gown catching the candlelight and blinding him briefly. 'That will teach you to meddle in state affairs.' She left the room, her disapproval lingering in the air long after she had departed.

The scene became fuzzy and transformed from a warm interior to an exterior teeming with turmoil. He knew where he was – Red Square was looming in the distance. He heard voices, drunken voices, angry voices, voices that were coming for him. He could feel their hunger, their desire to destroy him. He tried to fly, but someone had clipped his wings and, before he could go anywhere, they had pulled him down. A person – a boy, really – grasping a rock in one small hand, was about to use it when the peacock turned his head and jerked himself awake.

He shook his head. For decades, he had hated Catherine; not only had she proved him wrong by being an effective ruler, but she had also devised a brilliant way to make him suffer year after painful year.

But now, he was wondering if she had done him a favor.

After all, he was here, away from the unrest and violence that he had witnessed in Moscow. It would come to St Petersburg, of that there was no doubt, but here, in the Hermitage at least, he would be protected. It was, after all, a private refuge, safe from any danger. *She* had taken measures to ensure that.

He could appreciate the irony of this... centuries after her demise, she still had the potential to both destroy and save him.

Feeling secure, he closed his eyes and went back to sleep.

RA Mitchell did not set out to be a writer. She would have been a professional reader but, sadly, those didn't exist in the 90s, so she instead got her first job at an ice cream shop. The freezing store meant this job didn't last long, but it instilled in her a lifelong love of ice cream. Since then, she has worked as a library clerk, primary school teacher and, most recently, a university administrator. RA Mitchell's journey has taken many unexpected turns, including moving from the US to Australia where she lives with her husband and son, who keep her on her toes.

When she's not working, she is dragging her son on long walks, taking road trips, reading, trying (and failing) to practice Spanish on Duolingo, teaching herself new recipes, watching British murder mysteries, and writing.

She can be reached at : ramitchellauthor@gmail.com

Acknowledgements

There are so many people who made this book possible. During the writing phase, music by Luke Faulkner, The Paper Kites, fun., Chad Lawson, Gregory Alan Isakov, Matchbox Twenty, Brian Crain, Mr & Mrs Cello, Dream Alliance and The Cranberries provided much needed inspiration and motivation. The editing stage, much like the fictional (?) tunnel in Moscow, did go on and on...many thanks to the Ballarat writing critique groups for giving me such insightful feedback. To my main beta readers/developmental readers, AJ Lyndon and Roland Renyi, thank you, thank you, thank you. And to Rebecca Fletcher, the best copyeditor, who miraculously transformed my scribblings into something far more polished within a ridiculous deadline. Your input was invaluable. I honestly don't know what I would have done without you.

Many thanks to my friends Samantha and Tina, who gave me very useful feedback and maintained my sanity these past many years.

And, of course, thank you to my family: my mom whose arrival to Australia served as a kick up the bum to get this finished once and for all, my husband for holding down the fort when I had to disappear into my writing nook, and my son for taking it easy on me when I stayed up too late working on it.